NADINE CRENSHAW

Xena X-Posed

The Unauthorized Biography
of Lucy Lawless
and Her On-Screen Character

PRIMA PUBLISHING

Library of Congress Cataloging-in-Publication Data

Crenshaw, Nadine.
     Xena x-posed : the unauthorized biography of Lucy Lawless
and her on-screen character / Nadine Crenshaw.
         p.   cm.
     Includes bibliographical references and index.
     ISBN 0-7615-1265-9
     1. Lawless, Lucy, 1968–   2. Television actors and actresses—New
Zealand—Biography.   I. Title.
PN3018.L38C74   1997
791.45'028'092—dc21   97-40183
[B]   CIP

     99 00 01 DD 10 9 8 7 6 5 4 3
Printed in the United States of America

How to Order

Single copies may be ordered from Prima Publishing, P.O. Box 1260BK, Rocklin, CA 95677; telephone (916) 632-4400. Quantity discounts are also available. On your letterhead, include information concerning the intended use of the books and the number of books you wish to purchase.

Visit us online at http://www.primapublishing.com

To my warrior-hearted daugher,
Johanna Crenshaw

CONTENTS

PREFACE

Lucy Lawless is real. After studying everything available about her, I have come to the conclusion that here is a woman—an actress—who finds no need to create a myth about herself. She is quite confident that she is just fine as she is.

And it seems she's right. A review of her life has shown me a woman who has lived honorably, who has nothing to hide, and who continues to hold the values instilled in her by an honorable, open family.

A New Zealand Radio talk show host called her "a lovely person, nice to talk to."

Does this authenticity make her less interesting? Hardly. It is so rare among others of her profession that it is interesting in itself, and as refreshing as the first thunderclap of a spring storm.

I'm sure Ms. Lawless must have regrets. There must be parts of her life that she would live differently if she had them to do again. But it's hard for an outsider to pinpoint what those spots might be.

Would she not have married Garth Lawless? But then she wouldn't have her daughter, whom she refers to again and again as the most important person in her life.

Would she have studied opera with more intensity? But then she wouldn't have become an actress.

Would she have kept her admittedly exciting position as hostess of a travel and leisure television show? But then she would not have become Xena.

No, I must conclude that Lucy Lawless is one of those rare people who, when looking back, wouldn't have changed much at all. Few of us have lived so well.

Events have broadsided her on occasion, coming unforeseen and unimagined, such as her serious injury while filming a *Tonight Show* skit. But even the events within her control have given her life texture, because she has such a rich imagination, and apparently very little fear. She seems to be eager to see what will come next.

Only time will tell whether she remains as free of regrets as she is today, but personally, I have confidence in her confidence of herself.

Chapter One

A PRIVATE CATHOLIC EDUCATION

IT'S NOT HARD TO UNDERSTAND WHY *XENA: WARRIOR PRINCESS* HAS generated such a devoted adult following, including hundreds of shrines on the Internet. The show bursts with head-butting, butt-kicking action, sexy actors in tight costumes, quality special effects, hip and totally anachronistic '90s dialogue, sexy actresses in skimpy costumes, wonderful and scary beasts, comic and appealing secondary characters, and . . . oh yes, sexy actors and actresses in tight, skimpy costumes.

The person around whom all this excitement revolves is actress Lucy Lawless. Lucy surprises some fans who meet her in person. Her natural New Zealand–accented voice is higher and rather light, much different from Xena's deeper, more somber, Americanized timbre. And Xena is a woman of Amazon proportions. Lucy is not. Xena strides through life with an attitude that says, "Try me." Lucy comes across as demure and modest.

But make no mistake, Lucy Lawless is Xena. She is also a charming, dynamic performer, as comfortable with her character's smart-aleck comebacks as with her broadsword. The embodiment of Lucy's two personas tends to make her a very busy lady.

The Lucy who is Xena, television's formidable warrior woman, is a strong, confident champion, and the heroine of millions of women, men, and children—but especially to women. "I'm thrilled that the show has struck such a chord with women," Lucy told *Mr. Showbiz,* "because it's been brought to my attention that an awful lot of women need that." Many of Lucy's fans have been in situations in which they wished there had been a warrior woman close at hand. "A lot of women write to me after they've been through a rape or something." Lucy's role on *Xena: Warrior Princess* has helped them realize that they are not at fault for their victimization. "They're not going to let themselves be victims after the attack. They're going to bloody work through it. I have been thrilled that they get something out of the show."

Where did all of this commotion begin? With Frank and Julie Ryan, who had a daughter they named Lucy, in Mount Albert, New Zealand. The date was March 29, 1968.

Lucy would later say that from the hour of her birth, she led a charmed existence. Her father, Frank Ryan, was one of eight boys who grew up in New Zealand under the auspices of Catholic nuns. The Ryans were well known as a good, strong Irish-Catholic family in Auckland. One of Frank's relatives, Kevin Ryan, was a famous lawyer. Frank himself became mayor of Mount Albert the year of Lucy's birth. He remained in that office for twenty-two

years, until the community was absorbed by the growing city of Auckland.

Julie Ryan, Lucy's mother, played an important role in the mayor's office during all of those years. Always a strong supporter of her community, she was a female powerhouse, forever opening their family home to those who had no other shelter.

Lucy was the couple's fifth child, but their first daughter. She would later credit her parents as being wonderful people, tremendously supportive. They never said "You can't" to any of their children. Lucy's "daddy" in particular let her know there were no bounds on her or her imagination or on how far she could go in life. Lucy's mother took her to plays and did art projects with her, such as collages—sometimes late into the night. She mixed the glue that cemented the strong personalities and fired the creative side of her children. Lucy had much to be thankful for in her parents.

For a while, she held the high position of being the only girl after so many sons, but Julie Ryan gave birth to another daughter after Lucy, and then had yet another son—seven children in all. A considerable amount of traffic for one womb, but that was the norm in their Catholic sector.

With five brothers, young Lucy was exposed

> **"** You learn how to charm, wheedle, and manipulate [in a large family] . . . plus you learn how to keep coming back from the knocks. It made me a fighter. **"**

to an abundance of testosterone as she grew into a preschooler. If her parents were positively encouraging, she certainly received plenty of "knockbacks" from her brothers and sister. She believed that living in her large family provided the perfect training for an actor. "You learn how to charm, wheedle, and manipulate . . . plus you learn how to keep coming back from the knocks. It made me a fighter," she said on Starwave's Internet CelebSite.

Her parents characterized her as sweet-natured and trusting, but also a bit of a ham. "She used to get up on the coffee table with a seashell for a microphone and sing away," Julie Ryan told *People*.

"Lucy was a very special child to us," Frank told *Weekly*.

On New Zealand Radio, Lucy said, "They were kind of relieved to see me turn up. And I hear from the others that I was luckier than the other children, and I'm sorry to my siblings for that, but I didn't know any different."

A CHARMING CHILD

As a child, Lucy tucked her mother's scarves into her leotard to do her own version of ballet to whatever music was available. At a very early age, she announced that she wanted to be rich and famous. It became quite a joke in the family. Yet Frank insisted she was a charming child, and never any problem.

Julie took Lucy to a lot of plays at Theater Corporate and the Mercury

Theater. During the programs, Lucy always picked a person on the stage to admire as someone she could be herself.

Her family environment was traditionally Catholic and loving, yet it wasn't like the environment of other children she knew. Her family was liberal and trusting. Lucy's mother and father knew not to keep their children in a stranglehold, forcing them to hide their dreams. Yet that Catholicism—and the Irishness of the family—had tremendous influence on Lucy's life, too. She went to church at least once a week until she was eighteen. She credits the theatrical nature of the Catholic religion with giving her a love for pomp. It fit right in with her own dreams of greatness. Yet her religion also informed her, even as a little girl, that she was only mortal. Learning the "Hail Mary" prayer, especially the portion "pray for us sinners now, and at the hour of our death," struck her hard. Death? What exactly did that mean?

By the tender age of six, she realized she was going to die one day. Some day she would be an old woman with her life coming to an end. It made her feel she must hurry—hurry to achieve, hurry to soak up as much life as she could. Her resilient mind found a way to counter the morbidity of this notion of death: If she was going to grow old, at least she would be a cheerful and active old lady, with lots of family to love her and for her to love in return.

If religion was important in the Ryan household, rugby was certainly not scorned. In fact, Lucy was raised on just about equal parts of both. Rugby and religion—not a bad basis for a future warrior princess.

In the rowdy Ryan household, there was a lot of scrapping. Lucy particularly got into it with her older brother Tim. She would later admit that she was sometimes a bratty little sister.

The entire Ryan family often held mock battles on a back field, using grass clippings and rotten fruit. Some of Frank's happiest recollections of raising his seven offspring were these rollicking frays the family enjoyed around their sprawling home. Lucy was always in the thick of it, giving her all. She credited drinking plenty of milk with the fact that she never broke any bones. She learned early to give back what she got. "I've got a good kick, I can throw a punch, and I learned not to cry," she told the *News Times*.

The children didn't always keep their ruckus outside. Lucy first learned to do flips on her parents' bed. The Ryan children opened the bathroom door to get the longest run possible, then they sprinted through and tumbled onto the elder Ryans' bed.

That poor bed. Frank and Julie often found six or seven youngsters in bed with them in the morning. That poor piece of furniture just couldn't take the weight in the end. A leg broke, and from then on it was propped up with telephone books.

Until the age of eight, Lucy was very much a tomboy, following the lead of those four older brothers. Julie Ryan always joked that Lucy didn't know she was a girl until she was eight. Lucy claims she couldn't have known, that everyone in her family kept her in the dark about being a girl.

Having four older brothers served as good preparation for playing Xena. "Lots of battling," Lucy laughed to *Total TV*, "lots of battling. You had to be pretty wily to survive. Or fast. And I wasn't fast, so I had to be wily." She claimed she'd learned from the best of the best.

In New Zealand, education is compulsory for children between the ages of six and fifteen. Lucy attended a public kindergarten for a year before entering a public primary school. New Zealand's primary schools offer "infant" classes during the first two years, followed by six annual grades that are designated as "standards" and "forms."

Lucy attended public school for her first two years, then began a private Catholic education at Wesley Intermediate School. Though her intelligence was never in question, she told the *Orange County Register* that on occasion she chose to hide it, at least to some degree. "I went to a Catholic school where, at eight or nine, I discovered how cool it was to be a dunce, because you could get away with so much by just pretending to be a dummy."

A TOUGH BROAD
EVEN THEN

She was a tall tomboy, but graceful and always performing. Julie Ryan remembered the little gymnastic displays, recitals, and dramas that Lucy staged with her friends. They made all their parents come and watch their presentations.

"At age ten, in a play about the prodigal son, I was the woman who rips him off," she said in an interview with the *San Francisco Chronicle.* "I played a tough broad even then."

Between Lucy's third and sixth forms, she thought she wanted to be a pathologist. Coincidentally, she was a great fan of the television series *Quincy M.E.* at that time. She hadn't any real idea what a pathologist did, but it seemed glamorous. Marine biology also entered her thoughts as a possible career—because it had such a fascinating name.

She must not have played the dunce too often, for she topped her form during her last year at the intermediate school. She was also voted most likely to succeed. That was when

her parents recognized fully that she possessed the ability to excel at whatever she chose.

Lucy attended Marist Sisters College (high schools are often called colleges in New Zealand). Pursuing an interest in acting, she appeared in many musicals and dramas throughout her high school years.

"I always had this kind of bug to perform," she told *Cleo Magazine,* "but [was] always tempered by the Tall Poppy Syndrome. You have to be a very quiet achiever in New Zealand. They get behind you once you have succeeded, but nobody wants to hear about it on the way up." So that was how she played it.

Her parents fondly watched her star in *The Mikado, South Pacific,* and *The Pirates of Penzance.* She was a gifted youth. She also had a vivid imagination. "I got this idea in seventh form French once that I was going to go to Europe and pick grapes on the vine," she told WGN Radio, "'cause it sounded so romantic, you know."

"She had a fine singing voice," said Frank Ryan to *Weekly,* "but all she wanted to do was get into film and television." She took piano lessons for eight years, but never was much good at it. In fact, only a few years later she would claim she couldn't play a

> **"** At age ten, in a play about the prodigal son, I was the woman who rips him off. . . . I played a tough broad even then. **"**

note. She blamed it on poor eye-brain-hand coordination. Also, if something didn't move her emotionally, she was not likely to become excellent at it. Lucy could not spend hours a day working on something that didn't arouse her interest.

"When I was fifteen, I went on an opera tour of Europe with my mum, to see all the best opera, like *Carmen,* a million times. It really awakened my senses." Back home, she began to study opera; and as the ham in her family, she also continued to perform in class plays.

Lucy never idolized anyone as a teenager. She didn't put posters of heroes up on her bedroom walls. Pop culture didn't particularly interest her, maybe because she didn't lack people to admire in her everyday life, such as her own parents.

At five feet ten-and-a-half inches tall, with light brown hair and intense sapphire eyes, she was always popular with boys. Her family's phone rang often, and most of the calls were for Lucy. But her father was happy to see she was always respected. There was no "nonsense" allowed, and Frank never felt let down by her. Julie Ryan agreed that her daughter always behaved very sensibly. One of Julie's friends commented that Lucy was never a child, she was always adult in her manner.

She eventually became head girl of her convent school. When not studying to maintain her high marks, she loved to ride horses. And she also fell in love with Garth Lawless, a boy who went to high school with her.

AN OPERA SINGER'S LIFE WAS DULL

Lucy graduated from Marist Sisters College at age seventeen and entered Auckland University. She took courses in opera and languages—German, French, and Italian. She had a dream of a genteel show-business success as an opera diva. Then, after a year at university and about four years of opera training, she decided she didn't really want to be an opera singer after all. An opera singer's life was dull—she couldn't stay out late at night, she couldn't laugh herself to tears, she couldn't eat certain foods. Lucy also realized she simply didn't feel enough passion for opera to survive all the rejections she was bound to receive.

She knew she had a good ear. And she understood how music worked. Lucy would always appreciate the sensual delights of music. And she still loved to listen to and watch opera—but she didn't want to perform it.

So what was she going to do with her life? What about that old idea of picking grapes in Europe?

At eighteen years old, Lucy suddenly got what Kiwis call "a traveling Jones." (Note: "A kiwi is not a fruit!" Lucy explained in a KTLA television interview. In New Zealand, a kiwi is either a flightless bird with a long, slender bill and brownish hairlike feathers, or a citizen of New Zealand.) She was itching to get away from her little island country, located west of Australia, at the Earth's south end. "I was just desperate to escape my claustrophobic family and go and have a wild life," she told *TV Hits*. She wanted to see the rest of the world.

Though her parents didn't try to stop her, "My mother made me take this big, ugly, yellow suitcase—a millstone around my neck," moaned Lucy to *Parade*. Leaving her family for the first time in her life, she headed for Lucerne, Switzerland.

It proved not to be the wildest spot on Earth. "When I got to Lucerne, I found out it was a really upstanding and moral place. It's not the sort of place you go to have a cathartic, teenage rebellion at all. So, I went to Munich, and hung out at the cafes." She told WGN Radio that she met some strange characters.

From Munich, she let her wanderlust take her across Europe, where she occasionally found jobs. She even picked some grapes—beside Germany's Rhine River. But it was nothing like she'd imagined grape picking would be, nothing like her schoolgirl daydreams of it.

She traveled some more, and slept where she found herself at the end of the day. A self-proclaimed "rough diamond," she lived on coffee and cigarettes until she was skeletal. Lucy was too proud to ask for help from her parents. She missed home, but traveling was pure adventure. There was even some danger involved. After all, she had no cash, she was young, and she didn't have any friends. The journey taught Lucy at least one important lesson: It was a big, cold planet, but there was nothing much to be truly afraid of, because she could survive even if she was broke, hungry, and homeless.

The strangest spot she visited was the Players' Park in Prague, where they really championed the performing arts. She saw free plays there, which upon later reflection were mostly rubbish. The worst was by a group of Canadian students who whacked each other on the head with big mutton chops and screamed about a plague. Lucy sat there watching and realized she wasn't as pathetic as she thought, at least not in comparison to those poor "blokes."

Her Auckland sweetheart, Garth, eventually followed her to Europe. Perhaps they would never have had the nerve to live together in staid New Zealand, with their parents breathing hotly down their necks, but in Europe they were free to do as they liked. They went together to Greece, taking odd jobs along the way. When money got too scarce, they came up with a rather simpleminded tactic: Go to Australia, earn some more money, and come back to travel in Russia.

After eleven months of wandering about "the Continent," the couple flew to Australia, signing on with a gold-mining company. The work was in Kalgoorlie, a small village deep in the Australian outback, five hundred miles from Perth. Should anyone get romantic ideas that Lucy was soon going underground with a light on her head, picking chunks of gold out of the soil, think again. She and Garth wound up doing some very dirty work. And the company soon moved them to a mining camp another two hours away from civilization.

These "mines" were not tunnels and shafts, and workers didn't carry pick axes or need a canary in a cage. It wasn't like that at all. These were catskill mines, bloody awful things in Lucy's opinion. The company engineers laid waste to miles of the countryside with huge explosive charges. They literally detonated the landscape. Huge machines then sifted out microscopic particles of gold. Lucy never saw any gold in the ground.

A MOB OF RANDY MINERS

There were very few women workers in this mining company, and Lucy did the same punishing labor as the men— shoveling dirt, mapping the ground, driving trucks (which included changing a lot of tires), and pushing huge core samples of earth through a diamond saw. In other words, a lot of grueling, dirty, hard labor.

She never suffered any difficulty about being a woman in a predomi-

nantly male camp, even though the ratio of females to males was one to forty or fifty. It could have been an unhappy affair had she got herself into any bad situation. No woman out there wanted a mob of randy miners on her tail. So Lucy was careful not to put out any dangerous suggestions. She didn't want to draw unwanted attention. As a consequence, she never met up with any "bloke trouble" she couldn't handle.

In fact, she and Garth were largely alone. Often they didn't see anyone for weeks at a time. They were two hours from anywhere, living in a caravan (a trailer) with a cat named Basil. Their only companions were the native emus, kangaroos, and snakes.

"There's nothing a man could say to me that I wouldn't be able to give back," she told New Zealand Radio. "I don't mean chat-up lines . . . any sort of verbal abuse."

Altogether, she lived in Australia for eleven months. Her wanderlust partially satisfied, she satisfied another kind of lust with Garth. And while in Kalgoorlie in 1987, she discovered she was pregnant.

Chapter Two

A BIG FISH
IN A SMALL POND

THE PLAN OF RETURNING TO RUSSIA WAS CANCELED. INSTEAD, Lucy and Garth decided to get married. Their wedding was hasty. It took place in a registry office, located in a cement-block building. Lucy always hated cement blocks. She hadn't imagined getting married in this way, with the two witnesses' children screaming, "Mummy! Mummy!"

At the ceremony she stood beside Garth in her high school ball dress. "I don't know why I took that to Europe and Australia," she told *Cleo,* "but I had it on hand." It didn't fit right because she was three months' pregnant at the time. "It was a kind of sorry exercise . . . but I mustn't say that because it's not right. It was the way it had to be, and things have worked out for the best."

The implications of changing her name from Ryan to Lawless only dawned on her after the wedding. The first time she heard herself called Mrs. Lawless, she hid her face in her arms and sobbed. Most likely, it was a reaction to the tension of the hurried ceremony and the abrupt changes taking place both in her life and in her body. Yet at the time, it seemed to her that people would never take her seriously with a name like that. She pouted about it for a while. "And then I realized, if people weren't taking me seriously, it wasn't because of my name, and I better get on with things anyway," she said in a New Zealand Radio interview.

In fact, Lawless was an excellent name for an actress. No publicity department could have thought up a better appellation for somebody who would one day star as a warrior princess. But all that was in the future.

She and Garth returned to Auckland shortly after their marriage. Lucy had been away from home for two years. Her family welcomed her back in their typically hearty manner. Garth took a job managing a bar, and the couple moved into a tiny apartment. Their neighbors were peculiar old ladies with cats that drove Lucy insane.

In a few months, daughter Daisy was born. After that, Lucy voiced no regrets about not seeing Russia. In fact, she was perfectly happy to have a new baby instead.

Almost perfectly happy. But there was still something missing, something driving her. That feeling of hurry, hurry, still rode on her shoulders. To counter it, she took up yoga. That discipline helped her realize that she had to slow down, to enjoy what was in her life in the present and not always be striving for the future. She began to understand that now is all anyone really has. Inwardly, she grew in wisdom. She grew less hungry in some ways, or at least, less desperate.

But she also enrolled in various acting classes. Lucy now understood that behind her impulse to study opera had been a desire to perform. Opera hadn't been the right outlet. Though she'd had a certain rough talent for it, she simply hadn't enough love for music—and certainly did not want the life of a diva, with all the hours of intense training and discipline. Yet she had an uncontainable urge to perform. It had never left her, not during her travels, not during her gold-mining adventures in the boiling heat of the Australian Outback, not even after she'd married and had a child.

With her husband's support, Lucy started to go out to tryouts. She was often rejected, but she just kept going. She had decided to be an actress, whatever it took.

It was not really possible for New Zealand actors to work regularly in films. Although the world did take notice of the artistic content that came out of New Zealand, few films were made there and several years could easily pass between roles for any actor. The theater was the main source of steady work, but it often entailed "company" acting. Open slots were rare in such ensembles. Television also offered roles for the actor seeking work, and then there were always television advertisements.

Lucy won her first role in a series of television commercials for New Zealand's ASB Banks. It wouldn't exactly make her rich and famous; Garth couldn't quit his job as a bar manager. Nonetheless, it was work.

Lucy never thought acting could be a primary means of income for her. Kiwi Kevin Smith (not to be confused with the American actor Kevin Sorbo, star of *Hercules*) told *Whoosh!*: "Back when I was in high school, it was inconceivable that someone would make a living as an actor. Just of late, I guess because of the success of *Once Were Warriors* and *Heavenly Creatures,* the profession has kind of become legitimized in the

> " Back when I was in high school, it was inconceivable that someone would make a living as an actor. Just of late, I guess because of the success of *Once Were Warriors* and *Heavenly Creatures*, the profession has kind of become legitimized in the public's eyes. "

public's eyes." These two prestigious feature films had won New Zealand a certain movie-making fame.

A TYPICAL NEWCOMER'S CURIOSITY

Lucy first met Kevin Smith during this period. He would later play the recurring role of Ares, the god of war, in *Hercules: The Legendary Journeys* and *Xena: Warrior Princess.* When he was twenty-four and working as a professional rugby player, his wife put his name in for an acting audition. He was soon cast in New Zealand's first prime-time soap, a one-hour weekly called *Gloss.* Kevin remembered, "I had just met Lucy. It was just after she had gone back to work after Daisy was born. She was very young." Kevin had recently been promoted to a mid-range role on *Gloss,* and Lucy came on as an extra. With a typical newcomer's curiosity, she asked him how he had got started. Kevin saw her around often after that, because New Zealand's acting community was so very small.

For what seemed a long time to her, Lucy felt she didn't do well in her chosen line of work. Frank Ryan remembered Lucy crying on his shoulder, sobbing that she was working so hard but no one would give her a break. Why was it proving so hard for her to get work in Kiwi productions? Her loyal mother felt the producers had a group of actors they used over and over. Julie Ryan also feared that her daughter might be too tall. She would need a leading man at least seven feet tall.

In truth, however, Lucy didn't have to wait long to be discovered. It was a matter of months, not years. As a boost, she entered a beauty pageant—and won. She was crowned Mrs. New Zealand 1989. Soon after, she landed her first real acting job. She was just twenty when she was invited to join a comedy troupe that did a burlesque-style skit show called *Funny Business.* What followed was an assortment of guest-star roles on several television series, including *High Tide, The Ray Bradbury Theater,* and *The New Adventures of the Black Stallion* (in the episode titled "Riding the Volcano").

By 1991, Vancouver, Canada, had begun to beckon Lucy. That was where the William Davis Center for Actors Study was located. Garth agreed that it would be a good idea for Lucy to study there. So the family moved again.

Lucy studied for eight months with Bill Davis, who would later earn his own fame as an *X-Files* character, the Cigarette-Smoking Man. Lucy's classes at the school provided her with some fine training as an actor. She would always be thankful for it.

While in Canada, she also won a few small walk-on parts on Vancouver television. But the family's stay in British Columbia was short-lived; back in their homeland there were new acting opportunities for Lucy. They returned to New Zealand in early 1992, and Lucy began a two-year stint of cohosting *Air New Zealand Holiday,* a magazine show broadcast in Kiwiland and throughout Asia. It looked like her flare for drama had finally blossomed into a career. *Air New Zealand Holiday* also provided her with more world-travel opportunities.

She also appeared in a feature-length docudrama, *The Rainbow Warrior,* about an eponymous Greenpeace ship that was sunk in New Zealand's waters. (Two actors from *The Rainbow Warrior,* Allison Bruce and Simon James Prast, would later do guest spots on *Xena.* The New Zealand acting community was very small indeed.)

Lucy was hosting a second season of the travel show when *Hercules: The Legendary Journeys,* a new syndicated show for U.S. audiences, began shooting in various New Zealand locales.

Though Lucy's cushy job as the cohost of *Air New Zealand Holiday* had its advantages, she gave it up after only two years. She wanted to concentrate on the craft of acting, rather than host-

ing. "It paid okay," she told *Cleo Magazine,* "was fun, and took me to some thrilling locations—particularly Israel—but you often couldn't tell the whole truth. You'd really want to say, 'Wow, don't go here. It's crappy!'" Or, on occasion, she would have to work with a nasty dictator of a guide in some backward country. Yet it was fun for the most part. She got some wonderful photos of her travels and made some great friends.

But it was only fun, and that wasn't really enough for her. In the end, it wasn't hard for her to leave the show. She knew there was nothing available for her on the acting front, but hosting a travel show wasn't what she was meant for. Continuing would have made her heartsick. Lucy was either going to become a big fish in a small pond or lose it all.

So she quit the cohosting job. Right away, she looked for work in American television shows, because she felt they offered jobs she could obtain. She couldn't get New Zealand roles. It seemed she didn't have a typical Kiwi look. She couldn't fathom what was wrong with her, except that she simply did not have the all–New Zealand look that producers wanted. Much of her problem must have been her unusual height, but she only knew that she was being turned down time and again.

Kevin Smith recalled her working on a gambling drama, called *Marlin Bay,* around 1993. Kevin came on the series afterward as the bad guy and they worked together for a few weeks.

A LITTLE BIT OF A BOLSHIE

"I would always get cast for the American or Canadian–New Zealand co-productions. I'd always get those jobs and never the New Zealand ones, so my theory is that I didn't look right," Lucy told New Zealand Radio. "Perhaps the way I look, the way I behaved, was a little scary. I think I was always a little big for my boots perhaps, a little bit of a Bolshie." ("Bolshie" was New Zealand slang for an extreme radical, derived from the Russian word *Bolshevik.*) Her agent was told by one casting director that "Lucy didn't sufficiently fit within the parameters of the show." Upon later reflection, Lucy felt the

woman was quite right, that she would not have been the right person. For one thing, she would have grown tired of the format of the show in question very quickly.

Yet at the time these rejections perplexed her. And they were painful. Something good came from it, however. She learned that rather than feeling sorry for herself about the kind of jobs she couldn't win, she should aim for those she could win. She developed her American accent and decided to go for the American productions in a bigger way.

She got the accent down pat, through plain hard work and her natural talent for languages. After all, she could get along in German, French, and Italian, why not "American?"

When she won the part of Lysia, a vicious Amazon enforcer, in the television film *Hercules and the Amazon Women,* Lucy knew she had made the best decision. At the time, however, she was so low that she would have been excited just to get a job in another commercial. A casting director on the *Hercules* set championed her as Lysia—and helped her be excited when she got the role.

Hercules: The Legendary Journeys was the brainchild of Sam Raimi and Rob Tapert, whose company, Renaissance Pictures, had made

> " I think I was always a little big for my boots perhaps, a little bit of a Bolshie. "

the *Evil Dead* films, as well as *Darkman, Hard Target,* and *Timecop,* and the short-lived television series *American Gothic.* Sam and Rob had been production partners for more than twenty years. Sam left college to form Renaissance Pictures with Rob and actor Bruce Campbell, a longtime friend. Out of this association came the trio's first feature film, *The Evil Dead.*

Written and directed by Sam, produced by Rob, and starring Bruce, the ultra-low budget horror picture became an immediate cult hit at the Cannes Film Festival. It also became a theatrical and video phenomenon in Great Britain, Europe, and the Far East, firmly establishing Sam as a wunderkind director.

The Evil Dead was soon followed by the equally impressive sequel *The Evil Dead II: Dead by Dawn,* which was made under the auspices of the De Laurentiis Entertainment Group. Then came a mainstream fantasy thriller, *Darkman,* starring Liam Neeson and Larry Drake. *Army of Darkness,* an outrageously comic sword-and-sorcery fantasy, again starred Bruce Campbell. *Hard Target* starred Jean-Claude Van Damme. The two-hour pilot of *M.A.N.T.I.S.,* for Fox, led to a television series, but the Renaissance team was not happy with the terms, so they washed their hands of the project. Other endeavors by Renaissance included *The Hudsucker Proxy,* starring Paul Newman, Tim Robbins, and Jennifer Jason Leigh; *The Quick and the Dead,* starring Sharon Stone and Gene Hackman; and *American Gothic,* a critically acclaimed (but doomed) television series for CBS.

Universal approached Sam and Rob to do a bundle of two-hour movies, one-time television adventure yarns, to come under an "Action Pack" banner. They would begin airing in January 1994. These "Universal Action Pack" movies were to include *Tekwar,* from William Shatner's books; *Bandit,* based on the "Smokey and the Bandit" movies; *Midnight Run* and *Vanishing Son,* based on previous movies; *Knightrider 2010,* an update of the television series *Knightrider;* and *Hercules.* Six movies of original material—really top-notch stuff. The *Hercules* movies would be based on the Hercules legends, using up-to-date dialogue and cutting-edge CGi (computer-generated image) monsters.

THE TRICK WAS TO FIND THE PERFECT ACTOR

Making a feature based on Hercules was not a new idea. It had been done—and done—and done again. This latest version began filming in 1993, with the four Hercules features planned. The trick was to find the perfect actor to play the lead role.

"The studio put a great deal of pressure on us to put Dolph Lundgren in the role," Rob told *SFX.* "We approached Dolph with a big offer and he turned it down. And, boy, are we glad he did."

After auditioning more than one hundred prospective Hercs, the producers eventually cast a relative unknown, Kevin Sorbo, who had previously tried out for such roles as Fox Mulder on *The X-Files* and Superman in *Lois and Clark.* Anthony Quinn was cast as Zeus to give the project some much-needed credibility.

Now, where to shoot the movies? Another television special, featuring the snowcapped mountains, frowning cliffs, and beautiful beaches of Down-Under-Land, prompted executive producer Eric Gruendemann's decision to film in New Zealand. "Just four weeks before I had the assignment to find a location for the Hercules movies, I watched a *Good Morning America* special and was impressed by the beauty of New Zealand," Eric told Wellington's *Evening Post.* The producers wanted a location that would set the show apart from the 1950s, '60s, and '70s versions of Hercules, which were all filmed in the sword-and-sandal manner, with very arid backdrops. Renaissance wanted something dramatically different, something primordial, beautiful, with lush ferns and waterfalls, and light that fell like dazzling rain in the gardens of Eden.

> We approached Dolph [Lundgren] with a big offer [to play Hercules] and he turned it down. And, boy, are we glad he did.

New Zealand is situated in the South Pacific Ocean, a wee bit further than a hop, skip, and a jump from the majority of the human race—in time as well as in distance: Its time zone puts it an entire day ahead of the United States. It comprises two large islands, North Island and South Island, and many smaller islands. The total area, exclusive of territories, is about 103,740 square miles—making it about two-thirds the size of the state of California.

It is mountainous, but with several large regions of plains. The country has more than 220 named mountains. North Island has a very irregular coastline, particularly on its northern extremity, the Auckland Peninsula. In the vicinity of the city of Auckland, the peninsula is only six miles wide.

The climate is mild, and seasonal differences are not great. The northern end of the Auckland Peninsula has the warmest climate, with an average temperature that varies between 66 degrees (Fahrenheit) in January and 51 degrees in July. It is also wet; the average rainfall is 48 inches.

New Zealand plant life is remarkable: Of the two thousand indigenous species of plants, about fifteen hundred are found nowhere else in the world. North Island has subtropical vegetation, including mangrove swamps. The forest is evergreen, with a dense undergrowth of mosses and fern.

An interesting fact is that with the exception of two species of bats, no indigenous mammals exist in New Zealand. The nation has a large native population of wild birds, however, including the kiwi, from which the people take their nickname.

English is the official language of New Zealand. More than 90 percent of the people are of British descent. Approximately 7 percent are Maori, a Polynesian group who migrated to New Zealand in the fourteenth century. Officially, the population totals about three million, and approximately 72 percent of that reside on North Island. Auckland is the largest city, serving as a seaport and a distribution center for the dairy region. It also boasts the oldest art galleries and museums in New Zealand.

The national economy is largely dependent on wool production, a major export. New Zealand is predominantly an agricultural country.

Besides the natural beauty, Renaissance Pictures was attracted to the healthy economic exchange rate in New Zealand at the time—almost fifty cents on the dollar. The state of the New Zealand film industry was appealing as well. "We were looking for a place that would provide us with technically proficient crew and wonderful artisans," Eric Gruendemann

said. He found the New Zealand industry very much in the expansion stage. Exciting things were happening there.

Kevin Sorbo, cast as Hercules, had never carried the lead role in a major television series. He was glad to have somebody like Tony Quinn in the cast. The veteran actor kept both cast and crew alert, because he liked to ad-lib rather than always follow his script. Director Doug Lefler believed that Kevin's portrayal was enhanced by his apprenticeship under Anthony Quinn.

LIEUTENANT TO THE AMAZONS

Lucy Lawless also won a part in the debut Hercules movie. *Hercules and the Amazon Women* was released April 25, 1994. In it, Lucy plays a menacing renegade Amazon lieutenant, an "enforcer."

"I was sort of a Bolshie lieutenant to the Amazons," Lucy said to the *New York Times.*

The very next week, on May 1, *Hercules and the Lost Kingdom* was released. It costarred a little-known actress named Reneé O'Connor. Reneé's performance so impressed Rob Tapert and Sam Raimi that they signed her for a starring role in *Darkman II: The Return of Durant*, a feature to be released for home videos in July 1995.

Kevin Sorbo, after fifteen years in the business, became an overnight sensation. In fact, those first Hercules movies were such successes that Universal began talking about commissioning thirteen hour-long weekly episodes.

The record suggests that the decision to convert Hercules from telemovies to a weekly show was determined sometime between May and September of 1994. MCA knew it had a potential hot property in those two movies (which featured Lucy and Reneé). John Schulian, coexecutive producer, revamped the series, which would be called *Hercules: The Legendary Journeys*. The series would no longer

> *Hercules* is an action show, and we're going to have fights . . . [but] Hercules makes a point of saying he doesn't kill people. They may wind up dead when they're fighting him, but it's usually because they're being hoisted on their own petard.

feature Anthony Quinn, but would retain Michael Hurst as Herc's best buddy, Iolaus. For extra impetus, John also killed off Hercules' family in the story line, leaving the champion free to roam the land righting wrongs.

Then they needed writers. Bob Bielak, hired as a freelancer, wrote scripts for the initial season (and later became a coproducer). John Schulian told Bob to consider how a Western was written—for instance, *Butch Cassidy and the Sundance Kid*—when writing scripts for *Hercules* episodes. The producers wanted contemporary dialogue, yet nothing so hip as "Yo, dude!" That advice really helped Bob and the writers who later came to the project.

One of the show's quirks was its elaborate action scenes, which tempered fast-paced comic-strip violence with a healthy spoonful of humor. "That's one of our main calling cards," John told *SFX*. "*Hercules* is an action show, and we're going to have fights . . . [but] Hercules makes a point of saying he doesn't kill people. They may wind up dead when they're fighting him, but it's usually because they're being hoisted on their own petard."

That was a fine line to walk, and some episodes in the first season crossed it. They were much too dark, too violent, and too unpleasant to view. That was not what *Hercules: The Legendary Journeys* (HTLJ) was about. It was supposed to be about escapist amusement, the kind of stuff John Schulian had watched as a boy.

The show's other trademark was the cutting-edge special effects that created a virtual bestiary of mythological mutants. The visual effects team, a good many of whom were fans of Ray Harryhausen, one of the first special effects technicians, enjoyed dropping an occasional tribute to the master of stop motion, such as a skeleton fight in an Argonauts-reunion episode, "Once a Hero."

Success tends to spawn more success. The Hercules movies had spawned a series. Was that the end of Renaissance's run of luck? Hardly.

THREE MEASLY INSTALLMENTS

ERCULES FADED FROM SIGHT AGAIN UNTIL OCTOBER 17, 1994, when *Hercules and the Amazon Women* repeated, followed by *Hercules and the Lost Kingdom.* Afterward came three new Hercules tele-movies: *Hercules and the Circle of Fire, Hercules and the Underworld,* and *Hercules and the Maze of the Minotaur.*

Then the Hercules company began a weekly series format. Lucy Lawless was cast in a part for two of these early weekly episodes. As the lovely and courageous Lyla—the future consort of Deric, a centaur—she filmed "As Darkness Falls." In "The Outcast," Lucy's Lyla character gives birth to Deric's baby centaur. (Ouch!)

Lucy joked about this role with a *Playboy* reporter who asked her about interspecies mating and what exactly were the duties of a wife whose husband was half-horse. "First," she answered, "you've got to carry around a spade. It's like owning a dog in Los Angeles. You also have to pick stuff out of their feet and keep laying down new straw. When he feels his oats, you sow them, but *neigh* really does mean *nay,* even in ancient times."

For Lucy, these guest roles had no portent except as building blocks of her own acting career. She was busy auditioning and working elsewhere, such as on the short film, *Peach,* which would be re-leased in 1995.

The HTLJ producers wanted to end their own initial season with a bang, however. They came up with a trio of stories that introduced a warrior commander named Zena, a feisty warrior princess who would try to destroy Hercules. Zena would appear in a single episode, then reappear two months later in a dramatic two-parter to climax the *Hercules* season. The role was planned to end with the warrior princess' blazing death—a "big event" finale.

While the producers were still bandying around ideas for this story arc, Dino De Laurentiis advised Rob Tapert to spell the name with an X rather than a Z. Why? Simply because kids would like it better. Later, when Lucy learned of this change in spelling, she saw Dino's reasoning at once. She recalled clearly that as a child she'd thought the letter X was attractive. And unusual. And they were good symbols. On the other hand, what did the letter Z symbolize? Sleep, zzzzz, snoring. Xena spelled with an X, now that had kid allure, and everybody had a kid inside them somewhere.

But at the time, Lucy knew nothing about the Xena role. She'd done her stint as Lyla, and figured that was the end of it. She was much more concerned about her personal life. She'd begun to realize that she and Garth

had married much too young. The union simply wasn't working out as they had planned.

It's hard to believe that Lucy wasn't everyone's first pick for the role of Xena, that it wasn't a case of the studio powers taking a single look at her and saying "She's our Xena!" According to *Whoosh!*, Rob Tapert later told a Burbank fan convention, "She was always *our* [Renaissance Pictures'] top choice. MCA wanted us to cast someone else." It seemed that Lucy had appeared too recently as the centaur's wife. MCA executives feared viewers would be baffled to see her cast as a different character. Instead, they gave their stamp of approval to American actress Vanessa Angel. But after four weeks of training—and just three days before filming was to start—Vanessa fell ill. At that point, Rob and Sam put Lucy's name forward again. Arguments were made in her favor: She had already proved herself too great a talent to be wasted on minor roles; she certainly could be counted on to rise to this occasion.

But the studio still feared it wouldn't work. Rob Tapert told the

Los Angeles Times, "Since she already played two different parts in *Hercules,* the studio wanted another actress." MCA gave the casting directors a list of five American actresses.

> Since [Lucy] already played two different parts in *Hercules,* the studio wanted another actress.

, One after another, the actresses turned it down. Their reasons varied, but Lucy later speculated that they just didn't dare leave America during the January pilot season, not for three measly installments in an unknown series filming at the bottom of the globe. Better to stay in L.A. and score a pilot that would hopefully become a series.

These incredible mistakes in judgment led to Lucy's good fortune, however, because eventually Rob and Sam got their way. They continued to argue for her: She lived in New Zealand, and the studio had liked her previous work. In the end, MCA executives capitulated: All right, she would do.

Later, at a fan convention, Lucy would comment that the five women who had turned down the role of Xena were "probably kicking themselves," and she added with great fervor, "Thank you!"

FAME AND FORTUNE ARE WAITING

With eight years of acting experience behind her, Lucy had decided to take some vacation time over the New Year's weekend—a summertime holiday in New Zealand. "I'd just split up with my husband and was trying to work out how I was going to manage to support my daughter, Daisy, on my own," she told *Sky TV Guide.* While fighting a mild case of the flu, she was trying to give Daisy a camping experience. They were near some podunk town where the local newspaper was shut down for three days for the holiday. The last edition reported only the next three days' horoscopes.

As night gathered in the east, and the first white stars opened above, Lucy and Daisy got a small bright fire going outside their tent. They amused themselves by reading their horoscopes by the firelight. They both laughed over Lucy's forecast in particular. It read something like, "Fame and fortune are waiting for you. Overseas travel. This might be the big one. Expect a call from overseas." Given their rugged circumstances, and the sadness and worry attending the break up of their family, this seemed pretty far-fetched.

But she got a call from overseas that very night. The producers of HTLJ had literally hunted her down in the wilderness. They were in a terrible spot, they told her. They had to begin filming the *Xena* episodes in five days. Could she possibly take the part?

Two days into her "holiday," she clinched the deal. And she never looked back.

She didn't even have to audition, since they had already worked with her, and because time was so short. More important was conceptualizing the Xena character so that she would have the impact needed to climax the HTLJ season.

Dying her hair black was Lucy's suggestion. She told fans on America Online, "They wanted to go blonde, and I said, 'Whoa there, big fella! How 'bout if she was more like an Argentinean or Amazon princess—like the tennis player Gabriela Sabatini—except with brains. Bronzed, with a mane of dark hair.'" The producers agreed. Lucy was relieved, because bleaching her hair blonde would certainly damage it. Besides, she thought it was time that television viewers had an atypical female to look at for once.

Her newly black hair was then altered further, with hair extensions. Lucy hated them. "They're ghastly," she told *TV-Times*. "No one can run their fingers through my hair."

Lucy was fair-skinned, but she pushed for Xena to look bronzed. So the makeup people sponged Xena's tan on her. Lucy soon regretted that particular decision. Though it only took five minutes to apply the tan makeup to her body, it took much longer to get it off. Her bathroom would always be stained with it—and she hated scouring tile grout.

As for Xena's costume, Lucy donned a black and malevolent outfit. It had big claw-sized epaulets and a cape. She thought it very sexy, however, and it was comfortable.

All this revamping of her looks took place in two days. That was all the time they had. Filming was about to start.

Lucy saw this role as her first significant breakthrough as an actress. She felt the character was as strong as any woman had ever been—and could fight as well as any man. Xena was a woman who lived by her wits.

Lucy liked working with Kevin Sorbo. As a person, he was fabulous. As an actor, he was extremely professional. He learned his lines and didn't bump into the furniture. Of course, he looked good too. But Lucy wasn't interested in him in that way. In her opinion, he was a "good guy."

Meanwhile, the first weekly episode of *Hercules: The Legendary Journeys* aired on January 15, 1995. The television series took the U.S. syndicated television market by storm. Kevin almost immediately became a household name—and the figure behind a major merchandising line of action dolls.

The episode in which Lucy played Lyla, the centaur's consort, aired on February 20. But the production crew was well ahead of the viewing audience. They were already filming the first of the three episodes that would close the season. Lucy took to her Xena part so well that the producers reconsidered killing off the evil warrior princess in the final two-parter. Xena would see the error of her ways—and live on.

HER OWN SHOW

Even as they were making those episodes in early 1995, Rob Tapert began to discuss with Lucy the possibility of a series for Xena. Rob, in a live Universal Netforum chat, said, "I was inspired [in creating Xena] by a character in a Hong Kong movie called *Asia the Invincible* and [by] a series of Hong Kong movies called *Swordsmen I, II,* and *III.*"

Lucy at first thought he was joking. She had always hoped something like

I was inspired [in creating Xena] by a character in a Hong Kong movie called *Asia the Invincible* and [by] a series of Hong Kong movies called *Swordsmen I, II,* and *III.*

that would happen, but she hadn't really expected it for another five years at least. Yet it was happening now. As soon as she detected Rob's seriousness, she gave her verbal agreement. She was no fool. This was definitely the career move she needed: her own show.

On March 5, 1995, a hint came, like clear voices calling over silent fields: A reference to an internationally syndicated television series called *Xena: Warrior Princess* emerged in *Daily Variety.* This was no official press announcement, but merely a trailing idea in a paragraph that pondered MCA's consideration of international partnerships. Four days later, a *New York Daily News* gossip section used the phrase, "trying to spin off a new pilot," in reference to *Hercules: The Legendary Journeys.* This was fairly strong proof that a spin-off series was already envisaged in the wake of *Hercules'* wave of popularity.

Eight days after this article, Lucy's first Xena episode was aired. On March 13, the intrepid "Warrior Princess" appeared, proud with the love of Ares, the god of war. Xena was intent on Hercules' destruction. The plot portrayed her as wicked to the core, but the end of the episode clearly inferred that Xena would be back.

John Schulian was happy with that first episode of the trilogy. He had written it, as well as the third one. He thought Kevin Sorbo and Michael Hurst were good, being at odds over Xena, and Lucy made a great femme fatale. The episode was very simple to produce, with no special effects, though there were some wonderful fight sequences. And it was filmed well.

Lucy was thrilled with the overwhelming reaction to the character. "You always aim for excellence," she said in an official fan club interview, "because to aim for anything else is a waste of life, and to be well received is very encouraging." She added, with less seriousness, "It gave me a good buzz."

"The Gauntlet," the second Xena episode, was released on May 1. Sometime in this period, Lucy was officially approached with the offer of the lead in her own spin-off series. She said yes.

On May 5, 1995, the formal announcement was made by MCA: The series called *Xena: Warrior Princess* would begin production of twenty-two episodes. (This was later increased to twenty-four.) They would start filming in the last half of June 1995, and the first episode would air in September. Lucy's Xena would also appear in three Hercules episodes in the 1995 season.

"Unchained Heart" followed on HTLJ a week later, on May 8. Xena stormed the world of syndicated adventure television. Titanic, beautiful, and fierce, Lucy's Xena tries to kill Hercules in a quest for power. But a single act of mercy causes her own army to betray her, and she undergoes a radical conversion. Realizing she's lost sight of her own humanity in her obsession to establish herself as the ultimate warrior, she spurns Ares. As the story arc unfolds, Xena and Hercules became allies, then lovers. In the last episode Xena heads homeward to begin a new life.

John Schulian felt that the third and final episode of the trilogy fell just a little flat somehow. Xena merely rides away. John later wished he had come up with something better.

But Xena was engraved indelibly on the audience as a great character. The warrior princess was so evil and perfidious—and there was an outstanding scene at the end of the second act in which Hercules and Iolaus square off over her.

Lucy's appearance in the trio of episodes aroused such enthusiastic response from viewers that the producers, not surprisingly, knew they had a winner. Also, a rival series just happened to be on its last legs. *Xena* would make the perfect replacement. Everything seemed primed for Lucy to jump into her own show.

A WICKED CHARACTER

It is hard to imagine but fun to speculate about the job qualifications of a warrior princess. Like superheroines before her, she should be strong and fearless. If she's pretty, that's a plus. She must vow to defend the powerless and to battle evil. Superhuman powers are advisable, if not mandatory, and she must have the ability to save whole cultures in a single episode. A real-life Lucy Lawless might just do.

Xena: Warrior Princess, the series, picked up where Lucy's role on *Hercules* left off. But since originally Xena was a wicked character, there had to be some changes. The show's creators had to fashion a person struggling for redemption. Otherwise it might be really hard to get an audience to tune in. With *American Gothic,* Renaissance had tried to win viewers with an antihero main character, but they failed. Viewers naturally gravitate toward hope and want to see real heroism. So Xena had to change.

"Rob and Sam had always wanted to do a female hero and just didn't know where, when, or who," Lucy told New Zealand Radio. She added, grinning like a letter box, "And it was me, and here, and now!"

Xena, though still a dark, mean female character, was determined to atone for the sins of her past. As the series began, she defends a small village from soldiers dispatched by the heartless warlord Draco. There she encounters a spirited young woman, Gabrielle. When Xena leaves, Gabrielle secretly follows Xena, hoping for a more exciting life.

Xena next outwits a blind, man-eating cyclops; then she thwarts an ambush by Draco's men. She finally reaches her own village knowing that Draco plans to destroy it. Her offer of help engenders only hostility and suspicion from everyone, including her own mother, Cyrene, who cannot forgive Xena's dark history.

Ultimately, Xena and Draco meet in a spectacular contest, and she defeats the savage warlord. Though she has rescued the village and reconciled with her mother, she cannot obliterate the misery she has bred over the years. With the feisty and chattering Gabrielle at her heels, she leaves to find her father and re-sume her battle against the pow-ers of evil.

Xena's amaz-ing skills in com-bat are constantly tested as she trav-els the land. To defeat foes, she re-lies on tactics, agility, acrobatics, and martial arts. She wields a variety of weapons, most notably her chakram, a razor-edged discus-like weapon that she can hurl at her enemies with as-tonishing speed. Also in her armory is the "Xena touch," a two-fingered pinch on the neck that can either kill or act as a sort of truth serum. Smart, fearless, and mighty, she always tries to settle things peacefully, but once pledged to a particular course, she is unrelenting.

Lucy began to tire of telling how she won the role of Xena. She tried to understand that a Cinderella-like story always fascinates people, and that it was a logical starting point for inter-views. As with any fairy tale, listeners will not grow weary of hearing it again

> Rob and Sam had always wanted to do a female hero and just didn't know where, when, or who. . . . And it was me, and here, and now!

and again. It had such classic over-tones: someone else's misfortune opening the door of opportunity for the heroine. Lucy knew it was an as-tonishing story, but it began to lose its freshness for her. She had it down pat for interviews—but hated to sound so completely rehearsed. Yet the facts of the story remained, and she could only hope she was making the most of the good fortune that had accidentally— or fatefully—come her way. She be-lieved that if she strived to live her life with awareness, she would recognize the opportunities that had been cre-ated for her and try to make the most of them.

Asked if she thought from the be-ginning that *Xena* would be such a suc-cess, Lucy told *Mr. Showbiz,* "Absolutely!

I always thought the show would be a big hit, and maybe that's because I was totally green!"

But it was a hit. And so was Lucy.

THE ACTRESS BEHIND GABRIELLE

Xena had a spirited young sidekick in the character of Gabrielle, the young bard who recklessly follows the warrior princess in seeking a more exciting life. Reneé O'Connor, the actress behind the character of Gabrielle, first played Deianeira in the "Action Pack" movie *Hercules and the Lost Kingdom*. She quickly discovered that working a weekly *Xena* series demanded a lot from everyone. She had underestimated the number of setups they must try to accomplish every day for a regular series, much less the physical action that accompanied it. All this hard work took time to get used to.

Reneé was born February 15, 1971, in Houston, and was raised in Katy, a town just west of Houston. She decided that she wanted to be a performer at a very early age. By begging her mother, Sandra Wilson, she was allowed to join Katy's Theater on Wheels. "The rehearsals were in a nearby church, so I felt safe to let Reneé participate," Sandra Wilson told *Whoosh!*

Reneé's earliest stage role came when she was eight. She played a caterpillar, and she even made her own costume. Her role earned rave reviews from Sandra. "The moment I saw Reneé up there doing the best darn caterpillar in the world, I knew. Okay, this is it. This is really what Reneé wants to do."

Reneé believed that her dream of becoming an actress could be realized, but it would require persistence and determination. And she would need instruction. Putting that philosophy to work, she started, at age twelve, traveling to Houston to take acting instruction at the Alley Theater. At sixteen, she tried out for Houston's High School of the Performing and Visual Arts. She completed her sophomore and junior years there. Then she made her professional acting debut in 1989, starring in "Teen Angel," a serial featured on Walt Disney's Mickey Mouse Club.

Next, she starred in "Match Point," another serial for the popular Disney children's programming. That same year, she moved to Los Angeles and landed a role in the episode of TV's *Tales from the Crypt* that marked Arnold Schwarzenegger's directing debut.

Reneé then portrayed Cheryl Ladd's daughter in Danielle Steel's *Changes,* and starred as one of a group of students suddenly endangered in the NBC telemovie *The Flood.*

Before *Xena,* Reneé's most recent theatrical film role was that of Julia Wilkes in Disney's *The Adventures of Huck Finn,* starring Elijah Wood. She also guest-starred as the daughter of a slain couple in an *NYPD Blue* episode.

Reneé had come to Rob Tapert and Sam Raimi's attention when an "over-the-top" audition won her the part of the young Deianeira in the two-hour *Hercules and the Lost Kingdom.* They were so swayed by her performance opposite Kevin Sorbo that they hired her for a starring part in *Darkman II: The Return of Durant,* a feature distributed for home video viewing in July of 1995.

After *Hercules and the Lost Kingdom,* Reneé costarred with Ellen Burstyn and Sheryl Lee in the television movie *Follow the River,* portraying a young colonist captured by Shawnee Indians. She also starred opposite James Garner as a self-involved actress in "The Rockford Files: A Blessing in Disguise," which was first broadcast in May 1995.

Reneé auditioned for the role of Gabrielle after playing a somewhat comparable character in the Hercules movie. The part drew her. Gabrielle seemed very young and spirited, although a bit naive. Reneé felt she definitely had that in herself.

SOUTH OF THE EQUATOR

Reneé told *Spur* that on arriving in New Zealand to film *Xena* she "was surprised at how cosmopolitan Auckland is. It's quite a big city, and I was expecting it to be more rural." However, the people were more "British" than she had expected. She might have said more, but she showed more tact than *Hercules* star Kevin Sorbo. When *Total TV* asked him what was the biggest difference between the United States and New Zealand, he laughed, "About twenty years." He said he'd loved the '70s as well as anyone, but he didn't know if he needed to relive them. Reneé must have felt the same way. It was a common reaction of U.S. citizens, because trends in North American took such a long while to drift south of the equator. In fact, Lucy Lawless' speech reflected slang that had been popular in the United States ten or twenty years before.

But "she is fantastic to work with," Reneé told *Spur.* The two actresses hit it off well right from the start, and were destined to become real friends.

According to at least one of the *Xena* directors, Reneé was a professional to the core. She took her job seriously. The *Xena* cast and crew concurred: Her kindness and good-humor made her a favorite around the set.

Chapter Four

A COPPER-ARMORED BUSTIER

CREATING A NEW WEEKLY TELEVISION PROGRAM FEATURING XENA wasn't quite a matter of simply duplicating the best bits of *Hercules: The Legendary Journeys* and adding Lucy Lawless dressed in black leather. Xena was to be a much more complex personality than Hercules, who, according to the premise of HTLJ, must always do good. Doug Lefler, who directed the earliest one-hour episodes of both series, saw Xena as a much more tortured character. Lucy's series would have different tones from Kevin Sorbo's. *Xena* wouldn't be an inferior imitation of *Hercules.*

Rob Tapert told *Black Belt Magazine,* "When we pitched the idea for *Xena,* I made a demo reel of four Hong Kong movies to show the syndicators the kind of action sequences we wanted to do in the show. We also weren't afraid to break the rules of fight realism and go for action that's entertaining and something that the American television audience has never seen before."

Sam Raimi wanted to use a post-feminist heroism, as he had with the strong, silent gunslinger in the 1995 film *The Quick and the Dead* (starring Sharon Stone). That character, along with an evil hell-raiser portrayed by Hong Kong actress Brigitte Lin in *The Bride with White Hair* (1993), heralded Xena.

Clearly, Lucy would be required to do some pretty fancy sword tricks and stunts for her role as a very '90s "ancient" heroine. The swords on the set weren't really made of metal, but they could still be dangerous. When an actor got hit by one with enough energy, especially if it was unexpected, it could do considerable damage. Lucy needed to learn how to handle these props. And she needed to learn how to handle her body. Though she had practiced yoga for some time, she was not trained in martial arts, sword play, or stunt work. Because the intention was to create a semicomic action show that mixed ancient mythology with Hong Kong–style fight scenes, the decision was made to have Lucy study under Douglas Wong, a Kung Fu master in Los Angeles.

Lucy did have experience with animals, having ridden horses as a youngster. Though she denied vigorously that she had any natural aptitude for physical challenges, her role as Xena would demand significant physical skill.

While visiting the United States during the summer of 1995, she prepared with Douglas Wong, who had trained Jason Scott Lee for *Dragon: The Bruce Lee Story.* Doug taught her basic Asian martial arts moves and the techniques of fighting with swords and staffs. Later, she worked one-on-one with a trainer in Auckland.

The role didn't really require her to become an expert martial artist, but she practiced as much as she could. Her best training would come when she was actually putting her lessons to use on the set.

One part of her role as Xena came relatively easily. She had a natural flair for languages and accents. She spoke English, German, French, and some Italian, and had occasionally worked on U.S. coproductions that had required a Midwestern American accent. That wasn't easy for most New Zealanders. In comparison, it was much easier to pick up a Southern drawl or a New York accent.

Infused with the same action and production values—and the same humor—that had made *Hercules* a breakout hit, *Xena: Warrior Princess* combined mythology with martial arts action, movie-screen special effects, and that sensational New Zealand scenery.

Though she had helped develop Xena's look, Lucy had no direct input into the writers' development of her character. "I don't even read a script until four days before we begin to shoot," she told fans on America

Online. But the interpretation of the scripts were her responsibility, with some help from the directors. "There are a million ways to spin a line, and you have to make the strongest choice."

Lucy felt Xena was a very sympathetic hero. She knew the darker side of human nature since she had to contend with it in herself constantly. In fact, Lucy felt she could have been Xena if she'd had different parents.

Xena's trademark *yi-yi-yi* battle cry was all Lucy Lawless right from the start. Lucy felt it was a really good sound—though she made sure not to shout it in small rooms. The executive producers had wanted an Arabic warble, in which the tongue moves from side to side, then up. That was something Lucy couldn't master. Her own *yi-yi-yi* came easily, and she could sing it out loudly and for as long as needed, with no harm to her throat.

Some viewers hated it at first, but as Tarzan had needed his yodel and his vine-swinging, Lucy felt that Xena needed her battle cry and gymnastic flips. She could certainly have moved across the set by running, but

the genre in which they were working called out for a more dramatic approach.

A MINIMALIST MARVEL OF STRUCTURAL ENGINEERING

The producers decided that the outfit Lucy had worn on the *Hercules* episodes was too menacing for a heroine with her own show. They changed it to a tanned leather bustier and short skirt. The look was more audience friendly. Lucy preferred the original, which was sexier—and far more comfortable. The new outfit had a longer bodice, which made her feel as if her entire abdomen was in a cincher.

Once she donned the Xena trademark costume, however, there would be no reprieve from wearing it. Superheroes do not make fashion changes. Xena would have only one costume. Forever. And the producers decided that costume would be a minimalist marvel of structural engineering.

Lucy soon became accustomed to her outfit, though, on some days, it was the last thing she wanted to see. It was

> **"** I don't even read a script until four days before we begin to shoot. . . . There are a million ways to spin a line, and you have to make the strongest choice. **"**

uncomfortable—and cold. Although the North Island of New Zealand was subtropical, the winters were bloody miserable for someone stuck with wearing nothing more than a corset and a whip. It was no fun to walk around frostbitten in that mini outfit. On the worst winter days, it nearly sapped Lucy of her enthusiasm. The metal breastplate shaped the leather so that there were air spaces between the bodice and her "bod," and on some days the wind entered there and whistled all the way around her back.

But when the cameras rolled, she forgot the costume. She forgot the chill. She didn't feel the rain. She didn't even feel pain. Lucy entered her role so completely that she sometimes didn't even feel it when she got hurt. Those were the moments she lived for, when she *became* Xena, and was actually in the scene she was acting, unaware of any other life, or of the cameras rolling. It was what made acting so fulfilling.

As an actress, Lucy was inspired by Susan Sarandon, Helen Mirren, and Robert De Niro. Also, Bill Davis, *The X-Files'* Cigarette-Smoking Man, had inspired her profoundly when she'd studied drama under him in Vancouver. As in her teen years, all of her heroes were real people.

Though thrilled at this chance to do her own series, she had second thoughts when she began filming the second episode, "Chariots of War." The story required her to drive a chariot on a beach in the wind in the middle of New Zealand's winter—one of the harshest winters Lucy could recall. In fact, it was sleeting. Lucy's leather costume was soon soaked with freezing rain. Between takes, she cowered down in her chariot and repeated to herself, "This too shall pass, this too shall pass." And this was only her second episode! Series or not, stardom or not, it was among the most dismal days of her life.

Unfortunately, it was the first of many experiences of filming on cold days. Since the television audiences in the Northern Hemisphere expected September premieres, much of the series would have to be filmed during New Zealand's June-through-August winter months. But Lucy would never get used to working in her skimpy costume in the cold. It was the thing she most disliked about her work.

Once the production company had the first three installments of *Xena* in the cans, Rob Tapert ran a rough cut of them for the powers-that-be at Hollywood's Universal Studios. The powers said yes.

Lucy was delighted, naturally, but in the midst of her newfound success she suffered a personal defeat. Soon after she launched into work on the series, her seven-year marriage to Garth

Lawless ended. The reasons given were sadly commonplace: The two had married when they were both too young. As a consequence, Lucy had to find herself a new place to live. Wisely, she kept her groovy married name. With typical humor, she told *Playboy,* "I did toy with Rita Reckless for a time, but that's not as good as Lucy Lawless."

But humor aside, she had to act heroically in her own life now. Her work was demanding of her time and energy, and the split in her personal life demanded so much emotion that she felt at times as if she were forfeiting her relationship with her daughter. Also, things were being said about her that she couldn't rebut. She felt she was being persecuted, and that she couldn't defend herself. She feared that Daisy believed her mother just didn't care. Moments came when Lucy had to struggle against every instinct to strike back at what felt like personal assaults. The period served to deepen her understanding of Xena, whose goal was to simply get through each day without killing someone.

Though Lucy and Garth had separated before Lucy was offered the part of Xena, the two incidents became confused in Daisy's mind. Consequently, the child developed a real loathing for the show and her mother's success. Little Daisy wanted it all to simply go away.

A COMPLETELY EMPTY HOUSE

According to the arrangements worked out by Garth and Lucy, Daisy would live with her father and visit her mother on weekends. That decision came hard for Lucy, but during the week, she was simply too busy working and training. Daisy needed a more available parent. It would be best if she resided with her father.

So Lucy lived alone in her newer, bigger, four-bedroom home in Mount Albert. The new house had one big advantage: Its location made for an easy drive to work. But there were more than miles to consider. There was also the transition from the hours spent completely surrounded by her work "family" to entering a completely empty house, from being the star whose every need was served to having

to open a can of beans for herself or go hungry. "I'm in the curious position of finding myself a slight misfit outside," she told *Cult Times*. "When you have people to tie your shoes—literally—if you are not careful you forget your place in the world as a human being."

Another problem she had was with the role itself. At a glance, *Xena* had an aura of lowbrow embarrassment, featuring a buxom woman in a short leather skirt, fantasy plots of mythical dragons, and campy dialogue. Added to that was its place in the network's programming, usually alongside *Baywatch*. Shoehorned into her leather outfit and thigh-high boots, Lucy sometimes "felt like I'd become some kind of Anti-Barbie," she admitted to *TV-Times*. It was all so improbable: A leggy woman whose claim to fame was her prowess with an array of weapons. Was it a bit too cheesy for a modern, mature woman who was also a mother?

Those were the thoughts that occupied her when she left the world outside the door of her home. There, she met herself unadorned.

She lived casually. "Generally I kinda slop about in shorts," she told

KTLA's Morning Show. She didn't get phone calls about work, but "my parents do," she told WGN Radio. "People ring from New York saying, 'We really need to get a hold of Lucy, some important business from the States.' And my dad's just going, 'What the hell are you talking about?'"

Her life as a superhero/mom was a constant challenge. She wouldn't mind if her daughter grew up deciding she wanted nothing to do with acting. "But I'm afraid there's a lot of me in her," Lucy told *People* with a laugh.

In her spare hours at home, Lucy read books by Mary Karr, Scott Peck, Frederick Forsythe, Pam Houston, and John Ralston Saul. While reading, she might drink a glass of New Zealand Chardonnay or Sauvignon Blanc. Often there was some jazz music playing in the background.

Despite the fact that she had studied it for several years, opera was not her favorite music. No, Lucy loved jazz. Her favorite performers were Fats Waller, Nina Simone, Lyle Lovett, and k. d. lang.

Sometime during this period, Lucy met Vanessa Angel by accident. The actress, who dropped out of the Xena role before Lucy was asked to take it up, did not know who Lucy was at the time. And to Lucy's later shame, she behaved badly.

Vanessa was working on the Universal lot in Hollywood, acting in the *Weird Science* series. Lucy saw her, and leapt off a Universal tram to ask ingeniously if she could have a photograph taken with her. Vanessa agreed, with genuine friendliness. So Lucy got her photo, in which she was posed beside her rival with a definitely superior expression on her face. Vanessa was simply being very generous to a stranger, not realizing she was being made the butt of a private jest.

JUST WHAT TV FANS CRAVED

Xena: Warrior Princess debuted the week of September 4, 1995, with the episode titled "Sins of the Past." MCA Television distributed it internationally in syndication. In that first episode, Xena saves Gabrielle from a wicked warlord and gains herself a loyal sidekick.

Twenty years after Lynda Carter's Wonder Woman lassoed her last villain in the late '70s, it seemed Lucy Lawless was just what television fans craved: another raven-haired beauty of Amazonian proportions. The tall, leggy Kiwi was bound to be popular as a superheroine. Followers of *Hercules* who watched this spin-off were surprised that it was actually less silly than its parent program. Although *Xena* had its own brand of humor, Xena herself was immediately confirmed to be a more soulful, enigmatic character than Kevin Sorbo's droll, meat-and-potatoes hero. Rob Tapert deliberately gave Xena this more adult perspective. Hercules was decent—that was pretty basic and obvious. Xena, on the other hand, was a character who had something to say, yet she couldn't quite say it. That conception of her would deepen before it would be resolved.

Xena's weekly adventures unfolded with the help of an exciting mix of human action and cutting-edge special effects. State-of-the-art graphic-imaging techniques, including three-dimensional animation and digital composition, were combined with complex makeup and prosthetic effects to create a terrifying assortment of mythic gods,

fiends, and monsters. The production was further enhanced by elaborate and exceptionally imaginative sets and costumes that reproduced style elements from a broad range of historical periods and places. (As Lucy told David Letterman, "We have absolutely no respect for chronology.") The fresh, exotic, and spectacular scenery of New Zealand provided a backdrop of beauty for this imaginative blend of culture-spanning fantasy and reality.

In the "Xenaverse," Xena righteously battles barbaric tribes, slave traders, and the Earth's dregs in her mission to free the oppressed from injustice and cruelty. Jumping on and off horses, crawling through mud, and routing warlords would have most women limping to the doctor's office, but for Lucy, such grueling deeds of physical prowess were just another day's work. And she does it all in a copper-armored bustier and leather miniskirt.

Some of those early episodes indeed worked well, and the series was off to an excellent start. The richness of Lucy's character was based on that wonderful struggle she fought with her inner monster. When observers remarked that *Xena* didn't serve up as many monsters as *Hercules,* producer R. J.

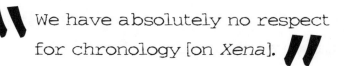

" We have absolutely no respect for chronology [on *Xena*]. **"**

Stewart answered that they served up a monster every week—the one inside Xena, the one she fought to suppress.

According to producer Steve Sears, Hercules was such a noble character that he was difficult to write. Xena had flaws—she had a very dark background. Light or fun plots did not easily suit Xena, but her strong character took the writers in a distinct direction.

Lucy became aware that the show was breeding a cult following fairly quickly. Indeed, almost from the beginning the show garnered good press. That success gratified the crew, who seldom experienced the excitement that Lucy encountered more directly.

She had to brace herself against earthquaking fame almost as soon as *Xena* hit American airwaves. But that was not the case in New Zealand. There, she felt barely a vibration underfoot. She might be celebrated else-

where in the world, but she continued to enjoy virtual anonymity in her own backyard because, *Xena* wasn't broadcast in New Zealand.

NO ATHLETE

On the set, the cast and crew continued to fly by the seat of their pants. The episodes they made were going to air as soon as they were post-produced, which meant within just a few weeks of when Lucy first read the scripts.

Despite the rush, Lucy portrayed the inner turmoil of her character admirably. Xena's conflict was evident in her eyes, in her face, in her mannerisms, in her very carriage. Lucy pulled emotions and conflicts from her own life experiences and applied them to her character. And she did it so well that many observers felt no other actress could have played the role as well.

> ❝ I don't want to give away too many secrets and say that really you could be a foot away [from the end of a swinging fist] and nobody would know. ❞

Lucy continued to maintain that she was no athlete. In fact, she considered herself physically uncoordinated. Nonetheless, she did the majority of Xena's stunts, putting aside her dislike and fear. Thankfully, not all of them were as dangerous as they looked on television. "I don't want to give away too many secrets and say that really you could be a foot away [from the end of a swinging fist] and nobody would know," she told WGN Radio. On the other hand, "I can do some pretty good stunts," she told *TV Hits.*

And sometimes she got knocked silly. It was an occupational hazard of her job. She got smacked, she got bruised, she got knocked down. Once she got hit hard enough to blacken her eye. That particular blow loosened every one of her teeth. As everyone gathered around to ask if she was all right, her words were slow, her reassurances furry. She called the experience "interesting." It happened during a stunt fight. She was tired, and she simply "collected one." Lucy flicked her head to miss the blow and came back to see the stuntman's fist traveling right for her face. The two connected solidly.

Once she recovered her wits, Lucy felt sorry for the guy, who was overcome with remorse. "Stunties," as she called them, did not like hurting people.

The makeup department took a prosaic view: They took Polaroid pictures of Lucy's colorful eye in case they needed to replicate a real shiner in the future.

Though it must have hurt, Lucy never complained. Perhaps she considered herself luckier that Kevin Sorbo, who once got a mean gash on the head with a metal sword. He needed ten stitches. "It was a really nasty hit, actually," Lucy told WGN Radio, "and the next week I [hit] him myself, and I just felt terrible."

The man responsible for cooking up these stunts—which usually did not go so wrong—was stunt coordinator Peter Bell, known for his work on the films *Savage Island, Mutiny on the Bounty,* and *Willow.* Although Lucy was not a serious martial artist, most of the stunt team were ardent boxers and martial artists—and they had to be good fall guys, too. In order for a fight to work, the stuntmen and women had to "sell" the hits. If viewers cringed after a fist collided with a cheekbone (or seemed to), then that was a good stunt. And flying through the air and somersaults made the skirmishes far more visual.

A GRUELING EXERCISE REGIME

Lucy learned to enjoy the show's fights. "Usually I get more enjoyment out of doing dialogue, but when I see the results of the fights on the screen, it's just so rewarding," she told *Black Belt Magazine.*

She admitted that the physical requirements of her role were exacting. It was incredibly hard work. It was a challenge to keep a balance between being rested enough to give a good dramatic performance yet remaining flexible enough for the fights and jumps. In fact, Lucy had embarked on a grueling exercise regime in a bid to turn her body into that of a warrior. She felt she didn't really look the part of Xena. She wasn't muscled enough. So for the next eight months, after her fourteen-hour workday on the set, she worked out privately for two more hours. Lucy did weight lifting, boxing, and took kung fu classes. She felt herself overcoming her ungainliness through the martial arts instruction, even after practicing only a few months. But this regime would nearly kill her before she finally gave it up.

Since Xena was supposedly ultra-strong, when she hit someone, she sent him flying. To accomplish this effect, the crew used either a "jerk harness," a "jerk ram," or an "air ram" to launch the stunt person through the air. The

> **"** It goes against the laws of physics, but nevertheless, we have even known Reneé to have eyebrow whooshes. **"**

air rams could throw a man twelve feet up or thirty feet out. When Xena picked someone up and dangled him by his ankles, or carried him around, they used wire rigs.

As mentioned, fights were filmed with stunt doubles. The first crew shot with the camera on the lead stars. For example, the camera would shoot Lucy from the front while she battled a stunt double with his back to the camera. The second unit then shot the fight from the opposite angle, filming the lead villain's face and Lucy's stunt double's back. Meanwhile, Lucy might be off working on the next episode.

She couldn't do all her own stunts, because many of them were too hazardous, and besides, they just didn't have the time to use her in shots that didn't require her face. So, if those

incredibly blue eyes weren't visible, chances are it was not Lucy. Geraldine Jacobsen filled in for Lucy then. A xendo kai blackbelt, Geraldine grew up in Paeroa, New Zealand. Her work also involved long days, but with lots of waiting time between shots. She liked the job, however, because she got to perform feats that many people would pay to do—such as bungee jumping. Geraldine was barely recognizable as Xena when not in costume. "We actually look nothing alike," she told the *Waikato Times*. "I'm a lot shorter. She's got blue eyes, I've got brown."

Geraldine had become Lucy's proxy after doing a onetime stunt as Xena in a *Hercules* two-hour movie. She was consequently hired to work at the job nine months a year for the *Xena* series.

There were actually two filming units at work at the *Xena* set at all times. Each episode typically took eight days of work by the first unit, which did all the filming of the principle characters. Then the second unit worked for another eight days filming scenes with the principles' doubles. The second unit would also shoot bits of action such as knife thrusts, sword thrusts, and their results, and close-ups of punching fists, kicking feet, and all the other minutiae of detail that added to the show's richness. Grunts and sword clangs were added still later by the sound effects people.

Since the second unit shot scenes in which the principle actors weren't involved, this maximized the efficiency of the first unit, where the main unit director and lead actors were devoting all their energies. And it wasn't uncommon for film editors Robert Field and Jim Prior, who worked at Camp Renaissance in Los Angeles, to call New Zealand with requests for specific "pick up" shots needed to complete a sequence. One example occurred in the filming of "A Fistful of Dinars." In it, Xena jumps across a chasm to rescue Gabrielle on a bridge. Robert Field discovered there was a shot missing between Xena at the bridge and Xena on top of the cliff. To fill in the hole, the second unit filmed a close shot of Lucy's double's feet as she climbed the rope. When inserted, it kept the sequence smooth.

Whoosh! is an Internet publication that took its name from the many scenes in which Reneé O'Connor, among others, turned her head with a whooshing sound. Film editor Robert Field commented, with a perfectly straight expression, "That actually happens. She actually makes that sound." He added, with typical Xena leg-pulling humor, "It is a very strange phenomenon. It goes against the laws of physics, but nevertheless, we have even known Reneé to have eyebrow whooshes." *Whoosh!* could get no serious comment on whose idea the trademark effect was. The editors blamed it on the producers, and the producers blamed it on the editors. It clearly was one of those elements that kept the making of *Xena* fun.

HER HEAD WAS CROOKED ON HER SHOULDERS

Though Lucy had Geraldine to do most of the dangerous stunts for her, she continued to gather war stories to set beside that tale of the black eye. In another episode, she got hit in a way that apparently misaligned the bones of her upper back. Her head was crooked on her shoulders for nine days, and her concentration was shot. Her sinuses felt stuffed, her vision was off. It took her a while to diagnose what was wrong, why she didn't feel up to par, why she had no energy.

But such things were bound to happen again and again. The company had to film extremely fast. There was essentially no time to rehearse, other than between takes. The stunt people were fantastic—and godsends. Lucy likened working with them to waltzing with a dancing partner. As time passed, she began to feel more comfortable with the swords and using Xena's chakram— her razor-edged discus-like weapon.

Stunt coordinator Peter Bell took great care to keep Lucy's fight scenes from cloning Kevin Sorbo's fights on *Hercules.* Their fights were different in their very nature. Lucy's used more martial arts, which meant using more wire rigs so she could run up tree trunks and flip backward, or run along walls sideways. The rigs gave Xena a hangtime that put Michael Jordan to shame.

Peter tried not to put in so many fancy kicks that it didn't look as if Lucy was really doing them. And for many kicks, he had her start them then used a double to complete them.

Peter was aware of Lucy's limitations. But as time went on, she more frequently forgot them herself, and just tapped into her body's instincts and went for it. In one episode's fight, she ran along the side of a wall and surprised herself by doing a fancy leg-pumping, flying kick. Often referred to as the Hong Kong kick, it was invented by filmmaker Ching Siu Tung to use when his hero fought against dozens of opponents. It was perfect for when Xena fought large groups of adversaries simultaneously.

Rob Tapert told *Black Belt Magazine,* "Although we wanted to emulate Hong Kong's style of action in *Hercules,* we quickly found out that we couldn't incorporate a lot of the acrobatics, because we felt it was out of character for Herc." Rob loved the fights he could incorporate in *Xena.*

He also loved the steely resolve Lucy gave her role. Soon, he would love the softer aspects of Lucy Lawless as well.

Chapter Five

A WOMAN OF MANY SKILLS

L UCY BEGAN TO VISIT THE UNITED STATES FAIRLY REGULARLY FOR publicity purposes. Americans couldn't get enough of her. Part of her charm in North America was her New Zealand accent. On her part, she was always amazed to come to the United States and hear people talking as she had heard them do on television. She informed *Playboy* that though Americans and New Zealanders technically spoke the same language, there were some words and phrases that might be innocent up north but were faux pas in Kiwiland. "Fanny pack" was one—New Zealanders called it a "bum bag," because in New Zealand "fanny" refers to the private anatomy "in the front." Also, "knickers"—boys short pants up north—were underpants in New Zealand.

On the other hand, all Lucy's life she had heard people say, "Oh, bugger off," or "bugger me." In New Zealand, no one thought what that really meant. It was just an expression, like "blow me down with a feather." But in America, "bugger" had a different meaning.

"Good on ya" was another expression used a lot in New Zealand. It meant "good for you." One of *Xena*'s producers thought the Kiwis were saying, "Get on ya." It took him a year and a half to figure out his mistake.

On one of her Stateside visits, Lucy saw the ten-inch Xena action doll sold in every Toys "R" Us in the country. Once again, she showed more tact than Kevin Sorbo, model for the Hercules doll, who told *Total TV,* "What's funny about being your own doll is kids get it at nine years old, and three years from now they're going to pour gasoline on you and put a firecracker up your butt—stuff I did with my G.I. Joes."

Actor Kevin Smith explained how the doll model of his character, Ares, was made. He had to sit in a chair while a laser was run around his head, gathering measurements to make a three-dimensional image. Evidently, Lucy must have gone through the same process. This image could be flattened out, like a globe, to make a two-dimensional pattern, quaintly called a "road-kill image." Kevin told *Whoosh!*, "It's a terrible thing to witness."

At that time, Toy Biz, the company that made the official Xena and Hercules dolls, was notoriously slow in making and distributing Xena dolls. They even required stores to take ten Hercules dolls for every two of Xena. The company's reasoning was that action figures were generally for boys. There really hadn't been a successful girl action line. Later, the company realized its error.

With a knowing, humorous look, Lucy told Rosie O'Donnell that the doll had a sort of sexy dominatrix thing going for it. She felt it revealed what viewers wanted from her. Sarah Dyer, editor of *Action Girl* comic magazines and a collector of action dolls, told the *Washington Post* why Xena was such a good female hero. "She's a big girl. She has big legs. She's not all waifish looking. She really appeals to young, post-feminist women and girls. She wears a skirt and she proves you can fight really good in a skirt. She has cool-looking hair, but she kills people."

Great hair and mayhem: the best of both worlds?

Actually, Lucy's hair caused some mayhem all by itself on the Internet. *Whoosh!* offered an entire article titled "Exploring Lucy Lawless Hair Color Myths." It quoted a *Los Angeles Times* reporter who wrote, "They dyed the naturally blond Lawless brunette." An *Entertainment Weekly* article quoted Lucy, "I love being a brunette." But on the *Mike and Matey Show,* she had said, "I used to have fair hair." *USA Today* quoted her as saying she had honey brown hair, "but they dyed it black, rather than make me a blond chickie whose hair would one day fall out."

People called it ash-blond, but honey brown was perhaps the best description of her natural hair color. In the *Rainbow Warrior* and *Peach* movies, made around the same time as *Hercules and the Amazon Women,* Lucy's hair color was a light honey brown. Just in case

> **"** [Xena] is a big girl. She has big legs. She's not all waifish looking. She really appeals to young, post-feminist women and girls. She wears a skirt and she proves you can fight really good in a skirt. She has cool-looking hair, but she kills people. **"**

fans thought the *Whoosh!* article had cleared up the issue forever, however, a later *Tampa Tribune* article reported: "She also dyed her red hair black for the role."

As for trying to look like a dominatrix—or at least like a warrior princess—Lucy continued to spend two hours a day in the gym, after working up to fourteen hours on the set. She looked like a different person, but she felt unhappy about it. Working out had made her obsessed with her body. She knew it wasn't healthy, and in the end her back gave out. "I used to overtrain tremendously to try and make up for a lack of athletic prowess," she told *Cult Times,* "and it just about killed me." Lucy had to stop punishing herself. So, instead of the gym workouts, she started walking and working out lightly with hand weights. She lost some of the muscle she'd built up, but she decided she looked just as good.

After the first flush of her success, Lucy realized she had to maintain a balance. She couldn't let her work take over her life. With a blue flicker of earnestness in her eyes, she told *Cult*

Times, "The best thing I can do to maintain energy and enthusiasm is to try and have a life outside of it."

Besides the brisk sales of Xena action figure dolls, fan clubs for Lucy and Xena sprang up everywhere, such as "the Xenite Club," which offered a membership certificate and a *Xenite Newsletter.* Then there were Xena trading cards. The Internet was a favorite meeting place for avid fans who used intriguing screen names, like "Jetthead."

Just as Lucy was charming Xena's fans in general, and in particular fans in the United States, she was in turn charmed by them. Considering differences of public behavior in the United States and in New Zealand, she told *Playboy,* "People down under don't understand the generosity of the American spirit. In America, if you catch somebody's eyes, you'll say, 'How are ya?' If you do that in New Zealand—and I've seen this time and time again with Americans who come down—people turn away quickly. They're embarrassed. Eye contact with strangers is impolite."

FRANKLY NAIVE

As *Xena* continued to gain an audience, Lucy became aware of one of the main reasons behind that popularity: the need for a strong woman figure among women looking for role models. Coming from a family of strong women, Lucy was frankly naive on that point. Oh, she knew that women were underrepresented in her own industry. There happened to be a lot of women in her crew, but she knew that was unusual. She thought it was only because most women, at some stage of their lives, found the calling to be mothers. Lucy felt that was an honorable choice, and one that might preclude them from following a profession, for a time anyway.

Although she characterized herself as a woman's woman, and loved hanging out with other women, "I didn't know there was such a need for a symbol of strength in women," she told New Zealand Radio. "I guess I have been just going around blinked my whole life."

She couldn't say why there were so few women heroes on television. But now she saw the world had been primed for Xena. It gratified her to find she had inadvertently stepped into a role that so many were ready to embrace. And she felt the public hadn't seen anything yet. She was really proud of some of the work they had done.

Still, she maintained that the show's appeal was simply that it was fun. Anachronistic, action-packed, sexy, cartoonish, multi-referential fun. Bam! Biff! It had traces of *Batman* and *The Adventures of Brisco County, Jr.* It was a style coproducer Sam Raimi had honed with *Evil Dead II.* The show's campiness—the swoosh of Reneé's head, of Xena's sword, the absurdly exaggerated stunts, the broad double entendres—was part of the appeal.

Viewers did appreciate that unique brand of humor. A lot of intelligent people, even professional people, had started watching it with embarrassed pleasure, only to later become devotees. Lucy called it high-common-denominator television. It wasn't all T & A. There was more content than technique, more technique than

sugarcoating. To be an action star had never been her ambition. The show represented what Lucy lived by, in that she wanted to make people *feel,* she wanted to pass vicarious experiences on to them. Even though she believed it was a completely noble thing to be an entertainer, she admitted that sometimes she questioned herself in private, asking, "What am I doing?" After all, she was only making a television show. But didn't everyone who really loved what they were doing sometimes wonder if it was worthy?

A FAMILY PERSON

Lucy certainly spent a huge part of her life working on *Xena.* That those long hours were spent in New Zealand, rather than anywhere else, made them easier for her. She was a family person, and a mother herself. There was occasional talk of moving the production to Hollywood or Vancouver. But that wouldn't fit in with her plans at all. She wanted the show to continue to be filmed in New Zealand—because her daughter, Daisy, was always nearby.

Garth considerately lived close to Lucy, so that she could pop in and say good-night to her daughter whenever possible. It would be too disruptive to Daisy's life to have to move with her mother, and her father was certainly going to stay put in New Zealand.

Lucy hoped she would never have to make Daisy choose who to live with and who to spend vacations with. The situation was as good as a divided family's could be. In fact, it worked very well.

Meanwhile, her series muscled its way into a hit, garnering legions of fans and solid ratings. "We knew we could make a better show than *Baywatch*," Rob Tapert told the *News Times*.

"It just seems to have hit the world at the right time," Lucy said. "The world is ready for a woman hero who is smarter and stronger than she is good-looking." Evidently Lucy didn't realize just how good-looking she was in that costume of leather and metal. In fact, she was beautiful. And she was getting lots of fan mail from some pretty peculiar male viewers. Lucy only slowly began to realize that there were a lot of judges out there who wanted to be

spanked by a warrior princess, and a lot of lawyers who would love to be walked on by Xena in her thigh-high boots.

That costume remained an affliction to her, however. Some mornings Lucy went to her camper on the set, saw that leather thing waiting for her and thought, Oh God, not again! She dreaded days when rain and hail poured down, when she had to work on a cliff side and needed to jump onto her horse while trying to look perfect all at once. But there was no getting away from it.

If the outfit was a bit exploitative for a feminist icon, and a bit breath-choking for a superheroine, well, that was one of *Xena: Warrior Princess*' little jokes. Some of its other jokes were:

Time   The show was placed "somewhere in the golden age of myth." Dialogue, however, foamed with hip double entendres reflective of *Melrose Place*. In the Xenaverse, characters spouted Shakespearean platitudes and Brooklynese wisecracks. Story lines didn't so much careen through eras as they commingled them, inventing a milieu that was at once primeval, medieval, and surfer dude. And somehow, hilariously, it worked.

Closing Credits Viewers who read the small print were likely to discover a guarantee than no centaur (half-horse, half-human) warriors were mistreated or killed during filming.

Sexuality Men loved Xena. So did women. So did lesbian women. Fans and producers alike snickered over Xena's friendship with young, blonde, hero-worshipping Gabrielle.

Continuity An episode could be completely slapstick in the beginning, then turn intense and dramatic with some fantastic moral predicament.

It was those moral quandaries, Lucy believed, that gave her character more gravity than the average superhero. Xena could make mistakes (though she was never made to appear stupid), and that allowed Lucy to relax a bit. She could ignore all those super-protective defenses that other actors liked to keep on their characters.

Consequently, Lucy's Xena showed distinct differences from past superheroines such as Lynda Carter's Wonder Woman. Former female action stories simply inserted a woman into the basic male archetypical narrative. At the same time, television producers made them almost too feminine. Wonder Woman's hair was always perfect—and worse, she looked as if she cared about such things. In contrast, if Xena were to have her clothes yanked off while fighting, she wouldn't shriek and try to cover herself. She'd just keep on fighting, probably with more fierceness and fury than before.

With her severe good looks, Lucy's Xena evoked a long line of pop-cult visages—Barbarella, Vampirella, and '50s pinup queen Betty Page. Lucy made good use of her comedy background, her training in music, plus a self-assuredness that stormed traditionally male strongholds. She told the *Baltimore Sun,* "I hope it does become the next great TV phenomenon. I think it has caught a wave, a need of some kind for a strong female hero."

But again, she quickly added that Xena's greater purpose was to make viewers laugh. "It's mainly a hoot."

A WOMAN KICKING BUTT

People, however, found Xena more than just a hoot; they found her empowering. And Lucy herself was fast becoming a role model.

At first, she rejected the idea—vigorously. It was one thing for Xena to be a role model. Xena was a mosaic of makeup artists, designers, writers, stunt women, and all the rest. Lucy had no problem with such praise as was given in *The Province* by Debbie Cassetta, a budget director of New York's Polytechnic University: "It's nice to see a woman kicking butt for a change. . . . We finally have a hero who doesn't always fall, sprain her ankle, and have to be saved. People underestimate the power this show has to draw older mature women."

"Her power doesn't come from her sexuality," said Jennifer Smith, a sociology graduate student at McMaster University. "It is not that she can seduce men, but that she can out-strat-egy them; that she is a good leader, a great sword person and is inspirational to others."

Lucy told *SFX,* "I don't mind if women think that way about Xena, but Lucy Lawless is a standard human being." To be somebody's ideal felt like too heavy a burden. It intimidated her. It frightened her. She didn't want to get on anybody's soapbox except her own.

By October of 1995, Lucy had begun dating a man she described as wonderful. But she insisted that her top priority was her daughter. She only wished she could spend more time with Daisy.

It was Xena that Lucy spent the most time with, however. Lucy had a notion of just how Xena should be: dark, menacing, riding wild unicorns, doing battle against skilled swordsmen, running against the gods, wading in rat poop . . . hey, wait a minute! Rats hadn't been mentioned in her contract. Yet, there she was, sloshing through a dank, stinking subterranean tunnel in order to assault some wicked king's castle. The ick-factor was high for that episode. "There were so many droppings on the ground," she told *People,* "I was slipping;

and then they dumped all these rats on me that were biting and scratching, getting caught in my hair. It was so vile; I had to get a tetanus shot."

Happily, her superhero health coverage was paid in full. Still, Xena continued to prove a curious job for a working girl/single mother. When it wasn't raining rats on her, some villain waited in ambush. It was the most demanding role for any actress then on television. But Lucy held her ground—and even renewed her childhood taste for "mixing it up" a little.

She particularly liked Xena's comeback, "I have many skills." Some of those skills were acquired, some came naturally. Many characters in *Xena* were parodies of real people the writers and actors had met or known in the past. Every now and then a line would come out of Xena's mouth that Frank Ryan, Lucy's father, recognized well.

 [Xena's] power doesn't come from her sexuality. . . . It is not that she can seduce men, but that she can out-strategy them; that she is a good leader, a great sword person and is inspirational to others.

Lucy didn't see the show as making a political statement. In her mind, it was absolutely not to be taken seriously. Nonetheless, viewers saw what they wanted to see and read what they wanted to read into each story and every character. Lucy admitted that the film crew tried to push the envelope a little, but only because that made life more interesting on the set. Like the episode in which Xena's lover is black.

More and more, people began to speculate on the nature of Xena and Gabrielle's relationship. Could they be lovers? Renaissance hadn't intentionally inserted that element into the series. On the set they laughed about it at first, then began having fun with it. Asked about the relationship, Lucy might answer enigmatically, "Xena is a woman of many skills."

No one wanted to shove it down the audience's throat, however. It could be alienating, and they didn't want to offend any sector of their growing base of fans. But they weren't above punctuating the relationship between Xena and Gabrielle with sly hints that attracted an appreciative gay audience.

"We are always winking at the audience," Lucy told the *Chicago Sun-Times*. "There is really a lot of satire and irony in what we do." No one wanted to make a middle-of-the-road show. No, they were trying to attract the highest common denominator of viewer.

IN THE REALM OF FANTASY

The little joke became an established part of the series. In interviews, Lucy explained the limits: Xena would protect Gabrielle to the end, but Gabrielle could not borrow Xena's cloak. She

could get on Xena's horse, but she couldn't touch the warrior princess' weapons. In particular, Gabrielle had to keep her mitts off the chakram. She might be permitted to rub Xena's shoulders, but she was not allowed to dally with that black fall of hair. She couldn't use Xena's toothbrush, either—that, Lucy joked, was being kept for the fourth season.

Since the series was placed in the realm of fantasy, Renaissance Pictures was allowed a little more liberty with it. Lucy gave credit for most of the show's vision to the producers and writers. She still didn't have a great deal of input.

In the beginning, Reneé found it harder to execute Gabrielle than she'd expected. After the launch of Xena's first season, the character started to change, at least in Reneé's mind. She started to find a sense of identity. Reneé hoped she would grow up quickly, but the writers made certain that Gabrielle grew at a believable pace.

Reneé wasn't concerned about being typecast as Gabrielle: Warrior Bard forever, "because Gabrielle is set in another time," she told *Spur*. "I could

probably do any-
thing contempo-
rary, and that
would be quite
different." But she
intended to film
Xena for as long
as they would
have her.

> **"**We are always winking at the audience. . . . There is really a lot of satire and irony in what we do.**"**

To do that, she had to live in New Zealand. She found the island country a virgin and naturally beautiful place. In fact, she often felt dumbfounded at how gorgeous it was. Yet she felt homesick, too. Kevin Sorbo, a native Minnesotan, explained his feeling of exile to *Total TV.* "I don't know what to call home anymore. I still feel like I'm living out of a suitcase in a way. I miss my friends. I miss the American lifestyle." Reneé was in the same boat. She missed her "mama" and her step-dad, who ran Treadgill's World Head-quarters, a restaurant in Austin, Texas, that called itself "the home of South-ern Comfort food."

When not working on the set, Reneé took up a book or watched a film to keep up with what was going on in the rest of the world. Her favorite movie of the time happened to be *The Piano,* also filmed in New Zealand. Holly Hunter was one of her favorite actresses. Reneé thought *The Piano* was wonderfully symbolic and beautifully filmed. And now she was working with many of the crew members from that production.

When she could, Reneé partici-pated in any sort of charity work that presented itself. She also liked sports—horseback rides, kickboxing, rock climbing. To stay in tip-top physical condition for her role, she got up before sunrise to work out.

The work that she and Lucy were putting into the series paid off. Millions tuned in every week to watch Lucy's swaggering Xena. Lucy quickly became as much a sex symbol as a femi-nist icon. Prison inmates met on the

Internet for *Xena* nights. Even critics as divergent as *Ms.* and *Playboy* magazines sang her praises. Everybody loved Xena. If viewers missed an episode, they could post on Crimson's XWP Trading Web Page and trade for tapes of Lucy, Reneé, home-taped episodes, etc. Those Web fans were about to take the warrior princess to places she never could have gone to alone on television. And to that end, the heroine's corporate owners let a thousand Xena stories bloom online.

The online following provided an example of just how computer technology was altering the manner in which fans and creators influenced each other. There was an intimate alliance between the Net and the Xenaverse. The producers stayed alert to Internet fan reaction to even such arcane issues as Lucy's hair color.

Another syndicated television success, *The X-Files,* exercised strict copyright observances. But Renaissance Pictures did nothing to warn or penalize fans who used their characters in fiction, or even used screen captures of the show on the Web.

"The Renaissance folks are very much aware of the large online community, the numerous Web sites, and the fact that these Web sites have screen captures and use images from the MCA/Universal Xena/Herc Web sites," Michael Martinez told *Salon.* Michael himself maintained the comprehensive Xena Online Resources Web site. Anybody could write a Xena story of their own, in any fashion they saw fit, including an outpouring of Xena/Gabrielle erotica.

LESBIAN FAN FICTION

In the world of pop cultural fan obsessiveness, underground "slash fiction" using previously copyrighted characters was not rare. In the Internet era, however, no underground existed. Every obsessive subcultural faction was easily accessible. But didn't use of copyrighted characters constitute legal infraction? Neither Renaissance nor MCA Universal seemed interested in probing that question. Some authorities claimed that slash stories were forms of cultural criticism and thus fell under the permissible notion of parody. The most controversial stories—the lesbian fan fiction—were plausibly the best protected from potential corporate-sponsored censorship.

Besides the parody defense, in order to repress fan fiction, a corporation had to prove financial harm. The truth was exactly the opposite. As fans saw it, online creativity had helped catapult *Xena: Warrior Princess* to huge popularity. It appeared that MCA/Universal realized the value of a few dedicated Webmasters spending ungodly hours creating Web pages that only helped advertise their series more. Universal monitored the Internet, however, and reserved the right to act against sites and contributors who stepped over the line into bad judgment—though even they admitted that bad judgment was an arbitrary notion.

And there was no doubt that bad taste thrived on the Internet—such as when a photograph of Lucy's head was digitally superimposed on someone else's naked body. Contemporary pop culture was far more accepting of conspicuous lesbianism than of gay male passion, but the lesbian Xena factor that flourished online pressed quite a few taboo buttons.

Still, Universal initiated no legal action. Though they reserved the right to make changes in the future, their official policy seemed to be "don't ask, don't tell."

Chapter Six

SHOCKED TO BE CALLED A FEMINIST

WHEN LUCY WAS FIRST LABELED A FEMINIST, SHE WAS surprised. Women's rights had never been an issue in her life. Women in New Zealand had already enjoyed nearly a century of suffrage: They had been given the vote before women anywhere else in the world. And Lucy's own mother had always been a powerful force in her community.

"I'm not saying that women in New Zealand are treated better than they were anywhere else," she told *Playboy*. "But I am saying that we're pretty strong, because it was a hard land to colonize. We've retained that get-on-with-it attitude."

To her, feminism meant nothing more than the continuing maturation of women, who made up 51 percent of society. She believed that someday women everywhere would be amazed that half of the species had ever been dominated by the other half.

It was Lucy's opinion that if her character were to wed Hercules, Xena would certainly require him to do his share of the household chores. Maybe she would even put him in a French maid's outfit, or make him wear a collar. However, that episode hadn't been written yet.

Actually, Lucy doubted the wisdom of such a match. After all, Hercules was inherently good-natured, and Xena's moods swung violently. It would be a vortex of woe. Lucy foresaw that Xena would whine that he wasn't passionate enough, that he was too nice. No, it would be a match made in Hades.

" I'm not saying that women in New Zealand are treated better than they were anywhere else. . . . But I am saying that we're pretty strong, because it was a hard land to colonize. We've retained that get-on-with-it attitude. **"**

In fact, Lucy saw Xena as a little dysfunctional, a woman with a devil on her shoulder. You had to keep an eye on her, she warned, because you could never know which way she might lunge next.

Lucy's divorce from Garth was settled by December of 1995, and she was falling in love again. The new man in her life made her terrifically happy, but she kept the romance under wraps. Lucy was cagey with the media, as when she answered a question from *TV Hits* with, "No, he's not an actor, no, no, no!"

What did this man have that attracted her? What was the greatest aphrodisiac for her?

He was somebody who was good at his job. Nothing made her angrier than somebody who was incompetent on the set of *Xena.* If he was no good at his job, or didn't like it, then he should do something else. He shouldn't waste her time and money.

Her idea of the perfect man also included a sense of humor, a high degree of intelligence, and a personality that was not needy. She wanted somebody who was unafraid of the world. He wouldn't have to be number one at what he did, but he did have to be courageous enough to get out and try. Lastly, she wanted a man willing to follow his dreams.

In 1996, Lucy's father, Frank Ryan, turned sixty-four. He was by then a councilor for Auckland City. Frank and Julie, who was fifty-nine, still lived in Mount Albert, the Auckland suburb where Lucy grew up. To millions around the world, Lucy might be the sword-swinging, man-bashing Xena, but to her parents she was still the sweet-tempered, trusting little girl they had tenderly raised.

The Ryans had heard that the series had a huge following in America. Julie felt Lucy was handling the fame extraordinarily well. Both parents were delighted with their daughter's success. She had worked so hard, she deserved it. But they hadn't actually seen *Xena: Warrior Princess.* The series still did not air in New Zealand.

In February, New Zealand viewers had a chance to see Lucy on the *Mike and Matey Show,* a light interview show produced in Los Angeles. Lucy felt much more comfortable doing interviews with foreign reporters and on talk shows to be aired overseas than in her homeland. She knew instinctively how the New Zealand publicity game had to be played: by staying low. The acceptable way was to succeed quietly,

and maybe afterward her fellow Kiwis would claim her as one of their own.

If *Xena* should air in her homeland, what would conservative New Zealanders think of it? Would the lesbian double entendres cause an outcry?

Lucy's own positive attitudes about lesbians and bisexuals were shown in her willingness to take her daughter, then seven, to a gay Mardi Gras. And Daisy wasn't the only one to accompany Lucy. Rob Tapert "just happened" to be on hand to escort the ladies. According to *Femme Fatale,* "The American producer was down here and couldn't believe all the women's breasts around. He said, 'This just wouldn't happen in the States!'"

THE REACTION IN NEW ZEALAND

The time came when *Xena: Warrior Princess* was scheduled to debut in New Zealand. Daisy Lawless dreaded it—she didn't even want to watch the premiere. Lucy was puzzled.

On Wednesday, June 19, 1996, just as the new episodes of the first season went into reruns in the United States, the first episode aired in New Zealand on TV3. It had thrilled viewers in the States, but what would be the reaction in New Zealand?

At that time, much of the television programming in New Zealand was still state run. The practice was to broadcast batches of ads during the commercial television hours. But the stations tended not to go to an ad in the spots where the program was edited for a commercial break. New Zealand stations rocketed right on through those provided pauses and instead cut to commercials in the middle of some poor actor's speech. And there was another practice that drove Lucy wild.

According to *Whoosh!* she told Kevin Smith that she hated watching the show at home because, imperceptible to most viewers, the local stations sped up the film a fraction in order to get in even more ads. "I think I sound like a chipmunk on the New Zealand show."

After the first episode aired, Lucy asked Daisy if the kids at school had mentioned it. Daisy said they really liked it "actually." (Daisy was fond of the word "actually.") In fact, they had liked it as much as *Hercules.* Lucy realized that her daughter had feared her friends wouldn't like it. Daisy's relief was palpable.

Julie Ryan gave it her seal of motherly approval as well. She and Frank soon became the biggest fans of the television show. Julie thought Xena was amazing, and a great role for Lucy, because it used all the things she knew, like horse riding and doing tumbles and flips, such as she'd done on her parents' bed as a child. And she got to give the boys as good as she got. Her mother thought it could have been written for Lucy.

"My mother loves it, and [so do] the kids at my daughter's school," Lucy told *Entertainment Tonight,* "so what could be better than that?" Lucy could let out a big sigh of relief.

Until the series' premiere in New Zealand, she had enjoyed complete anonymity, but that was all over now. The series succeeded there, though not as hugely as in the States. Lucy joked that a real advantage of playing an intimidating character was that people just left her alone. But "*I am not intimidating,*" she was quick to tell *Parade.* Nonetheless, she had a certain don't-mess-with-me smile that tended to make even aggressive types back up quickly.

" My mother loves [the show], and [so do] the kids at my daughter's school, so what could be better than that? "

"People are so indiscreet. I go into a restaurant and they all turn around," she would later tell Rosie O'Donnell, "they all look. They think you can't see them." Lucy had a hard time with that kind of attention. For one thing, it was hard to understand what made her so interesting. And the huge numbers of people who watched *Xena* represented an abstraction for Lucy—she just couldn't fathom it.

After the New Zealand debut, a cameraman for *American Journal* found out where Garth Lawless lived and waited for him to get in the car with Daisy, to drive her to school. The cameraman stuck his camera in her face, right into the car window. It frightened her badly.

Garth was also offered money to participate in a tell-all about Lucy. He turned it down. Despite the failure of their marriage, they remained loyal friends.

But these events served as an abrupt awakening for Daisy about what it meant to have a "mummy" who was a star.

For Lucy, the biggest problem was trying to counterbalance her stardom with her responsibility as a mother. And she suffered a lot of guilt over it. It was by far the biggest stumbling block of her newfound success. She was afraid of what Daisy would throw at her when she reached her teenage years. Lucy remembered her own teenage inclination to confront her parents with painful truths. Every child, in passing on to adulthood, needed to air out what they believed their parents had or had not done for them. Lucy could only hope she wouldn't come out too badly in that period of Daisy's life. She was certainly striving to be a competent mother. But now she was learning what all parents must learn: that it wasn't easy.

One day after the series started airing in New Zealand, Lucy was suddenly startled to see a huge photograph of herself, as Xena, plastered on an enormous billboard. Her jaw dropped, literally. She was uncomfortable with it, not only because she felt the photo chosen was very uncomplimentary. This huge billboard was in her hometown, in New Zealand, where people were expected to be modest about themselves and their accomplishments.

In reality, the debut in her home country did not much change her life. She worked from early in the morning to early evening five days a week, and on the weekends she was more interested in being at home with Daisy than out in public. She only got out to take the dog for a walk. Still, now that she was famous, Lucy could no longer do business in downtown Auckland in her Xena regalia. (She claimed that once she'd run to the bank between takes on the set, explaining to curious onlookers that she was dressed in leather because she was an exotic dancer.) Those days were gone for good. Being out in public now led to ogling and intrusions.

At about the same time that Gillian Anderson, the star of another syndicated television cult hit, *The X-Files*, was nearly mauled while visiting Down Under, Lucy Lawless's short film, *Peach*, was showing in New York. *Peach* was one of eight lesbian films from around the world shown in an anthology called "Girlfriends." In it, Lucy appears as a sexy tow-truck driver.

GIRLFRIENDS

By the end of its first year, *Xena: Warrior Princess* had reached as high as eleventh in rankings of syndicated shows, now and then even beating out *Baywatch*. The next season, with twenty-two original episodes, the series would try for the top ten. Success seemed imminent. If Xena could save Titans, couldn't she pummel David Hassel-hoff? *Yi-yi-yi-yi!*

By June of 1996, the show had finally started airing in New Zealand. They were up to episode eight when Lucy made a trip to New York in August. A grinning Lucy raised Xena's sword on the cover of a summer issue of *Ms.* magazine. That was flattering. But in the text of the article, her political correctness was questioned. That was irritating.

Meanwhile, the "Girlfriends" anthology continued to attract attention. Although labeled "lesbian," these films had a broad appeal to women in general. Rarely did they pointedly refer to or feature material that was lesbian or gay, and even those references were often peripheral to the plot.

The final film in the anthology was Christine Parker's *Peach,* which recalled Lee Tamahori's *Once Were Warriors.* It portrayed a young Maori, Sal (Tania Simon), who resides in a tough neighborhood with her jerk of a lover Mog (Joel Tobeck). A grocer gives Sal a fresh peach, which she is resolved to preserve and protect. It comes to symbolize Sal's attitude toward life. An at-

traction of the film, and of the entire program, was the appearance of *Xena* star Lucy Lawless as a tow-truck driver who offers Sal needed advice about the peach, life, and whatnot.

Peach had won prizes at various film festivals and was a little gem, fully deserving of viewing without any gender-specific or lesbian-oriented categorizations.

People Daily reported in June that a spokesman for *Xena*'s distributor, MCA Television, said the company wasn't fazed by Lucy's steamy kiss with actress Tania Simon, but "There won't be a sequel. That I can promise you."

Xena: Warrior Princess was produced by Renaissance Pictures and exclusively distributed by MCA Television, which was a division of MCA Inc., a unit of the Seagram Company, Ltd., the global beverage and entertainment company. In July 1996, Neil Hoffman, of USA Network Programming, revealed that the USA Network had bought the domestic off-syndication rights to *Hercules: The Legendary Journeys* and *Xena: Warrior Princess.* USA had exclusive rights to all episodes, which included seventy-two from *Xena.* In September 1998, USA

Network would begin broadcasting the companion shows as a strip, Monday through Friday. "We're delighted with these terrific additions to our action/adventure programming," said Hoffman in a USA press release, "particularly as they contribute to USA's counter-programming strategies. Both shows draw a strong family audience as well as balanced demographics, and we already know that their repeat performances are outstanding."

Jim McNamara, president of MCA's distribution, felt that USA was the ideal match for the two series. He expected the two to establish themselves as staples of USA's schedule, and to reach the same ratings success they had in their initial syndication.

A BEAUTIFUL VOICE

"These are the best days of my life to date," Lucy told WGN Radio in August 1996. No surprise, considering her soaring stardom.

Appearing on the *Rosie O'Donnell Show,* taped in New York, Lucy was so excited she laughed about the nervous quiver in her voice. Nonetheless, she

revealed to the studio and television audience that she had wanted to be a diva when she was younger. Without prior planning, Lucy sang a cowboy song. Rosie, in turn, talked about her own performance as Rizzo in the revival of *Grease!* She also made a joke that, of course, the producers wouldn't even consider casting Rosie O'Donnell in the lead role. But Lucy and Rosie agreed that Rizzo was really the best part in the play. Rosie told Lucy, "You could do Broadway. You've got a beautiful voice."

Rosie told her that they had gotten more requests to have her on the show than anyone else. "The most," Rosie emphasized. "People have been faxing, they've been calling, they say, 'We want Xena.'"

"It's amazing," Lucy replied. "When you're the object of that kind of attention, it's hard to believe."

Afterward, Lucy meandered to New York's Ritz-Carlton Hotel for a press interview with *Total TV.* She made her way through New York's traffic anonymously. "People don't look twice. They're expecting to see some enormous woman. This muscle-bound, leather-clad wo-man." If Lucy had belted out her *yi-yi-yi,* maybe the crowds would have recognized her.

> **"** It's amazing. When you're the object of that kind of atten-tion, it's hard to believe. **"**

Actually, she was getting recognized more often. Sometimes someone would look at her, then look again. If she were to re-main standing still, she thought they just might recognize her. So she kept moving. Those who recognized her on the first look were by and large ex-tremely nice. They left her alone. Per-haps, she laughed to herself, it was because Xena was so scary.

Lucy confessed she wasn't worried about being typecast as Xena. "I get to do wacky comedy," she told *Total TV.* "I also get to play other characters. No, it's not a huge concern. I'm so stretched. It's the most amazing grounding I could ever have for my career." She explained that when you did something daily, it simply had to improve—unless you were a cretin. The entire cast had come along, had learned a lot through the past season.

The quality of shows in the forth-coming second season would bear that out.

Reporters inevitably found the ac-tress behind Xena very soft-spoken—and that New Zealand accent inevitably charmed. For the *Total TV* interview, she wore a purple sweater and black skirt—nothing remarkable, except for her pale blue eyes, which stood out just about anywhere. The star of television's number one syndi-cated series presented herself as just another single, working mom. In restaurants, Lucy did not bust heads Xena-style if the food didn't come promptly.

But she didn't like being quoted out of context, and was quick to jab back at a recent unflattering *Ms.* article, which had been based on a telephone inter-view. She felt that what she had said "in a certain tone" over the phone had not carried over into print. In fact, she thought *Ms.* had made her sound like an idiot.

The ruckus was centered on her being quoted as saying she was shocked to be called a feminist. Well, she hadn't meant "shocked" as in appalled and disgusted. She'd meant "shocked" as in astounded, because she had never considered *Xena* a political show. The *Ms.* interviewer had also asked Lucy if she was political? What was meant by *political?* Lucy countered that her father was a politician, her mother had been a suffragette. Was the interviewer asking if Lucy voted? Or if she would rather leave politics to others? There were so many ways a question like that could be interpreted, and an answer based on the wrong interpretation could easily seem flippant.

Another reason that the *Ms.* interview went poorly was because Lucy was still so frightened of the whole role model thing. Though she knew that Xena was an imposing character, the heartfelt mail from fans, the Internet discussions, and the *Ms.* cover article

hailing her as a feminist icon amazed her.

Yet, during her visit in New York City, she was meeting many women who seemed incredibly inspired by her show—not inspired to make themselves into replicas of either Xena or Lucy, but to be themselves. "They use the word *empowered*," she told *Total TV.* "It feels kind of new-agey to me. But it's a great word, and it's a perfect expression for what they're feeling. A woman goes out and buys a Harley because she's always wanted to, that's great. As long as she doesn't kill herself."

A CERTAIN RIVALRY

The New York trip made her more comfortable with being a role model. The responsibility didn't feel as weighty to her as it once did. She was glad to play someone who could help others in real life. She felt it was good for little boys to see a strong woman in a leading role, a woman who was multidimensional.

Lucy felt it was probable that Xena would appear in a *Hercules* episode during the up-coming second season. The two characters had an intriguing kind of devotion to each other, along with a certain rivalry. They were at-tracted to one another, but it was a volatile mix. If Xena and Her-cules were ever to fight, who would win? Kevin Sorbo had been known to say that Lucy herself—not Xena—could "whip his butt."

> **"** They use the word *empowered.* . . . It feels kind of new-agey to me. But it's a great word, and it's a perfect expression for what they're feeling. A woman goes out and buys a Harley be-cause she's always wanted to, that's great. As long as she doesn't kill herself. **"**

Was Daisy enjoying Lucy's rise to stardom? Not surprising, she had mixed feelings. Tabloid types had followed her. *People* magazine asked Lucy if young Daisy was awed when she saw Mom wearing all that armor? "Yeah, I think she is, but she's too cool to show it." While the little girl was proud of Lucy, and liked Xena, her joy was moderated by the menace of photographers invad-ing her privacy. And she grew irritated by the kids who always asked her, "Is your mum Xena? Is your mum Xena?" Even worse was the next question: "Is your dad Hercules?" Part of Daisy was quite proud—up to a point. After that, she didn't want any part of it.

Daisy, like most children, kept Lucy's feet on the pavement. She was not above telling her famous mother that she didn't know up from down. Lucy saw the humor in that, and felt it kept her sane. Lucy also felt fortunate that her daughter didn't want a performer's life. She was not the attention-grabbing kid Lucy had been.

After the New York trip, Lucy had no other upcoming projects. So she made plans to vacation in Turkey. The past year had been a huge push for her. Now was her chance to take time off and kick back.

She had mentioned to *Total TV* that she was going to be yachting off the coast of Turkey (the place to go at that time) with her mysterious and so far unrevealed male companion. That relationship was deepening in secret.

When shopping ashore during her well-earned vacation, Lucy searched for unique musical instruments for composer Joe LoDuca to use on the show's music. Lucy believed Joe was a true genius.

Despite the fact that Lucy's horoscope had predicted that she would get the call to be Xena, she was loath to believe any New Age mumbo jumbo. She did not regularly "consult the stars," and unless her gaze lighted on it when she looked for the comics section, consulting her daily horoscope wouldn't occur to her. Coincidences continued

to happen, however. While in Turkey, she and her companion were told that her guide's wife's cousin had an exceptional fortune-telling talent. She "read" coffee grounds.

Turkish coffee is not filtered. The thick brew is drunk from small cups in which there is always a residue of sludge in the bottom. The young fortune-teller told Lucy to put her saucer on top of her finished cup and flip both over. After it cooled, the girl lifted the cup off the saucer. The more suction, the more potent the information, and Lucy's cup would hardly part with its saucer. Reading the grounds, the girl said Lucy would achieve many things, and make a lot of money. She also warned of people dying and things Lucy had no desire to believe—like something about a man with a big chin or long face who would come into Lucy's life bringing pain.

AN ELECTRIFYING NEW BATCH OF EPISODES

On the set that autumn, Lucy had the same problem she would have every time she took a vacation from the show: She slipped back into her natural New Zealand accent and had to re-learn her "American."

Although *Xena: Warrior Princess* was a success right from the start, its producers and leading actress continued to tinker with their formula. It constantly evolved. They twisted a line here or a plot there. The writers also felt freer to experiment as time progressed. They didn't aim for political correctness. Just when the audience got comfortable, they liked to turn things around.

As the second season got well underway, Xena's producers promised an electrifying batch of new episodes, including the return of Xena's rival Callisto and an episode featuring Poseidon.

R. J. Stewart told *Whoosh!*, "You know, all of the writers here are able to be as ambitious as we are because we have those three great actresses—Hudson [Leick], Lucy, and Reneé. We are really very, very fortunate to have them."

"We had an episode dealing with an evil Bacchus and the Bacchae too," said Steve Sears in an *SFX* interview. "And also a huge episode coming up which

Rob Tapert directed. It's going to deal with what made Xena who she is."

As if keeping two series going wasn't enough, the producers also had a one-off young Hercules feature in the works, and a video animated adventure. Bullfinch would have been proud. Rob Tapert was a little disgruntled about the coming Disney Hercules animated feature film. He felt it was a shame that Universal had a four-year lead on the release of the Disney movie and wasn't able to do something more with it, particularly in merchandising.

The episode Reneé O'Connor most liked came in the second season. In "A Day in the Life," she got to interact with Lucy throughout the entire episode. There were very few other characters, which kept the plot concentrated on their relationship.

Lesbian fans particularly liked that episode, too. After making it, *Whoosh!* reported that Lucy—with a megawatt smile—told a fan, "You're gonna love what's coming up. I just spent the past week filming in a hot tub with Reneé, playing 'Where's the soap?'"

But at least one of the writers was not happy with that episode. "He felt

Xena's character ballooned over what it should be—it became too large, too broad," said film editor Robert Field to *Whoosh!* Robert's personal feeling, however, stated with a laugh, was that Xena could be whatever Xena wanted to be. "Obviously, this is a choice of the producers and the writers and how Ms. Lawless interprets her character for that episode."

Those able to attend conventions where Robert appeared could enjoy a reel of outtakes from "A Day in the Life," featuring every shot of Reneé being whacked in the head by the fish thrown at her by Lucy.

WHEN SHE PUT ON THE COSTUME

Lucy thought at the beginning of the second season that she would like to see the warrior princess get a little harder. She worried that the sharp edges of the character were perhaps getting a little dulled. But Xena seemed to evolve with a life of her own.

Yet Xena was a product of Lucy, and the character was connected to her own

history. In that respect, the Xena that viewers saw on screen *was* Lucy Lawless. But how much of Xena was Lucy? What personal character traits extended into her portrayal? People rarely saw the side of Xena in Lucy when they first encountered the actress. But Xena was there. The summoning of the Xena aspects of her personality happened partly when she put on the costume. When Lucy shot the episode in which Xena goes undercover at a beauty contest, quite a different sort of Xena came out of her, one who looked gorgeous and dainty. It made her realize how much the "clothes maketh the man"—or woman.

She continued to dislike Xena's costume, however, especially on days when the wind licked her bare skin like a wet tongue. She wished the warrior princess could wear caftans—but you can't karate-kick in a caftan.

And besides, Xena was fairly ignorant of feminine fashion. When a woman character in the episode "A Day in the Life" has difficulty because her man is in love with the warrior princess, Xena gives the woman some tips. According to that counsel, she next appears in a Xena-esque dominatrix outfit.

As the days rolled toward the new year, Lucy told *SFX,* "I don't look like Xena when you meet me. She's a bronzed, leather-clad beauty, and I'm pale, and not that large." But interviewers found Lucy much saucier than her stern, spoilsport television character. For instance, when *TV Guide*'s David Rensin asked her what modern comfort Xena would kill to have, Lucy came back immediately: tampons!

She argued that Xena could be fun, too. In the episode in which the warrior princess enters a beauty pageant—

> **"** I don't look like Xena when you meet me. She's a bronzed, leather-clad beauty, and I'm pale, and not that large. **"**

undercover, of course—viewers behold a dumb blonde Xena, a Xena who pivots on her toes, flicks her hips, and even gives viewers a look right up her skirts. That last incident was in reality an accident, but viewing the film later, Lucy saw that the angle was good, so she didn't mind.

With the first half of the second season in the cans, Lucy felt she could promise fans some interesting new episodes.

Chapter Seven

GOOD CHILDBEARING HIPS

LUCY WAS TAKEN ABACK TO LEARN ABOUT THE *XENA* GROUP-viewing nights in various prisons. Although she and the rest of the cast and crew hoped to win over every possible constituency, they never hustled any particular section of audience. They simply wanted to make something they might want to watch themselves. They did like to shock—mildly—but they were careful not to alienate. *Xena: Warrior Princess* was simply trying to entertain, not change the world. It delighted them to twist things just when the audience was feeling comfortable. They wanted to jar people. For instance, the first couple of episodes of the second season had gentle, emotional heartrending stories; then they shot a fast-paced, almost MTV-video girlie-vampires Halloween episode, with Gabrielle biting Xena's neck. They used half-speed close-up shots—and they chuckled as they did it.

Meanwhile, Lucy was proving herself a versatile actress. Within the space of the series' first two seasons, she had played four characters besides Xena: Diana the Princess, Meg the Tramp, Callisto, and Xena's distant offspring, Melanie Pappas. She gave each role a distinctive slant and focus. The most difficult character to portray was, naturally, Callisto, who had been so well interpreted by Hudson Leick.

"She's a beautiful person, and a joy to work with," R. J. Stewart said of Hudson in *Whoosh!* Heidi Hudson Leick (pronounced "Like") was born in Cincinnati, Ohio, in 1969. She grew up in Rochester, New York. While still a teenager, she worked as a model in Rochester and Tokyo before attending a New York City acting school. She later

> " The first time I saw her was when she auditioned for us. And she was good . . . when Hudson came in, sat down, and started reading, there was no doubt. "

graduated from the prestigious Neighborhood Playhouse. At the age of twenty, Hudson started acting at the Community Theater in Rochester. She lived briefly in Vancouver, Canada, during the filming of the television show *University Hospital*. She lived in Los Angeles, where, prior to playing Callisto, she had been enjoying a rich and varied acting career.

"The first time I saw her was when she auditioned for us. And she was good," recalled R. J. Stewart. Renaissance casting director Beth Hymsen brought in about ten actresses for that part. "Eight of them could have done it," R. J. said, "but you know, when Hudson came in, sat down, and started reading, there was no doubt."

Rob Tapert agreed. He said, "That's her." He also sang Hudson's praises on a Universal Netforum chat. "The character of Callisto, played by Hudson Leick, brought a villain to life greater than anything we ever imagined."

Some actors on the series garnered more criticism than acclaim. Ted Raimi, who played Joxer, was one. It made Lucy's hackles rise. She felt that such criticism was an affront to a wonderful actor. The show needed him for comic relief. Certainly, Xena could not fill that capacity. Nor could Gabrielle. They weren't allowed to appear silly. Joxer was intended as a pleasant vent, and Lucy didn't like the hatefulness toward him that circulated on the Web. She would even go so far as to bring up the matter at a later fan convention, where she asked the crowd to be more welcoming of Ted, who really added to the show.

That was her maternal impulse at work. There was no doubt she liked

Ted, but many fans truly felt that his recurring character, his big witless face crimped into a self-satisfied grin, detracted from the show. He appeared too frequently, they complained. And there was a certain cloud of nepotism hanging over him. It was no coincidence that his last name was the same as executive producer Sam Raimi's. According to a casual survey taken by *Whoosh!,* Joxer was one of the aspects of the show that heterosexual women most disliked.

Theodore Raimi was born and raised in Detroit, Michigan. He started entertaining others as a deejay in high school, and started his acting career with industrial films in Detroit. His unique ability landed him roles as both good guys and villains. He had guest roles on *Baywatch, Twin Peaks, Alf, Alien Nation,* and *American Gothic.* In *seaQuest,* which ran from 1993 to 1995, Ted played a bashful but smart and capable officer named Lt. Timothy O'Neill. He was also known as a stand-up comedian. In *Xena,* Ted's Joxer was a total incompetent with a heart of gold. Joxer drives Xena crazy, yet she tolerates his foolishness.

Ted wrote screenplays when not acting. He coauthored a script for *seaQuest,* but had not written for *Xena* yet.

TOO EXTREME

One of Lucy's favorite episodes of the first season was "Doctor in the House," a blend of *ER* and *M*A*S*H,* filmed in a temple. It called for five fervent days of shooting—what Lucy would call the most intense five days of her entire life. The episode had to be edited, however. The advertisers were scared by all the blood. Even Universal felt it was too extreme, and would later bury the episode amid summer repeats. Lucy was heartbroken. Many of the excised bits were things they had worked hard to shoot. "There was a lot of heart put into the episode."

When she saw the final dub, however, along with the background music, she realized that composer Joe LoDuca had successfully pulled it together. She told *Total TV,* "He really made up for it, because the music just subconsciously really works on an audience. And it gets such poignancy and urgency. I feel like he saved it."

Joe was the composer for both *Xena* and *Hercules.* Sam Raimi and Rob Tapert both believed that a film world without music could not seem real. Joe's music, like the great god Prometheus, breathed a living spirit into the celluloid characters the producers were trying to portray.

By the age of thirteen, Joe was warming up Bob Seger and Ted Nugent in smoke-filled Detroit clubs, and sneaking into Jeff Beck concerts. He got his formal training in jazz and classical music at the University of Michigan and in the Big Apple. Later, he performed for Montreux Jazz Festival audiences. He submerged all his senses in jazz and ethnic harmonies. When asked to play with violinist Jean Luc Ponty, Joe declined. He preferred composing, which gave him more freedom.

One day, Sam Raimi and Rob Tapert suggested that he would be great at scoring films. Not too many years later, not only had he racked up an awe-inspiring list of film and television credits, he was named Horror Film Composer of the Year. He'd collected nine Emmys as well. Obviously, Sam and Rob had been right.

Writing music for television is not something mere mortals should attempt. Incidental music and themes must work with specific images and enhance a preplanned mood. The music couldn't create a mood of its own, as music usually did. But Joseph LoDuca was good at both kinds of composing.

Lucy also admired Bruce Campbell, who played the recurring role of Autolycus, the King of Thieves. Bruce had played the hero in Sam and Rob's *Evil Dead* films. He relished the chance to ham it up with both Hercules and Xena. And he was one of the most popular guests on both series. In his first appearance on *Xena,* in "A Royal Couple of Thieves," he is enlisted by the warrior princess to help steal back a valuable coffer.

Steve Sears wrote that all-out farce, jumping at the chance to write for Bruce's character. Steve wanted to do a comedy episode, so he put Xena in an absurd situation in which she is subjugated by the conceited Autolycus. The beginning of the episode is quite funny: As Autolycus runs up stairs, Xena pulls the rug out from under him. He falls, and says, "This is not good!"

"That was an interesting episode," Rob Tapert, the boss of bosses around Renaissance Productions, told *SFX.* Fans were frustrated because Xena couldn't get back at Autolycus. "They didn't like seeing their hero put as the second fiddle, to constantly be hit upon sexually and not be able to strike back. But our intent was to do a farcical comedy."

While Autolycus fans talked about a possible spin-off, Rob said the chances of that happening were pretty slim. Bruce was pursuing his career elsewhere, recently appearing in the movie *Escape from L.A.,* starring Kurt Russell.

MORE OF THE ANTIHERO

With the first half of the second season completed, Lucy had already identified her favorite episodes, like the one in which Xena and Gabrielle dress as Bacchae. "It's quite an exciting Halloween episode," she told *SFX,* "and in the best tradition of vampire movies, it has that very sexual energy."

She also liked the story in which she played three roles, "Warrior . . . Princess . . . Tramp." "I play this raunchy bar hag who's got a real thing for Joxer, Ted Raimi's character. He and I were just firing off one another."

Lucy still wanted to see Xena a bit grimmer, that is, to display more of the antihero—stern as rock, gnawed by nameless things. Lucy thought a schism between Xena and Gabrielle would help. She wasn't worried about losing fan approval with such a move. She'd found that even when Xena was bad, people loved her.

Episodes aired in New Zealand during September 1996. It wasn't as popular there as in the United States and Europe. As for Lucy, she spent part of that month doing promotion work in the United States. Earlier in the year, *News Times* reporter Dennis Anderson referred to Xena as "a kind of she-hunky leather queen who sails through the air like Bruce Lee and could be a dream date—as long as you surrender the car keys." But Xena and Lucy were not the same person. Another reporter for the same publication, Christy Slewinski, wrote that as Lucy strolled through the door to meet her, light as swan's down, Christy couldn't help but

> **"** [Xena is] a kind of she-hunky leather queen who sails through the air like Bruce Lee and could be a dream date—as long as you surrender the car keys. **"**

look to see if Xena had, by some mistake, been left behind in the lobby. Yes, Lucy was nearly as tall as Xena, but having substituted her trademark leather for an ultra-delicate lavender lace shirt and black miniskirt, her graceful presence put even the most favored catwalk striders to shame.

At that time, *Xena* frequently appeared in the top spot in the weekly syndicated drama ratings, sharing the position with *Hercules* and *Star Trek: Deep Space Nine.* Lucy maintained that she was being constantly stretched in her role, "because the writers go, 'Wow, if she can do this, then let's try this.'"

Lucy also did an *Entertainment Tonight* segment while in the States that Sep-tember. Again she was shown a Xena action figure. The doll wore a little bikini, which Lucy said was good because the weather in New Zealand was a bit nippy just then. "It is winter down under in New Zealand, but that isn't enough to stop Xena. Xena rides in chariots in 2 degree weather, and gets very wet in hardly any clothes, but she does it for you."

Xena's second season opened in the United States on October 1. During yet another visit to the States in October, Lucy regretted that there were no Xena Halloween costumes available.

THE HORSE MISSED ITS FOOTING

Lucy's life in leather included facing hordes of enemies and getting plenty of bruises (and the occasional black eye) on the set. A television bloopers show ran a behind-the-scenes segment showing Lucy/Xena falling off her horse. Lucy couldn't remember falling off any horse, so the shot probably was of her stunt double.

But a fall was in the cards—or in the Turkish coffee grounds. It came while she was "horsing around" for Jay Leno's *Tonight Show*. The statuesque actress, then twenty-eight, was taping a comedy sketch in which she was to ride through the show's Los Angeles parking lot to the theater door. All at once, the horse missed its footing on the painted concrete and fell.

The horse came out fine. Lucy didn't. It was the most painful and terrifying experience of her life. The ambulance, the hospital—it was all like a bad dream. Her pelvis was broken in four places. Would she walk again? Would she have a limp for the rest of her life?

She told *Playboy* that as she lay in the hospital, she was reminded of her trip to Turkey. "My traveling companion came to see me . . . and said, 'How about that fortune-teller?' I said, 'Well, she talked a lot of crap, didn't she?' He said, 'But remember how she said

there would be a man with a big or a long face and that pain would be involved?'" Lucy immediately envisioned Jay Leno's face, and cried out, "Oh my God!"

She would later claim that she never doubted she would get up and walk again—and do it as she always had. Yet she must have been worried. Perhaps that was why she made herself stand up just eight days after the accident.

Thousands of "get well" cards flooded the Renaissance studios, flowers from admirers filled her hospital room, and bulletins about her recovery were followed breathlessly by worried fans. Seldom did even major American television stars get this kind of attention, this kind of outpouring of concern. It just went to prove again that everyone was nuts about this Kiwi.

After the accident, *Xena* producer R. J. Stewart told *Whoosh!* "I was devastated for Lucy, because I love her. She is a wonderful human being, and to see her in the hospital in pain like that really sent me for a loop."

Rob Tapert was, of course, the unnamed "traveling companion" at

Lucy's bedside. Despite the fact that he was so close to her, he stayed very levelheaded. Tempering his concern was the fact that he had a filming company looking to him for leadership. And he supplied superb guidance for the cast and crew during the first twenty-four hours after Lucy's injury.

XENA WOULD BE DEAD

The key question was how to stay in production. A script, "Ten Little Warlords," coincidentally tied into an existing episode in which Xena and Callisto switched bodies ("Intimate Stranger"). The proposal was made to leave Xena in Callisto's body.

This decision came within twenty-four hours after the accident. Then others in charge scanned their memories for further episodes they could use to make up for Lucy's absence. They had one, "Destiny," in which Xena dies at the end. In the first version, Xena was brought back to life by the woman M'Lila. They scrubbed that ending, and extended the story line. They would do something along the lines of the Steve Martin and Lily Tomlin movie, *All of*

Me, in which the two characters share the same body. Xena would be dead, they would place a "to be continued" at the end of the episode, and proceed with the *All of Me* plot.

No episodes were refilmed entirely. They simply re-opened the endings. R. J. Stewart credits the postproduction people—Bernie Joyce and her crew—for skillfully reworking episodes that had already been completed.

To follow "Destiny," the producers wrote and filmed the episode titled "The Quest," in which Xena shares Autolycus' body. Chris Manheim, Steve Sears, and R. J. Stewart banged out the first draft. They had to work quickly. R. J. thought they'd come up with an amusing episode, but he was disturbed as well. They had made a comedy of Xena being dead. Chris and R. J. had to rush off to other things, so Steve was left to refine the script. His task, which he did brilliantly, was to furnish it with tenderness and grief. They really dodged a lot of bullets, thanks to Steve.

All of this troubleshooting would have been for nothing and the future of the series would certainly have been in doubt without Reneé O'Connor to carry the episodes during Lucy's absence. In R. J. Stewart's mind, as he told *Whoosh!,* "She is gold."

Another episode was quickly written—a farcical plot titled "For Him the Bell Tolls." It too was fashioned to bridge Lucy's absence. In it, Aphrodite turns the doltish Joxer into a dashing hero who steals a princess's heart away from her betrothed. For once, Joxer had all the women falling for him. It gave Ted Raimi a chance to show his abilities, and helped improve his standing with *Xena* fans.

Rob Tapert had nothing but praise for everyone connected with the series. They really pulled together during this difficult time. "They shined like the golden scribes they are," he said of his writers on a live Universal Netforum chat.

Hudson Leick's career got an unexpected boost from Lucy's injury as well. While episodes were being juggled and rewritten, Hudson was flown down to New Zealand to do another episode in which she played Xena's character in Callisto's body. As a result, Callisto—and Hudson—began to draw their own fan following.

Lucy usually relied on Steve Sears, *Xena* writer and supervising producer, to post her letters to fans on the Netforum. Known online as "Tyldus," Steve was a self-proclaimed computer geek. But Lucy, recovering in her hospital bed, grew sick of being sick and completely bored. So she went online herself. She entered a cyberspace "chat room" where Hercules and Xena were being discussed. She typed in some smart-ass comment that Xena was not real, as opposed to Hercules, who was really cool and very real. One of her fellow chatters, a woman who called herself "Ephany," got very snotty and "froze" Lucy out of the chat. Lucy thought it all very funny. And the laughter helped her mood. The very next day, she received a "get well" card in the hospital from Ephany.

She would later meet "Ephany" The woman made the excuse that she was just a "newbie," Net slang for "inexperienced." But Lucy blamed herself . . . well, not really. "It was stupid of me to dis on Xena on a Xena channel," she was quoted in *Whoosh!,* "and anyway, it was Rob's idea to say that."

Lucy was released from her Southern California hospital on Wednesday, October 18, after four agonizing weeks of recuperation. News releases said she would resume work on the series when production started up again toward the end of the year.

Back home in Auckland, her doctors assured her that her health and her recovery were certain. In fact, they were astounded at her rapid improvement. But she would need time to convalesce. She told her fans on the Universal Netforum that she was "crashing about the house with my zimmer frame, taking plaster off the scotia!" (Translation: She was crashing about with her metal walker, taking the plaster off the wainscoting.) It would take Lucy a long time to learn to walk properly again. But she had good bone structure—good childbearing hips, as she called them. And hadn't she always drunk plenty of milk as a child?

In the meantime, she realized she actually had a unique occasion to rebuild her body. Because she had been almost totally immobile for weeks, all her muscles had atrophied to some de-gree. She decided to rebuild them in a smart way. She had no delusions of becoming physically perfect, but she could always use a more functional form.

As her recovery progressed, she went from using a walker to using crutches. "I can walk without crutches, but the specialist doesn't want me to go without them completely yet," she told the *Denver Post* by phone. "It's a box of birds, as we say down here." (Translation: "It's a day at the beach," but delivered with heavy irony.) "I can take the car to shop and muck around a bit, but I can't walk even half a kilometer."

She agreed with her doctors that she should heal in the optimum amount of time. Mending the bones wasn't much of a worry, but damage to the soft tissue was cause for great concern. Lucy took every precaution for a complete recovery.

RECOVERING

Xena had aired from September through October in New Zealand, but then was dropped. It would return several months later. That was standard practice for New Zealand television. They would often show a network series for two or three months, then put something else on, then bring the first show back. Because they didn't have many channels, this was a form of channel surfing.

> **"** I've really learned about the indomitable human spirit. Happiness is a choice. You grieve, you stomp your feet, you pick yourself up, and choose to be happy. **"**

While continuing to mend, Lucy told the *Denver Post,* "I've really learned about the indomitable human spirit. Happiness is a choice. You grieve, you stomp your feet, you pick yourself up, and choose to be happy."

Resting at home, she read *The Liars Club,* by Mary Carr, and listened to Nina Simone. Though injured, she more or less lived a normal life with her daughter, Daisy. In fact, the time spent recovering brought her closer to Daisy simply because they had more time together. And Lucy treasured that opportunity. If Daisy really did believe her mother didn't care about her, Lucy now had a chance to prove her wrong.

She claimed that when she was in New Zealand she lived as a simple working woman. She didn't attend openings. Lucy didn't want what she called "schlebrity"—as opposed to fame. (The first was hollow, the other was hard-won.) Celebrity and fame were both hers for the time being, however, while her focus of attention was physical therapy. Lucy was a cooperative patient. After all, she wanted to be a happy, agile old lady one day.

She put herself on a serious exercise regimen for three hours everyday to recover her "grit." Mostly she worked out in her pool, wearing a flotation belt so she could have full range of movement. Rather than weights, she employed polystyrene dumbbells made for water exercises. They floated, and she had to push them down against the resistance of the water. It gave her a good workout.

Lucy planned to return to the set the week of November 20. Although she had built up a high tolerance to pain, and felt she now could suffer all sorts of torture without complaining, for the time being she would only do light duty—like playing dead. In the episodes planned around her injury, Xena's voice or spirit was present, but Lucy did not often have to appear on camera.

Daisy began to visit the set on Fridays. She handed out "biscuits" (cookies) to the crew. And Lucy began to understand the empowering theme of Xena, particularly for juvenile viewers. Xena was a different sort of hero. The show's fastest-growing audience was made up of women, in part because everyone who worked on *Xena* strongly opposed brutality against women, and would never allow the program to descend into degrading sexual violence.

It was undeniable, the show had caught a wave. The recent premiere of *Xena* in France had earned a fifty-share viewer rating, meaning half of the sets in use were tuned in to the warrior princess.

Despite her injury, Lucy flew north again in November, to appear once more on the *Tonight Show.* No horse was present this time. Instead, she was carried onto Jay Leno's stage by two musclemen in loincloths. Although she looked great for her big post-accident appearance, she later told *USA Weekend* that she was in pain during the filming. "I had to lie down afterwards."

Jay had been extremely nice to her, however, and his staff had been "bloody fantastic" about handling the medical insurance and such.

As she told Jay, some good things had happened as a result of her accident. She'd discovered that every cloud really did have a silver lining. She felt she'd managed to get her life sorted out in many ways, and she was much more content as a result. In fact, she felt the accident had been meant to happen.

Chapter Eight

RECUPERATING

JUST IN TIME FOR THE CHRISTMAS HOLIDAYS, LUCY'S OWN composition, "Burial," was released on a CD soundtrack of the *Xena* series. Most of the music on the CD was composed by Joseph Lo-Duca, but the cover of the jewel box featured a photo-embellished painting of Lucy, Xena's sword held firmly in her right hand, her left hand raised palm outward. Inside, a pullout booklet had more pictures of Lucy in Xena's clothing.

In the *Lucy Lawless Fan Club Newsletter* of December 1996, Lucy sent her devotees some Christmas advice: "Be good to the Earth and to one another, laugh a lot and always, always . . . wear a seat belt."

It was a serene and rather motherly message from someone who didn't always feel that serene. The trappings of fame had taken Lucy by surprise—"completely, and it's only been a year and a half," she told *Cult Times.* She couldn't imagine what it was like for children who acted in the soap operas. Were they screwed up for life? "I'm not out in the real world, not at all. I don't go to the supermarket anymore; somebody does it for me. I employ somebody to do my real-life stuff. I do not know, I'm ashamed to say, how much a pint of milk costs."

Lucy "appeared" in cyberspace on December 6. America Online hosted a live cyber chat "attended" by 1,166 participants. AOL Live was the largest gathering place on the computer service, bringing celebrity guests right onto home computer screens. Participants keyed in questions that were presented to Lucy, who responded online.

She started off by calling herself a computer retard. She wasn't afraid to push buttons, but she didn't have the time to become computer literate. Besides, as she had admitted to her official fan club, she was a bit shy about what people might be saying about her out in cyberspace. She had friends who kept her posted, and messages often did get through to her.

Lucy did the AOL question-and-answer session while lying on her bed in her New Zealand home. She had a glass of New Zealand's excellent Sauvignon Blanc in her hand. Bright sun fell in shafts from the windows. They were having a very hot, dry December down under. Unlike in the Northern Hemisphere, there was no Christmas snow.

She told fans who asked about her musical ambitions that she had no current plans to perform as a singer. She hinted there had been some recent feelers sent her way, and even though the notion intrigued her, she was working such an intense schedule that she really couldn't consider such an option at the moment.

When AOL fans asked her about her singing voice, she said she really would like someday to sing the "The Stars and Stripes" at a Detroit Red Wings' hockey match. That would give her enormous pleasure. It would be a real highlight in her career—that is, if she did it well, if she didn't botch it. (Only a few months later she would get just that chance, and she would botch it—in a way she could never have foreseen.)

A question was put to her: "How does it feel being able to beat up guys?" She answered, "It's make-believe, nitwit!" and added the :) symbols—a grin in computerese. "I personally do not derive any great joy from violence inflicted upon other human beings. . . ." Which proved that her 1995 comment to *Entertainment Weekly*—"I've hit plenty of people on the set, and it's great because stuntmen don't cry"—was completely tongue-in-cheek.

Lucy did keep a sword in the trunk of her Alfa Romeo. The sword, which was made of rubber-encased metal and quite weighty, was used to practice her sword-fighting techniques. But there was no violence in her. That didn't mean, however, that she wasn't above kidding about it in various ways. She told a *Mr. Showbiz* reporter, "I don't know what I would do if I was faced with violence . . . I would probably go into automatic Xena mode!" And on the *Regis and Kathie Lee Show,* she said, "I've always thought it's a very courageous or a very stupid man that takes me on." She joked with *Playboy* that she kept some breakaway Grecian urns in her house, for smashing people over the head.

NOT THE TYPE OF PERSON TO LET HER HEART BLEED

Lucy hadn't considered doing any writing for the series. She told fans on AOL that she didn't have the desire. Since she wanted to be a fine actress one day, she was content to work toward that end. She didn't see herself as a writer or director, at least not in the foreseeable future. And if she did, *Xena: Warrior Princess* would not be her medium anyway.

She also told her fans that she wasn't the type of person to let her heart bleed over her work. She felt she just had to do what she was capable of,

using all the integrity she could muster, and then present it to the world.

Another online fan asked: Was a Xena movie in the works? Lucy replied that she labored so hard on the television show that she needed her break time to recharge. If she worked on other projects during her break from *Xena,* she would not be rested enough to give the series her all. She admitted that she would probably make a lot of money by working on a movie, but she preferred to support the series. Also, she had her child to consider, as well as parents and siblings, and they were more significant to her than money. They deserved any spare time she had. If she were to work year round just to get rich, she might lose her family and loved ones in the meantime, and she would certainly regret that long after her career was over. Work came *second* in her priorities.

Fans learned that Lucy had come to like doing her own stunts as Xena. Her body actually enjoyed the challenge. She got a "high" from the physical exploits required of her, partly out of pride that her hard work and long

> **"** I will not have anybody invade the four walls of my home. Not phone calls, not faxes, not e-mail. Anybody who is not invited is not welcome. But, I have to say that people are pretty bloody wonderful. I don't get too much unwarranted attention. **"**

training had been successful. Yet she promised her AOL fans that she would never make a Xena workout video.

And for now, while still recovering from her injury, her life was shifted down into low gear, giving her time to put it in some order and simply appreciate her growing mobility. Without a doubt, the kind wishes of thousands of fans had helped cheer her.

For a long time, she reported, Daisy had hated having Lucy come to her school. The little girl hadn't liked the way the kids flocked around Lucy and yelled. She hadn't liked the way they would "bug" her about her mother all day long, either. As time passed, however, things got better. Lucy was one day graciously invited to the school concert. She knew then that her daughter had become more comfortable with her fame. In fact, Daisy showed signs of being proud of her mum, rather than embarrassed.

There were some aspects of her fame that Lucy could live without, she told the AOL crowd—like having her privacy invaded. She had been forced to develop ways to disregard what she didn't enjoy, but there was one thing she would not tolerate: "I will not have anybody invade the four walls of my home. Not phone calls, not faxes, not e-mail. Anybody who is not invited is not welcome." To soften this, she added, "But, I have to say that people are pretty bloody wonderful. I don't get too much unwarranted attention."

Another topic that came up during the AOL exchange concerned how Lucy's native New Zealand retained the codes of behavior and mannerisms of its colonial mother, England. Whereas the United States had made a clean break with England, New Zealand had not. Even the table manners of Americans were quite unlike those of New Zealanders. Lucy believed that the leaders of the American Revolution wanted to thumb their noses at the English, and so had changed many of their habits purposely. New Zealanders remained more reserved. However, Lucy enjoyed the bigheartedness of Americans, and felt she had enjoyed more hospitality in America than in any other country—and that was saying a lot, considering how extensively she'd traveled.

Asked what she would choose if she could have a single superpower, her answer was always the same: None! She believed people were made as they were for some purpose, and to have more than what she was given would defeat her function. She couldn't identify that purpose, yet she trusted in it. Once, while imagining what it would be like to be immortal (because of a script she was working on), she shuddered at the idea. It would be a nightmare, seeing all your friends grow old and pass away. Such thoughts tempered any wish for supernatural powers.

IN HER ABSENCE

Lucy's stunt double, Geraldine Jacobsen, had a lot of extra work while Lucy continued to convalesce from her broken bones. It would be two months before the lead actress reappeared on the set of *Xena*. In her absence, writers rescripted a whole batch of installments that had Lucy in the prime role. They also refilmed the end of the "Intimate Stranger" episode in which Xena and Callisto switch bodies. At the end of the original episode, the two women switched back, and all was fine (except for Callisto, who was later sucked into the bowels of Hell). They did a quick refilming and a bit of a reshuffle so Xena would remain in Callisto.

Kevin Smith told *Whoosh!*, "It is amazing when the two women play

> **"** It was Lucy Lawless who hooked me on the show, from the first moment I saw her," a fan reported to *Whoosh!* "And Lucy alone, with her portrayal of Xena's complex moral dilemmas, is enough to keep me watching. **"**

each other. It is funny watching Hudson doing Lucy doing Xena, and then Lucy doing Hudson doing Callisto. It is extraordinary." The way they moved their arms, walked, made gestures, spoke—the two actresses had studied each other very well.

Hudson had a wicked sense of humor. At a convention, *Whoosh!* reported that she complained because she'd never got to kiss Lucy, as Gabrielle had. "I tried to lick her once, but she leaned away."

As Lucy's absence continued, worry fused like an overcast of clouds among the series' fans. They were concerned that she might be leaving the show permanently. "It was Lucy Lawless who hooked me on the show, from the first moment I saw her," a fan reported to *Whoosh!* "And Lucy alone, with her portrayal of Xena's complex moral dilemmas, is enough to keep me watching." Without Lucy's presence, would the series founder?

Her popularity certainly wasn't foundering. She received 1,054,780 votes in *People* Online's admittedly highly unscientific year-end poll for the Most Intriguing Celebrity of 1996. She came in second, and Reneé O'Connor came in third. (For those who are interested, the Least Intriguing Celebrity category was headed by O. J. Simpson, Barney, and Madonna.) Web fans also made Lucy a finalist for the *People* Icon of the Year Award.

Lucy's fans complained of multiple voting in the *People* poll. They suspected that enthusiastic fans of the winner, Adrian Paul, star of *The Highlander,* may have stuffed the ballot boxes. Tom Simpson, who maintained a comprehensive Web page for *Xena: Warrior Princess,* said, "We did all our voting by hand." The poll was taken quite seriously by Xena's faithful followers. "There are some really devoted fans," Simpson said, "men, women, and a very large lesbian following."

The cast and crew of *Xena* often talked about the divergency of their audience. They were well aware that different sectors of the audience perceived the show differently. Surprisingly, Renaissance Pictures and the producers weren't afraid of the homosexual element. And Lucy frankly saw the relationship between Xena and Gabrielle as a love between two people. What they did privately was none of the rest of the world's business.

The producers promised an episode that would chronicle the daily lives of the Warrior Princess and her side-kick—what happens between the fights. Lucy looked forward to it.

FANS POOLED THEIR MONEY

As December 1996 edged closer to January 1997, a message to the Chakram mailing list on the Internet mentioned that it was possible to buy stars (the actual astral kind) and have them named for their "owners." Fans pooled their money to purchase stars for Lucy and Reneé, the "stars" of *Xena: Warrior Princess.*

The chief architect of this "Stars for Stars" project, Laurie Blankenship, arranged the purchase and made sure that Lucy and Reneé each received a twelve-by-sixteen-inch document naming their stars, along with sky and constellation charts, and an astronomy book. Lucy's parchment redesignated Cassiopeia RA 1h 33m 1sd 62' 24' as "Lucy Lawless." Unfortunately, that particular star has a magnitude of only 11.4, which means that one needs a very strong telescope to see it.

The company that recorded such purchases was the International Star

> **❝** I have been in a relationship for just over a year, and am terrifically happy. We do not live together because of the long working days on the series—in fact, we're a hemisphere apart. He likes to come down and visit me every month, but we'll see how that works out. **❞**

Registry. Their directory of stars was derived from the standard astronomical catalog. The two stars named after Lucy and Reneé were duly registered with the U.S. Copyright Office and the information was stored in a vault in Switzerland. The new names thus recorded, however, were not recognized by astronomers.

About this time, in an interview for *Cleo Magazine,* the divorced Lucy talked a little about the new man in her life. "I have been in a relationship for just over a year, and am terrifically happy. We do not live together because of the long working days on the series—in fact, we're a hemisphere apart. He likes to come down and visit me every month, but we'll see how that works out."

She still refused to tell who he was, or go into details, except to say he was an American, and the finest man she'd ever met. She considered herself a very lucky person. Despite her reticence, though, fans had guessed who her secret lover was: none other than Rob Tapert.

The Dallas StellarCon, a small convention focusing on science fiction programs such as *Star Trek* and *Babylon 5,* rallied on December 27 through 29. It had the distinction of being the first convention to host a *Xena: Warrior Princess* cast member. Walking through the dealer's room, fans fingered the wares offered at various booths, such as Xena T-shirts and Xena novels (published by Boulevard Press). Three of the popular Xena books were written by Ru Emerson and one was by Stella Howard.

Thanks to efforts by a group of fans, Robert Trebor, who plays Salmoneus, made an appearance at the event. Before *Xena* and *Hercules,* Robert was best known for his abrasive role in the movie *Talk Radio.* According to attendee Cynthia Ward Cooper and reported in *Xena Media Review,* No. 21, "He looked just as I'd expected—a regular guy, slightly apprehensive at the prospect of being quizzed by people . . . but determined to enjoy it." Asked what his relationship with Lucy was like, Robert said he and Lucy had a fun, flirtatious friendship.

While still recuperating from her fall, Lucy was interviewed by *Playboy* magazine. The reporter discovered that though she had an American accent on the show, in person she spoke flawless New Zealand English. She met him at her door in a wheelchair, and welcomed him cheerfully. She took him

into her kitchen, and asked him to get her a rolling office chair. After switching seats, she prepared him a delicious brunch of garlic and tomatoes on toasted shepherds' bread.

SKIN SELLS, BABY

When she was well enough to travel back to the United States, Lucy appeared on the *Late Show with David Letterman* and joked that her friends and family in New Zealand had hardly noticed her big success. "I hint, but nobody is really interested."

David evidently wasn't "hip" to how popular the tall Kiwi actress was. He had to ask her who Xena was. Lucy's answer was succinct: "Xena is a bad-ass, kick-ass, pre-Mycenaean girl who traverses the time lines."

With the smile that had launched a thousand Web sites, Lucy demonstrated the "Xena pinch" on David. The audience cheered, and David finally seemed to understand that Lucy, like her television alter ego, was not a woman to be trifled with.

She also got in an appearance on the *Regis and Kathie Lee Show* during her trip north. Commenting on her costume, she told her hosts, "Skin sells, baby, skin sells." She said she wasn't allowed to tell people her real height anymore, but then whispered, "Five-ten and a half."

Lucy also appeared at the first *Hercules/Xena* convention, held in Burbank, California, on January 12 and 13, 1997. The gathering drew thousands of guests each of its two days, but only the Xena day sold out—and still hundreds of people waited outside. They came from all over the country: Seattle, Boston, Miami, North Carolina, Indiana. They spent between $50 and $900 to attend. Most of them arrived in medieval costume, hoping to win a contest. Unofficial estimates claimed that between 50 and 80 percent of the attendees were lesbian.

Chapter Nine

LEFT DUMB, SPEECHLESS, AND LIMP

WOMEN, BOTH LESBIAN AND STRAIGHT, STATED THAT THE primary appeal of the show for them was Lucy Lawless herself. Both as a professional actress playing Xena and just as a person, she struck very deep emotional chords in her fans. The chance to see her in person was the nearly unanimous reason for attending the Xena convention in Burbank.

There were other reasons, however. If it hadn't been evident before, it certainly was now. *Xena: Warrior Princess* was a favorite television show of lesbians. They loved the relationship between Xena and Gabrielle.

One lesbian told *Whoosh!,* "I love Lucy's ability to speak to my heart with her eyes and her body language. She crosses the line between male and female character traits while never losing her feminine appeal." A heterosexual woman said, "She personifies everything that a woman could be, and I find it rather gratifying to watch her in action." Fans spoke of her amazing charisma in her role, of how her expressions and acting range captured the duality of Xena.

Lucy would later tell the San Francisco *Bay Guardian* that she felt Xena's gender was beyond the point. "It's a warrior living her life. The fact that she's a woman is incidental."

The lesbians felt valued by Renaissance Pictures, the producers of *Xena,* and by Lucy herself. Their appreciation was evident during the onstage presentation at the Burbank convention and in the interactions with Lucy at the autograph tables. Almost every lesbian woman present wanted to express her thanks to Lucy for being aware

" I love Lucy's ability to speak to my heart with her eyes and her body language. She crosses the line between male and female character traits while never losing her feminine appeal. **"**

immensely popular character. In person at the convention, fans found her as gracious and charming as Lucy.

An auction was held, so that fans with money might take a little piece of Xena home with them. One bidder paid $8,500 for an official copy of Xena's chakram.

Hearts pounded as fans waited for Lucy to appear onstage. The excitement was so high that some attendees felt faint and sick. Then . . . there she was, bounding onstage dressed in a rather amazing outfit—blue skintight pants the color of her eyes, a matching sleeveless (skintight) top, black high heels with blazing red toes, a simple necklace and earrings, two simple bracelets on her left wrist, and a gaudy blue-and-white costume-jewelry ring that she'd received as a gift a few days earlier. She was both svelte and sexy. And the outfit proved to her fans that she was in fine shape.

of them, for including them, for bravely portraying a character who could be perceived as lesbian. All the women were grateful for Lucy's depiction of a strong, self-reliant woman who did not feel the need to justify that strength or her skills.

Critiques of the series were part of the reason for the fan gathering. According to *Whoosh!*, neither the heterosexual nor the lesbian women liked the Joxer character, but several stated that as long as Lucy and Reneé were in the show, they would tolerate almost anything. Other things they merely tolerated were the *whooshes* and the stunts. On the other hand, Hudson Leick was an

The audience reveled in her warmth, and was more than willing to obey as she gave them a few orders. "Say Exxxcelent!" They did. "Say Sssplendid!" They did. Then, "When things aren't going quite right," (insert a big grin from Lucy here) "say Exxx-crement!" They did, laughing along with her.

They were hers to command—all in good fun, of course. She gave her war cry, with a mischievous flourish, and then talked about it. She called it a bastardized version of the ululation that Middle Eastern women employ in a variety of circumstances. The sounds were not actually *yi-yi-yi,* used so often in print (including here), but since no one knew what they really were, that was how it was printed.

The crowd was given leave to ask her questions, and it was as if they'd been re-minded, When your sun shines, make your hay. Someone asked her if she wanted to impart any secrets from her private life. Her answer was immediate: absolutely not. A pause followed, every-one wondering if she was offended. She merely gave them a shrug, as if to say, Well, there's your answer.

She sang a portion of "Deep in the Heart of Texas." Lucy didn't know it all, even though she'd been given a plaque signed by the governor making her an honorary Texan. Later, she burst into "I've Got a Loverly Bunch of Coconuts." Periodically, throughout her appearance, she would slyly say, "I feel a song coming on . . ."

SOME WOULD DIE HAPPY NOW

The crowd let themselves be enter-tained by her. And she proved to be an extraordinarily entertaining person. When a boy asked a question, Lucy said she was glad that boys could admire a woman hero, which brought a burst of applause.

A student commented that men were held in low regard at her all-girls school. Lucy replied with directness and strength that she hoped they got over the anti-male bit quickly, since men comprised half the human race.

She settled a major debate among her fans by admitting that she was not naturally blonde. Some fans felt vindi-cated, others betrayed. Some would die happy now, others would go to their graves sadly.

Asked if she liked children, *Whoosh!* reported that she replied, "Yes, I love them, because they are so honest. If they like the show, they tell you the truth; if they do not like the show, they tell you that as well."

She revealed without hesitation that her favorite actor was Susan Sarandon. Great actors, Lucy said, had an almost physical pull on their audiences. Susan had that, and Helen Mirren as well. Lucy felt they were both sensual and fiercely intelligent—and "bloody good" at their jobs.

Lucy, it seemed, also had that visceral impact on her fans. That she didn't consider herself in the same league as actresses like Susan Sarandon was not feigned humility. Her standards were very high, and she was not content to simply surf the crest of current fan adoration. Keeping a clear perspective on her talent and craft presented Lucy with her most formidable professional challenge.

Asked about New Year's resolutions, she revealed that she didn't make them. But for a long time she had been in a frenzy about pursuing her career. She had made the point on several prior occasions that she'd once had a "fire in the belly" about acting. Pursuing her dream had been everything. Now she wanted to slow down a bit and relish where she was, both in her career and in her life.

Someone asked her if her masculine role on *Xena* actually enhanced her sense of her own femininity. It was a good question, and she paused before answering it. She said thoughtfully that she'd actually struggled in the past to feel feminine. Having six brothers was a big influence on her. Some of her ability to play Xena stemmed from the masculinity she had acquired in the mostly masculine circle of her immediate family.

Yet she seemed at ease with her femininity then—or else she might have come to the convention in dungarees instead of in spandex.

Lucy saw Xena as a woman who did not view her femininity as a handicap. Lucy's ability to transmit her combined masculine and feminine sides effectively through Xena was precisely the greatest strength of the series.

Her personal appearance triggered terrific letdown reactions after the convention. "I was not expecting the event to trigger strong envy, regret, and such intense longing to be among Lucy's personal friends . . . to be her lover . . . even to BE HER," wrote Michael Evans-Layng in *Whoosh!* A middle-aged man, a husband of twenty years, a father, and a university administrator, Michael revealed that there had been times when Lucy's beauty on television had so struck him that he had to wonder at her effect on him. "But none of that really prepared me for the fact that Lucy's even more beautiful, even in that larger sense, in person." He confessed that he was "struck dumb, speechless . . . left limp" by her.

ENVY REARED OVER ROB TAPERT

Michael's envy reared over Rob Tapert, the potent producer who had won

> " I love [children], because they are so honest. If they like the show, they tell you the truth; if they do not like the show, they tell you that as well. "

Lucy's love (and access to her body). In fact, Rob was probably responsible for more regrets than anyone else at the convention. He had appeared the day before, boyish and shy, yet a font of information on all things Xena. According to *Whoosh!,* he was asked about his relationship with Lucy. "I see the cat's out of the bag," he said ruefully. Asked if they were planning to marry, he pretended not to hear. But his old friend Bruce Campbell, signing autographs nearby, yelled, "Answer the question!" Rob, blushing, replied he couldn't say, but that the crowd would be the third to know.

More envy arose when fans like Michael witnessed Lucy's powerful carnal and emotional impact on others. They had to share her though each

> **"** After three hours of waiting, about a hundred feet away from [Lucy], my heart started beating faster, and I got excited and nervous. Once in front of her, all remaining shreds of coolness disappeared. I couldn't have spoke to her if I could have remembered something to say. **"**

alone had developed very intense internal relationships with their conceptions of her. She preserved her private life, but Xenites longed for real intimacy with her, for an intimacy of shared experiences and mutual knowledge.

A large part of Lucy's popularity was due to her natural honesty—it had bridged at least a portion of the distance that separated her from her fans. She had shared with them some personal secrets, that she got tired, hurt, overwhelmed, and just plain needed help sometimes. It wasn't real intimacy, but it was a taste that tantalized.

There were heterosexual men in the world, and women too, who were uncomfortable with Xena's male-female combination. The masculine side of the warrior princess could be seen as an outright challenge to the conventional female stereotype. Straight men attracted to her femininity, yet unable to separate it from her masculinity, might be confused or worried about being homosexual. For women, Xena's masculinity could be uncomfortable because it seemed incongruous, or because of the discomfort of feeling attracted to another woman. Besides being "groovy," Xena challenged viewers' thoughts and feelings.

After Lucy's onstage appearance, she signed autographs. What was it like to stand in those long lines waiting for a turn to actually interact one-on-one with the idol? As the line inched toward Lucy, fans reported pounding hearts, feelings of exhilaration, dizzy sensations. Adults, teens, and children clutched color photos, posters, even shirts. They smiled, and nervously rehearsed what they would say when they finally had their twenty seconds of Lucy's attention.

One person told *Whoosh!*, "After three hours of waiting, about a hundred feet away from [Lucy], my heart started beating faster, and I got excited and nervous. Once in front of her, all remaining shreds of coolness disappeared. I couldn't have spoke to her if I could have remembered something to say."

Lucy asked one fan about a script she was carrying, "Where did you get it?"

"At the auction."

"Where?"

"At the auction." The fan felt weak, and couldn't tear her eyes from Lucy's.

"Oh. Well, good for you."

A LITTLE "X" FOR A KISS

Fans were limited to asking for one autograph only. One woman asked her to sign something odd. "I'll sign any damn thing you like," Lucy said. The fan whipped off her shirt and handed it to her idol. Lucy laughed, signed it, adding a little "x" for a kiss.

Cameras flashed almost constantly. Lucy ignored them, giving her attention to each and every person who came through the line.

Another fan took deep breaths to keep from fainting—or weeping. She was so wound up that when she got to Lucy and handed her a picture for signing, all she could whisper was, "Thank you." Lucy, seeing that the woman was terribly nervous, looked deeply into her eyes. "No . . . thank *you*." The woman walked away vibrating like a tuning fork.

When an autograph seeker introduced herself as "Ephany," Lucy looked up and said, "You! You kicked me off!" Ephany was the fan who had kicked Lucy out of a chat room during her recent hospitalization. Lucy

> **"** We never lost one second of production time due to star misbehavior. **"**

good-humoredly gave the woman a hard time. Ephany got her poster signed—and got a great story to tell her friends. (She also confessed to *Whoosh!* that, like many other fans, she broke the one-autograph rule, and went through the line three times.)

Lucy took extra time with the children, asking their names, where they grew up, what they wanted to be. She reminded them that they could be anything they wanted when they grew up, anything at all.

Her handwriting grew increasingly erratic and cramped. Though the "line bosses" began warning fans that she might be too tired to stay much longer, she did stay, until every fan who wanted an autograph got one (or more). It took three hours. She probably wrote her name and "Xena" more than two thousand times.

"If I was not a complete Nut-ball before," one fan told *Whoosh!*, "this gracious gesture by Miss Lawless would have convinced me." Many fans would not think of leaving as long as she was still in the room. Supervising producer Steve Sears and editor Robert Field were also around, along with Rob Tapert. They graciously chatted with fans, allowed photos, and signed programs.

Across the room from Lucy, Hudson Leick and Ted Raimi also withstood the hours of autographing. They grew woozy from the fumes of the permanent markers they used to sign their names.

When the ordeal was over, Lucy didn't even seem tired. Perhaps after eighteen months of fourteen-hour days, filming in unpredictable weather, and sustaining a fractured pelvis, signing a few thousand autographs was "a box of birds." She cheerfully went backstage to take pictures with the convention volunteers and the costume contest winners. The room was small, filled with people, tables, chairs, and a big spread of food and drinks. Lucy stood with Rob. "At one point, she leaned on his shoulder for a moment. It was the first time I saw her give any sign of being tired," reported Ephany to *Whoosh!*

Still, after the photographers were finished with her, she sat at a table to sign another huge stack of eight-by-ten photos. She signed one personally for a fan she was told was so sick she literally could not get out of bed. When *Xena* came on the television, friends dragged the woman's mattress out to the living room so she could watch. Anyone who believed that *Xena* was "just a television show" were mistaken. People's lives were being affected.

Lucy attended another convention in New Orleans before flying home. The appearances had given her a first-hand idea of just how firmly she was now "on the map." She felt over-whelmed by the attention, but she also loved it.

However, all this popularity, which was propelling her to international stardom, didn't mean that Lucy wouldn't have to return to the *Xena* set eventually. Soon she would once again be working long days.

But she always felt it was worth it. She wrote in the January *Lucy Lawless Fan Club Newsletter,* "I want to know that somehow I made an audience feel."

A TYPICAL DAY OF FILMING

On a typical day of filming *Xena: Warrior Princess,* Lucy rises at 5:30 A.M., drives to the set, and parks her car by 6:00. Lucy has a wonderful reputation for promptness and dependability. "I'm blessed unlike any other producer on television," Rob Tapert reported in a rather fatherly fashion during a Universal Netforum online chat, "because the leads of both shows (*Xena* and *Hercules*) are the nicest people you'd ever want to work with. We never lost one second of production time due to star misbehavior."

Most of the filming is done on a farm outside Auckland, located on Sturges Road, where the landscape is always changing. There might be a castle one week, a street market the

" There's a reason she has metal breastplates, but I don't know what it is. **"**

next. Heading for makeup, Lucy is greeted by the guys who lay out the coffee cups. In the clutches of the makeup crew, she is costumed and coated with bronzing cream as she hurriedly spoons down a bowl of steaming porridge and a couple of eggs. She told the *Globe,* "It's dull, but it sticks all day long." She needs something that will stick, because from now on it will be talk, talk, talk, fight, fight, fight, talk, talk, talk.

For our fictional day, filming takes place in a hilly parklike area, cleansed by buttery New Zealand sunshine. Two women, deep in debate, stroll up a path—pursued by a boom mike and a camera-mounted crane. Reneé O'Connor, fair and small, is clothed in a simple tunic. Lucy, however, is dressed like a walking saddlery. As the

zaftig and leggy Xena, she wears the usual leather wrist gauntlets, bicep bracelets, leather boots and knee protectors, leather miniskirt, and a leather bustier embellished by breastplates with brass swirls.

"Lucy is, umm, it's funny to say," Reneé paused during a KYSM Radio interview, "because I just think so highly of her that it's hard to put into words. She's just one of my best friends, and my best mate."

The two are always on the set together—probably twelve hours a day, if not longer, five days a week. Sometimes six days a week. So it is hard not to be friends. Reneé feels it is lucky that they get along so well.

Suddenly the sound man starts to waggle his headphones and adjust dials. The director calls out "cut," and turns to him. He says he is getting a little creaking from Lucy's costume. Lucy's expression changes from stern warrior to smiling showgirl. The sound man approaches, and reaches cautiously to adjust the offending metal on her bustier.

"There's a reason she has metal breastplates," Reneé O'Connor told *TV Guide,* "but I don't know what it is."

During another interview with KYSM Radio, Reneé joked that she might pull a prank on Lucy one day by spreading the inside of those breastplates with Ben-Gay. Then she thought better of it: "She's bigger than me, and she's a tough cookie."

The truth is, those squeaking breastplates don't make much practical sense, yet they seem to fit in with a goddess surfing on a giant clamshell and Xena vanquishing six or so bad guys by using two fish as her weapon.

During a break, Lucy stops to chat with another woman on the crew about their children, comparing their situations as working mothers. She draws strength from her coworkers. Some are the mothers of two and three children, and yet they work incredibly hard. They are dedicated to their jobs and their families, and Lucy takes courage from their strength and poise and grace.

NO JEALOUSY, NO BACKBITING

While Lucy takes a break, most of the crew is still busy. All the crew members support each other. There is no jealousy, no backbiting. Cast and crew are all dedicated to putting out the best series possible. Gaffer, grips—everybody does their job to the best of their ability. It is a great working environment. Lucy feels it shows in the high quality of the product.

"Everybody cares," she told her official fan club. "Everybody lends a hand. It's not like in the States [where] you're only allowed to do your job. If somebody's struggling with something, it's a family, and someone will be there to lend a hand."

Another cast member, Sharon, stops to speak to Lucy during her break. According to Lucy, Sharon has a special quality called "mana," a Maori word for inner pride and esteem. She is, in Lucy's mind, the real model for Xena—the strong, silent type. In the early days of filming the series, Lucy would often look to

> **"** Lucy and Reneé adore each other. What you see on screen is real—the real thing. **"**

Sharon to see what her portrayal of Xena needed.

Lucy must get back to work. She is not the strong, silent type. She feels more of herself has come out when she portrayed some of the other characters. Though she told *People* magazine, "Xena is threads of my character taken to extremes," Xena remains just an offshoot of her personality, one facet intensified.

She joins Reneé for a scene in a village. Lucy bends her head down to murmur something private to her "sidekick." Reneé grins and nods. "Lucy and Reneé adore each other. What you see on screen is real—the real thing," Reneé O'Connor's mother, Sandra Wilson, told *Whoosh!* The relationship between them is indeed wonderful. Lucy doesn't tell anything to anyone whose loyalty she doesn't trust, but she feels she can tell Reneé anything.

"They all have a ball at work," said Sandra, "laughing and joking and truly having a good time."

During her lunch hour, Lucy has a big midday meal, possibly of lamb shanks, her all-time favorite, to give her the stamina to make it through the rest of her long day. But she also makes time for some exercise. Three times a week she takes a run. Today, she heads out from her trailer for a walk with hand weights.

Toward the end of the filming day, Lucy goes into the studio for some "looping." They need her to redo the dialog during a scene when a plane flew overhead. She often sees an episode three times before it airs.

When the day's work is over, she goes home alone. She doesn't go to a gym anymore. She has given that up, and is much happier for it. In fact, she has never been happier in her whole life. And it seems to keep getting better.

Lucy eats a moderate dinner of more meat and vegetables. She might have a bowl of frozen yogurt for dessert. She has a weakness for fattening frozen yogurt, but her active lifestyle and intensely physical work burn the calories.

Afterward, she might call her "mum." Then she grabs her car keys and drives over to her ex-husband's home. There, she tucks her daughter into bed. Back home, she takes a quick swim, as therapy for her post-injured pelvis. Occasionally she does some yoga. Yoga has taught her the value of simplicity. When she does yoga, she is aware of nothing other than breathing and what her body is doing. She finds it very contemplative, which seems to straighten her out in more than a physical sense. She regrets that she doesn't have more time for it these days. Nonetheless, that value of simplicity stays with her, in all sorts of ways.

Soon, she tucks herself into bed, reading a few pages of a book until her eyes droop, then turns out the light. Our typical day ends, but tomorrow will begin early for her, as usual.

Chapter Ten

STRETCHED IN EVERY DIRECTION

WITH LUCY BACK ON THE SET OF *XENA: WARRIOR PRINCESS,* the pace returned to quick time. As she rode back from her accident, she was more popular than ever.

And how popular was that?

She was popular enough to inspire no fewer than 190 Web sites by January 1997. That was more attention than Teri Hatcher and Winona Ryder could generate combined.

Though Lucy had always expected the show would do well, and felt the audience approval through the good press that *Xena* had garnered from the very beginning, now her popularity started to seem vast. She knew the temper of the United States well enough to joke that if the American Midwest caught on to *Xena,* she'd know she had really conquered the market.

Her sense of humor wasn't above teasing her own family in print. When *Cleo Magazine* asked her which of her family members was most like Xena, she mentioned her older brother Tim, saying he liked to wear miniskirts. The joke was funnier to those who knew that Tim was a driller in an Australian gold mine at the time—and a lovable man, according to Lucy. But she remembered the trouble they'd given each other as children, when she was the little sister who made life miserable for him. Tim did most resemble Xena, though, and had given Lucy a lot of material to work with.

When the *Los Angeles Times* mentioned that Lucy had the best sneer ever seen on an actress, Lucy said, "That Xena look—sometimes

> **"** I'll be producing my own material. I'm not going to lie down and whine about being a 'victim' of typecasting. **"**

when I see her doing that sneer, I see my oldest brother so clearly. It's just his face when he was an angry young man. That's how much we look alike."

"My one and only sister is studying languages and working as a translator in Amsterdam at the moment," she told *Cleo.* "We're very close, but look nothing alike." Her sister had naturally dark hair, whereas Lucy said hers, before she'd dyed it dark, "used to be mousy brown."

Another brother was a money manager in London. Two brothers were plumbers in Auckland, and one was a builder. "I love having them around . . . because I'm remodeling my kitchen and bathroom right now."

There was no more rough-and-tumble among the Ryan siblings now. They were all grown up. Lucy felt a bit closer to them since she'd got her show, especially the brothers working with her to renovate her house. Her success hadn't changed her relationship with her family in any important way. It was still loving.

Of course, most of all she loved Daisy. The separations and long hours of work were hard on both her and her daughter, but no matter how guilty or pressured Lucy sometimes felt, she knew she would not be a better mother—and certainly not a happier woman—if she were to relinquish her career. She sincerely believed that someday Daisy would credit her for sticking to it.

She had offers for other television and film projects, and she would love to do a role that didn't require a leather corset, but for the time being she didn't want to star in anything else. That would leave her too tired to give *Xena* her all.

She still wasn't worried about being typecast. David Duchovny, star of *The X-Files,* suggested in a speech given at the Museum of Radio and Television that Lucy might have good reason to worry. He succinctly summed up which types of roles led to typecasting: namely, archetypical figures or action heroes. But Lucy insisted it wouldn't happen to her. "I'll be producing my own material. I'm not going to lie down and whine about being a 'victim' of typecasting." With Rob Tapert at her side, she had a good chance of overcoming the typecasting that had ended the career of Lynda Carter, television's *Wonder Woman*. (And the chances of having him by her side looked good. Lucy described their relationship as happy and stable.)

One day, she would like to play someone who was intellectually challenged, or at least slightly thickheaded. But she intended to play Xena for a long time to come. The role was challenging and allowed her to work in various styles: farce, intense drama, and action. There were few women, even in the States, who got the opportunity to play action roles. She felt stretched in every direction. It was as versatile a part as an actress could find, and she felt very lucky to have it.

WHAT A BUMP ON THE RUMP CAN DO FOR A CAREER

If imitation is the sincerest form of flattery, then Lucy was being flattered by some pretty big stars. Her character was being used in such other series as *Roseanne,* where, in a goofy episode, the show's star dressed as Xena.

But Down Under, Lucy continued to be treated to "New Zealand cheek." An Auckland *Sunday Star-Times* reporter wrote, "Lawless recently flexed her tonsillar muscles on the *Regis and Kathie Lee Show,* singing to a flabbergasted studio audience. Amazing what a good bump on the rump can do for a career." Another magazine commented that she had scored worldwide publicity as a result of her accident—not because of her role in *Xena*.

Lucy didn't object to these types of comments. Instead, she agreed that falling off that horse had helped to put her on the map. She told *Women's Weekly,* "Before it happened, there were a lot of people out there who had never heard of me or Xena. The publicity all over the world about my accident changed all that, and now a lot more people are watching the show. So, in a way, it was a blessing in disguise."

That didn't mean she'd ever want to go through such a painful ordeal again. No way. It was much too frightening to repeat. She didn't even like to think about it. And that "bump on the rump" still caused her trouble. She told *TV Guide,* "I'm not quite 100 percent. In three months I will be."

However, she was fit enough to fulfill a girlhood fantasy. She appeared in the U.S. sitcom *Something So Right,* in which she plays herself and accuses Stephanie (actress Christine Dunford) of ripping off *Xena* with a fictional "Thena: Warrior Goddess." The gag closed with Lucy charging after her rival in classic Xena fashion.

These seventeen-hour-long plane flights to North America could not have been comfortable for someone recovering from a pelvic injury, yet she couldn't afford to miss her chances now that they had arrived.

"She went straight from her plane to the set," a Universal Television publicist told *Area 52,* "and had—literally— an hour to tape her appearance."

The newly ambulatory celebrity then dashed off to do several more personal appearances before again returning to the *Warrior Princess* set in New Zealand.

There, scripts were still being revised to give Lucy more healing time, allowing her costars to carry the lead for several more episodes until she was fit. Lucy jested that "they covered my ass when my ass was broken."

She still refused to climb back on a horse, forcing the producers to employ doubles in her riding scenes. She would not let anyone push her into it prematurely. Lucy wanted a full recovery.

SEVENTY-FIVE REASONS NOT TO GIVE UP ON TELEVISION

In a documentary for television, *The Making of Hercules,* Lucy said, "Xena's a mystery. There's a certain mystique. She doesn't give out too much. You don't know too much about her thought processes." At this point, she didn't think of Xena as a warrior. She considered her as just a working woman—"a working stiff." Lucy explained that she and her coworkers were trying to make something that pleased them. They had to enjoy their creation and laugh a lot; after all, it was their life, fourteen hours a day. And life went by pretty quickly if you weren't careful. Lucy felt that in any creative endeavor you had to make something that you believed in, and they believed in a show that made them laugh.

Sometimes even the reviews made them laugh, like the one by the *Vancouver Sun*'s television critic, who gave readers seventy-five reasons not to give up on television. Xena was included in reason No. 36, which was "'B' TV, like *Hercules, Xena,* and *Star Trek: Deep Space Nine:* Wholesome, harmless, hooey."

Coincidentally, there was a strong revival of interest in all things classical in the entertainment world. It was not clear whether the *Hercules* and *Xena* television shows had precipitated that interest or simply had had the good luck to jump aboard a train that was about to leave the station. Even the *New York Times* noted the trend. Suddenly the word "classic" was synonymous with "popular" and "profitable." For example, Scholastic Books mar-

keted *Mythic Men: Guardians of the Legend,* a mass-market book and trading-card series directed primarily at boys ages four to eight. It used cartoon graphics to narrate famous Greek myths.

Meanwhile, Marvel Comics was still doing well with the previous summer's *The Incredible Hulk: Hercules Unleashed.* Of course, *Hercules* and *Xena* were among the top-rated syndicated television shows of the year. In early February, *TV Guide*'s cover shouted, "America's Hot for Hercules!" NBC, meanwhile, prepared to broadcast *The Odyssey* in May, which cost some $30 million to produce. And the trailers were out for an animated Hercules feature coming from Disney in June.

A WOMAN FANTASY FIGURE

As if in echo of the *Vancouver Sun*'s seventy-five reasons not to give up on television, one fan wrote an essay, "Why I Watch *Xena: Warrior Princess,*" for the *Xena Media Review, No. 21.*

The author wrote that the initial attraction was that the show "was about a woman fantasy figure who was not waiting around to be rescued or accompanied by a man, but was doing it for herself." Of course, no woman could do what Xena did. But then, no man could really do what male heroes did on screen, either. Clearly, television viewers had been socialized to accept the hero archetype—a larger-than-life metaphor—as only a role for men. Women need not apply.

Beyond that factor the strength, appeal, and rapidly growing viewer dedication to *Xena* was a result of the interweaving of several other features of the show:

- The show's action, from the cartoonish fights to the mythic critters. *Xena* was first and foremost an action-adventure romp.

- The humor, which was campy, self-referential, and mired in pop culture.

- Xena's search for redemption, which was a foundation of her character and provided the main subject matter for the series.

- The relationship between Xena and Gabrielle, which tweaked the deep wish many people felt for a close friend (or a lover).

- The depiction of free women, which flaunted traditional beliefs that women were too weak and/or too dumb to be independent.

- The immense, vivid, gorgeous landscapes, the wonderful sets, and the multiracial cast.

- The casting of a woman in the lead role, an actress who was not afraid to push beyond traditional female stereotypes.

- The creative and well-crafted scripts, and the superior production qualities.

Xena: Warrior Princess was essentially a morality play, similar to the original *Star Trek* series of the 1960s. Like *Star Trek*, *Xena* discussed current events in a seemingly innocuous manner, by employing mythological backgrounds. For instance, in the episode titled "Beware of Greeks Bearing Gifts," Helen is finally given a chance to voice her opinion on all that Trojan War nonsense. The plot offers a Helen who has interests beyond war. Likewise, "Altered States" successfully demonstrates assorted views regarding religious tolerance by retelling Abraham's sacrifice of his son. "Is There a Doctor in the House" bravely follows the idea of comic-strip violence to its rather explicit end, showing what really occurs when someone gets sword-skewered. "The Path Not Taken" and "Mortal Beloved" both show an interracial relationship that is not a plot point of the show.

Regardless of whether or not some critic thought it was "hooey," *Xena* and *Hercules* were popular—and they claimed responsibility for a new wave of fantasy fare on American television, including *Tarzan: The Epic Adventures, The Adventures of Sinbad,* and *The New Adventures of Robin Hood.*

Lucy told *Sci-Fi Buzz,* "It just seems to have caught a wave. I am hoping it will be the next sort of media phenomenon . . . and, with any luck, it's going to endure to be the last one of the century. And it's a good way to go into the next century, I think."

One issue *Xena* did not take lightly was the victimization of women—

Lucy had no tolerance for that. She told a reporter for *Sky TV Guide* about sitting at a restaurant table biting her lip with anger as she watched a man hit a woman outside the window. Her screen character might have given the brute a reason to think twice about his behavior, but Lucy didn't know how to respond. In real life, she was no Xena. "I wanted to intervene, but I can't really fight."

Instead, she later found a way to talk to the woman privately, to tell her that no one had to take that kind of treatment. She may not be a real-life warrior, but she still hated seeing women be mistreated.

THE WOMAN WHO PLAYED XENA WAS AFRAID

Even though she was taking things easy at work, Lucy managed to jar something during filming while running across some uneven ground. It set her recovery back a bit. Once she rebounded from the incident, she took up walking with hand weights. She trekked the mountains and stony

> **"** I don't think I'll ever get on a horse again without thinking of Christopher Reeve. **"**

streams around her house for about an hour at a time, going at a good pace.

Running, as she had learned the hard way, was not really within her ability yet. It wasn't until March 1997 that she was back to executing her own fight scenes—only toning down the kicks a little. And she was preparing to remount her faithful horse. The only reason she wasn't back in the saddle already was her continuing psychological rejection of the idea. The woman who played Xena was afraid.

It had to be a scary thing after taking such a hellish fall. She later told the *New York Times,* "I don't think I'll ever get on a horse again without thinking of Christopher Reeve," referring to the *Superman* actor who was tragically paralyzed after a fall from a horse. She had already given up downhill skiing because she'd thought it best not to risk an injury that would let down so many who depended on her. But she had to get back into that saddle, sooner or later. It was important to her. Lucy looked at it as a test. Could she overcome her fear, or would she be frightened forever?

Her diet hadn't changed substantially since her accident. As far as her weight was concerned, she wasn't careful about what she ate, and she didn't even own a set of scales. She relied on the test of whether or not she could fit into her clothes. If she could, then she consumed everything. She had a sweet tooth, but it was manageable. She did like wine, however. And Scotch. She didn't smoke anymore—but she sure would like to.

Lucy had some quirky eating habits; she liked to eat beans in the morning—out of a can, with sausages. Her garden was laden with organic vegetables that she often picked and ate. She still loved lamb shanks, too. Otherwise, she wouldn't care if she ever saw meat again. She needed some meat, however, because without it the bruises she got at work seemed to stay around longer. She was usually extremely bruised at night, so she made a point of eating some red meat and dark green vegetables.

Lucy had learned that in her kind of work she was going to get hit and going to get bruised. But her pain tolerance was very high. Interestingly, she did not consider the bruises, or the Xena costume, or even her broken pelvis as the worst downside of her work. Instead, what stood out in her mind was two weeks of filming in the cold and the rain, up to her shins—no exaggeration—fighting in the mud. Sometimes she was out in that kind of weather for eight hours straight.

CHAMPAGNE ROSES

In March, after long hours of work on the show, Lucy treated herself to an evening on the town. She didn't get home until nearly two in the morning, which was truly late for her, but she'd had great fun. Lest *Xena* take over her

life, Lucy needed to treat herself now and again.

The personal Lucy Lawless loves champagne roses. And among her favorite colors are rust brown and emerald green. She likes color in general, and plenty of it—"Tiffany colors."

Meanwhile, her mythic heroine strode across the entertainment landscape in truly legendary fashion, single-handedly raising the platform of women on television. Xena was throwing spears of branched lightning at her competition. Midway through *Xena*'s second season, the series regularly beat syndication champions *Baywatch* and *Star Trek: Deep Space Nine,* not to mention *Hercules: The Legendary Journeys.* Earlier in the year, the show had even prevailed in its Saturday prime-time hour against network competition in New York and Los Angeles.

Like *Star Trek* and *The X-Files, Xena* was speeding toward the oxymoronic distinction of being a "mainstream cult" hit. Evidence included conventions, Xena-fests, Xena-themed apparel, collectors' cards, fanzines, action figures, computer CDs, and innumerable Web pages. *People* Online users, who had voted Lucy one of the "Most Intriguing People of 1996," voted her one of the "Most Beautiful People of 1997." *Entertainment Weekly* quoted thirty-seven-year-old feminist schoolteacher Dana Eskenazi as saying, "There hasn't been a female television character who is totally independent of a male figure in her life. This is a woman who can fight—and beat—men, who walks the world like so many male adventurers have."

But Xena's invasion of the staunchly male domain didn't offend the guys. Hardly. "Xena's a total babe. Not only that, she's a babe who likes other babes . . . it's a babe-fest," said a twenty-year-old online devotee. "I watch her in action and think 'Wow, she could kick my ass,' and I kind of dig that."

Lucy was surprised to be called a sex symbol, however. "Hmm, I feel very impersonal about it," she told her official fan club. She was quick to turn that obligation over to her character: "But if Xena is a sex symbol, well, she's probably not a bad one to have, because she's in control of her situation. And totally unashamed of her body."

There is one scene in which Xena comes naked out of a waterfall. Lucy chose to play it as if the warrior princess was totally unconscious of being naked. Men attack her, "and she just goes in and fights . . . with no self-consciousness."

But what about Lucy Lawless as a sex symbol? Well, she just doesn't seem to have that view of herself.

EYED FOR SOME PRETTY MAJOR FILM AND TELEVISION ROLES

Lucy couldn't deny her fame, however. How did she keep her feet on the ground? Even she admitted that it was a problem. Her way was simply to refuse to believe it was real.

Yet it was real. Offers continued to come in from Hollywood movie producers willing to pay her lavishly to star in films during her three-month hiatus from *Xena.* Whether she admitted it or not, she had dramatically established herself in the American consciousness, and was being eyed for some pretty major film and television roles.

Some of those offers were tempting, too. But she turned them down for two reasons. First, she had real loyalty to the series. "This is the show that made me famous," she explained to *Women's Weekly.* "If I spent my hiatus making a movie, I'd be exhausted by the time it came to filming *Xena* again. And that wouldn't be fair to the show." Of course, one day she wanted to make movies, maybe even move to America temporarily. But for the time being, she was content to stay home and give *Xena* all her concentration. Even though she could earn millions of dollars with these outside projects, she stood firm.

The second and more significant reason for turning down the offers had to do with her daughter, Daisy. Lucy's work was only the second most important thing in her life. Her eight-year-old was number one. Because of the long days Lucy had to work on the set of *Xena,* she was committed to spending her hiatus as a mom.

"I know I've made a bundle of money," she told *Women's Weekly,* "but that's not everything. I wouldn't be a happy old lady if I hadn't spent pre-cious time with my daughter, Daisy, while she was growing up."

Daisy continued to have very mixed feelings. On some days she was proud of Lucy, yet other times she wanted things to go back to the way they had been. She didn't enjoy sharing her mother with so many people. She didn't often get to watch *Xena,* because she and her mother were always out on Friday nights when it aired. And it seldom occurred to Lucy to turn on the television anyway. She'd already seen the episodes at work three times.

Though Lucy told the *Mirror* that Daisy "can't understand why anybody should make a fuss of boring old mum," others understood perfectly. Fans held another Xena convention in New York City on March 11, 1997, which included events from costume contests to martial-arts self-defense training for women. Like the one in Burbank, it was so crowded that they had to turn folks away at the door. "There's nothing new or exciting about a big, beefy guy saving the world," said fan Betsy Book. "Xena's one of a few strong women characters."

> " If I spent my hiatus making a movie, I'd be exhausted by the time it came to filming *Xena* again. And that wouldn't be fair to the show. "

As hard as it might be to imagine the fist-swinging, leg-kicking, horsewoman Xena daintily dabbing on some fingernail polish, Lucy showed up for an interview with a *Chicago Tribune* reporter with one silver-polished fingertip. While getting in some shopping during a visit to the windy city to pump up her show, Lucy had sampled some nail polish in a store on her way to the interview, and without any remover, the polish had to stay. The fact that the writer reported this incident suggested that fans and media-types alike were having trouble separating the actress from the television character. The truth was, however, that Xena wouldn't be caught dead doing some of the things Lucy loved. Like laugh, for instance. And Lucy loved flowers. And she loved providing a pleasant home life for her eight-year-old daughter. And do you think Xena would ever name a child Daisy? "Xena's not into that frou-frou stuff," Lucy told the *Tribune.*

Lucy, on the other hand, especially loved children. If there were kids around, she always felt at home.

Chapter Eleven

HEROES, MONSTERS, AND SINGING, TOO

Fans of *Xena: Warrior Princess* debated Xena's sexual preferences with growing heat. Heterosexuals shouted she was *not* a homosexual! Two women were not necessarily lesbians just because they were pals, just because they were close friends, just because they laughed and did things together. Homosexuals shouted back that they *were* lesbians, that there was something more in Xena's touchy-feely relationship with cutie-pie Gabrielle. Also, there was much made of the fact that one of the show's producers, Liz Friedman, admitted to being gay.

The sexual ambiguity of these characters became a major draw for the series. Renaissance Pictures knew exactly what they were doing, creating one hell of a conversation piece, drawing people in without disgusting them. Rob Tapert and Sam Raimi played media interviewers like fiddles. "They're worse than lawyers, these guys," wrote Ken Parish Perkins of the *Star Telegram*. "They'll neither admit nor deny Xena's sexual orientation." Liz Friedman was almost as bad. She told *Entertainment Weekly*, "I don't have any interest in saying they're heterosexuals."

Lucy played this game, too. Asked by *Playboy* what was Xena's vacation fantasy, she answered, "a biennial sailing trip to Lesbos."

Those who watched the series knew that Xena had slept with men about as often as she knocked their heads together. On the other hand, the producers played with certain amusements, like the installment where Xena and Gabrielle latch lips. It's supposedly not

> The audience is not afraid of watching some women break out of the conventional mold. "

Xena at all, but a man carrying Xena's soul in his body. And in the episode in which Xena poses as a contestant in the Miss Known World beauty pageant, she kisses the winner, Miss Artifice—long and wetly. In the plot, the beauty queen is revealed to be a man. In actuality, she was triple-X film star Karen Dior, a.k.a. Geoff Gann, a drag queen, a gay rights activist, and a recent inductee in the *Adult Video News*' pornography star hall of fame.

These are lesbian scenarios fulfilled. The gay crowd stays.

Yet they are fulfilled without saying Xena is a lesbian. The straight crowd stays.

It's clever. It's the game of Television Tease played to perfection.

It seemed the series was so unique, so different from everything else, that the company could do some pretty contro-

versial things. Yet they were wise enough to be sly and not downright naughty, which kept it family oriented and advertiser friendly.

Xena: Warrior Princess definitely represented a refreshing change from the mawkish movie-of-the-week brand of female heroism, à la Danielle Steele, that had proliferated throughout the early '90s. With *Xena*'s success (and the success of *The X-Files*' Gillian Anderson and *La Femme Nikita*'s Peta Wilson), Sam Raimi felt the people had spoken. He hoped his newest television series, *Spy Game,* starring Allison Smith, would benefit from the growing taste for kickboxing heroines. "The audience is not afraid of watching some women break out of the conventional mold," he told *Entertainment Weekly.* Ruefully, he added, "the Hollywood establishment may not be aware that the audience really wants that."

Throughout its fifty-year history, television had produced a mere handful of successful, strong female characters: Emma Peel, the Bionic Woman, Cagney and Lacey—and most of these appeared in the more politically strident 1970s. Hollywood's brand of television was a medium of the familiar, not of social change. Predictably, blame for this status quo has been directed at the male-dominated ranks of television executives. Because of them, even successful actresses playing forceful women (like Gillian Anderson of *The X-Files*) navigated a tightrope between strength and femininity. These executives justify that balancing act by saying it was what television watchers of both genders wanted to see.

Xena happily, slyly, solved that problem—through subversion. Liz Friedman told *Entertainment Weekly*, "The best way to convey more challenging ideas is to make something that functions on a mainstream level but that has subtext that people can pick up on—or not." Add a Trojan horse, and you've got a *Xena* episode.

VERY QUIET DOWN THERE

Though Lucy had been tasting the nectar of *Xena*'s success during her trips north, Reneé was slower to realize her own fame. During her first visit north in nine months, she told an interviewer from KYSM Radio (in Minnesota), "It's so strange for us in New Zealand. The show just started a couple months ago again, and it's very quiet down there. So we have no idea that it's so popular. Every now and then one of the producers might say, 'Hey, you know, we're not doing too badly.'"

She wasn't bothered in New Zealand by overly avid fans. If the Kiwis said anything to her when she was out in Auckland, it was only a polite "I enjoy the show."

On April 29, 1997, Lucy's cameo appearance on the NBC sitcom *Something So Right* aired. Such prime-time spoofs told her just how well her own series was doing. "It says our show is really having an impact," she told *TV Guide*. "Of course, my personal goal is to totally infiltrate popular culture."

But seriously, the whole fame thing didn't make her feel empowered so much as it just plain made her giggle. Her previous sober attitude, her fear of being renowned, of being a role model, was gone. She was determined to enjoy her time of being on top.

She had learned to relax about her success, perhaps because she finally realized that a role model only encouraged people to be themselves—not her. "Before, it was too much responsibility to bear," she told *TV Guide.*

Her role models remained Susan Sarandon and Helen Mirren, but now she also thought Madonna was an admirable creature. She wouldn't want to fashion her own career on the singer's, however. No need to worry, the warrior princess's breastplates would not suddenly become pointy.

Out of the blue, Lucy got a completely unexpected offer—to play the role of Rizzo in the Broadway production of *Grease!* Apparently, the play's producers had just happened to be watching the *Rosie O'Donnell Show* in the fall of 1996 when Lucy had wowed the audience with her singing.

But that wasn't the only coincidence involved. *Grease!* had been slated to close in February, to make way for an *Annie* revival. But the unexpected closing of Andrew Lloyd Webber's *Whistle Down the Wind,* in Washington, D.C.,

allowed *Annie* to switch to the larger Martin Beck Theatre, which in turn allowed *Grease!* to continue at the O'Neill. It reopened in April after all, with comic Joe Piscopo and Olympic gold medalist Dominique Dawes in the featured roles. Did the gods have anything to do with that fortuitous chain of events?

The only musicals Lucy had done before had been school plays. "But I'm a quick study," she told *Parade.* "You have to be when you do a series."

She told *TV Guide,* "I think it's ironic that even in my time off from being a bad girl who wants to be a saint, I play a bad girl." Ah, that refreshing New Zealand bluntness.

Her fans were just as happy about the *Grease!* offer as she was. In fact, her fan mail had become too much to handle, not only in the number of letters she received but in the content of the messages. "It got to the stage where I was reading things, and I would break down and cry. I would get seven letters in a pile of forty, of people with just awful ailments—like a kid in Turkey who's going to Moscow because he's got to have a brain cancer operation, please Xena can you help?" she told New Zealand Radio.

She became overwhelmed by it. These people seemed to think she was actually a hero, that she could stage miracles that would help them. Too many had suspended their disbelief totally. They really believed Xena could come and fix things. It was too much for Lucy. She couldn't get up and go to work joyfully every day and carry the weight of the world on her shoulders, too.

Such letters made up only about 10 percent of her mail, but 10 percent of four hundred letters was a lot of letters. If she responded even to the fans who weren't asking so much of her, she simply wouldn't have time to do the show that gave them such enjoyment. So she responded to as many as she could, but knew when to let a service take care of the rest.

Kevin Smith, who played Ares, began to feel some of that surrealism

> **"** I think it's ironic that even in my time off from being a bad girl who wants to be a saint, I play a bad girl. **"**

in his own life. "In fact," he told *Whoosh!,* "a guy came up to me on the street the other day—we had a couple of quakes here about a week ago, quite decent ones, sort of fives—and this guy comes up and blamed me for it. 'Ares, you sonofa—, that was you, wasn't it?'"

ON A WILD RIDE

When Lucy looked around at her life, she realized that *Xena: Warrior Princess* had changed its landscape totally. There was not one thing that was the same. She joked that maybe she had one jersey sweater leftover from her old life, but that was all. Perhaps that was overstating it, but not by much. Even her daughter was a different person, though that surely had as

> **"** Everything [in New Zealand] is close because the place is small. There is desert, jungle . . . Quite often some of these things are frighteningly close to each other. **"**

used to be very close to two for one," Kevin Smith told *Whoosh!*, "so you would get double for your money. But it is like seventy U.S. cents to the New Zealand dollar now."

As for the Kiwis, most felt that the two Renaissance filming projects were great for the local economy. The film and television industry had pumped an estimated $670 million into the Kiwi economy during the last financial year alone. Not all of that was Renaissance money—*The Lost World*, Steven Spielberg's sequel to his blockbuster *Jurassic Park*, had also been filmed in New Zealand that year.

But the two Renaissance adventure series did spend lots of American dollars in New Zealand. The shows also served as tourism advertisements for the country, showing the diverse locations available within a small area. "Everything is close because the place

much to do with Daisy's growing up as with Lucy's change of fortune.

Most of these changes were positive. What hadn't been good, Lucy was learning to accept and not struggle against.

By May of 1997, *Xena: Warrior Princess* was well on its way to becoming the most watched program in the entire world. It was shown in Europe, the United Kingdom, and Australia. In Germany, it was a particularly huge hit. Lucy was on a wild ride. Considering all this success, the studio didn't worry too much that production of *Xena* in New Zealand had become less of a monetary bargain. The New Zealand dollar had strengthened. "It is small," laughed Kevin Smith to *Whoosh!*. "There is desert, jungle . . . Quite often some of these things are frighteningly close to each other."

Other New Zealanders were not cheering so loudly about the influx of U.S. dollars. There were those who worried that the foreign productions dominating the local industry were compromising New Zealanders' abilities to tell their own stories. Also, what would happen to the inflated economy when and if *Xena* and *Hercules* should move or end?

A WOMAN WHO COULD GRAB ARROWS IN MIDFLIGHT

Lucy, in her Xena costume, appeared on the cover of *TV Guide*. Inside, photographer Gary Heery showed the voluptuous actress in clothing much less menacing—a deep red formal sheath with spaghetti straps, and a rich golden full-skirted gown. Lucy's laughing face gave evidence that she thought the contrast was a hoot. And somehow she still looked like a woman who could grab arrows in midflight

and hurl grown men across a forest clearing.

Meanwhile, her program finally trounced *Star Trek* in the ratings competition, a feat that some thought mere mortals could not achieve. Since 1987, the intergalactic dynasty had controlled the syndicated-drama charts. The *Star Trek* franchise seemed invincible. Even *Baywatch*'s leggy lifesavers had only bobbed in second place during their four seasons. The triumph of *Xena: Warrior Princess* and her big brother show, *Hercules,* over *Star Trek: Deep Space Nine* seemed, well, Herculean. When executive producers Rob Tapert and Sam Raimi had launched *Hercules* in 1995, they really hadn't thought to reach that high. "Our initial goal was to bump off *Baywatch* as the number two show," said Rob to *TV Guide.*

Even director Charles Siebert had frankly never expected *Xena* to be such a phenomenal success. But, as the producers of *Ellen* could also attest, statistical probabilities often failed to take into account the enormous impact of gay and lesbian viewers. It came back to that game of Television Tease.

> It's something that Lucy and I have a good time with. We know that people read whatever they want to see into the show. "

"They're great," Lucy said of her lesbian fans to San Francisco's *Frontiers Newsmagazin,* "they're really loyal fans.'" But "loyalty" was not the word for it. Obsession might come nearer the mark. At the Chat House, on Eighth and Minna Streets in San Francisco, Tuesday nights featured two solid hours of *Xena*—a taped episode at 8:00 P.M. followed by the regular broadcast at 9:00. And there was a *Xena* contingent planned for July 1997's Dyke March, as well.

Lucy projected a refreshing lack of coyness about the gay connection to *Frontiers Newsmagazin:* "We do have fun with that aspect. We talk about it on the set. One of the best parts of the job is getting to throw in references that [gay] fans will pick up on."

Reneé O'Connor, however, seemed a little embarrassed about it. She told KYSM Radio, "It's something that Lucy and I have a good time with. We know that people read whatever they want to see into the show." However, she added, "For the most part, we're just good friends, and as long as we keep the friendship of Gabrielle and Xena true and honest, then anything we do that might be a little more intimate . . . it's just very honest, very natural, and just sweet."

Back home in New Zealand, Lucy herself seemed to be losing some interest in the game. She told a New Zealand Radio interviewer, "We are no longer humored by that particularly. What she is, is what she is. And what the relationship between those two characters is . . . is their own business."

HER MOTHER WOULD WEEP

Lucy might play a mythic champion on television, but she lived in the modern world. And according to her comments, she seemed to be finding the perfect balance between the facts and the fictions of her life. For instance, Xena might have had only a horse for transportation around her ancient earth, but when Lucy Lawless traveled, she rated a limo. Xena might sleep on the ground; Lucy, however, liked the Four Seasons Hotel in Chicago.

Luxurious or not, a trip north to the States now meant a more jammed-full schedule than ever. In one day she might do a long outdoor photography shoot, do some movie promos, make an appearance on a television sitcom, and give an interview. All she really craved after such a long day was to have a rum and cola followed by a relaxing dinner with lover Rob Tapert.

But all that publicity work was effective. Her face began to pop up everywhere. She was in "The World's 50 Most Beautiful People" edition of *People* magazine, wearing nothing but a black body stocking. Yet the world was soon to see even more of her than that.

Being a big-time Detroit Red Wings fan, Lucy had in the past been like any other fan, requesting posters and memorabilia from the team. She thought that her heart's desire had been answered when she was asked to sing the U.S. National Anthem at a play-off hockey game in May between the Red Wings and the Anaheim Mighty Ducks. For the appearance, she dressed in another skimpy bustier-style, tight-fitting costume—inspired by Uncle Sam and the Stars and Strips. In red, white, and blue she went out onto the ice. She concentrated hard on keeping her footing, afraid that the awkward shoes of her costume would cause her to slip, possibly injuring herself all over again.

"O-oh say can you see . . ."

Yes, everyone saw. While singing, she removed her blue blazer and lifted her arms to hit the concluding high note.

"In the home of the brave . . ."

The stadium audience, and those viewers lucky enough to be watching the game live on television, were surprised as the bodice of her costume failed to rise with her lifting chest, revealing her left breast. Lucy went on, completely unaware. She finished her appearance and left the stadium.

Television Channel 50 in Detroit received eleven phone calls about the incident. One was a complaint. Ten asked for the anthem clip to be re-broadcast. In fact, stills and film captures of the event were to be a popular item with fans for months after. Her performance made several sports highlight shows—but always with the exposed portion of her anatomy tastefully covered by a black bar.

The day after the event, Lucy learned the shocking news. As reported in the *Detroit Free Press,* she was first told of it by radio interviewer Dick Purtan (WOMC-FM). "You mean I've been flashing on national TV?" A deeply silent pause. Then, "I am horrified. It did not really come down, did it?"

She wanted to believe that only a little of her breast was exposed. Of course, Purtan and his morning radio colleagues happily gave her a specific explanation of exactly how drastically her outfit had let her down. She pleaded with them to tell her they were lying. Flabbergasted, she babbled that she didn't need that sort of public-

ity, she was getting plenty already, that the costume was too bloody small, and that her mother would weep.

NO SUCH THING AS REDEMPTION

What about the soul of Xena? Had she really shed her dark side and become good? Lucy felt that the character was still corrupt. There were murky cravings buried inside the warrior princess that she still must resist. Xena's agenda still was just to get through the day without killing someone. There was no such thing as redemption for her, because she could never reconcile with those she'd harmed in the past. They were dead. Like the sword that hung over Damocles' head by a single hair, self-condemnation always hung above Xena. The day the warrior princess found peace with herself would be the series' last episode. She was doomed to keep wandering her ancient world, to keep moving. The warrior princess would never have a hearth to call her own. She was a misfit.

Lucy too felt like a misfit, in that she had chosen such a rarefied atmosphere in which to live her life. Everyone reacted differently to her now that she was on the "telly." She grew into more of

> **"** We just did a funny, full-on musical number in the Busby Berkeley style for a *Xena* episode, and it worked so well that we've been marching toward an all-musical episode. **"**

a misfit with each day that passed—yet she wouldn't want it any other way.

Lucy's personal religious philosophy was gradually undergoing renovations with the rest of her life. Under the pantheism of ancient Greece, if you angered the gods, you needed a good escape route, which was not hard to provide, considering that the gods were an argumentative bunch. The smart mortal could wheel the gods' attention to something else by provoking internal squabbles. Monotheism was simpler—only one god to annoy you. But pantheism had advantages, because people could ascribe their behavior to lots of outside influences. She

told *Playboy* that she was personally dealing with the concept of a deity. She called herself a "recovering Catholic"—someone who was re-evaluating the Catholic faith given to her as a child. Still, she didn't wish for more gods. She couldn't image having to soothe all those egos. Even one was more than she could deal with.

On a more earthly plane, Lucy worked on an animated Hercules and Xena video, titled *Hercules and Xena: The Animated Movies—The Battle for Mount Olympus* (not to be confused with the Disney Hercules cartoon shown in motion picture theaters). It would arrive in video stores in the fall of 1997. Lucy not only did Xena's speaking voice, she also crooned a song—a real fan-pleaser, she promised. Could the public expect an album of Lucy Lawless singing Greek classics? In jest, she quipped that she was thinking of performing Sappho's greatest hits. (There it was again, that Television Tease. Sappho was a Greek lyric poet in the early sixth century B.C. She lived on the island of Lesbos—from which the word *lesbian* was coined.)

Working on the animated video whetted producer Rob Tapert's appetite for more music on the live-action series. "We just did a funny, full-on musical number in the Busby Berkeley style for a *Xena* episode," he told *ITV Guide Entertainment Network,* "and it worked so well that we've been marching toward an all-musical episode." Something decidedly Wagnerian, with gods, heroes, monsters, and singing, too. Television viewers wouldn't see the all-musical *Xena* until January of 1998, by which time fans would get to sample Lucy's singing in both *Grease!* and the animated video. It was something to look forward to.

Chapter Twelve

A CROWD OF ADORERS AT HER FEET

AT THE BEGINNING OF THE SECOND SEASON OF *XENA: WARRIOR Princess,* Lucy had feared that her character was getting too soft. But by the end of the season she felt that a shrink would advise Xena to lighten up. The devil was on her back and the angels were in her heart, and her head had to get them together. Her gut response was fight, not flight.

Lucy liked the way viewers thought they knew Xena more intimately than she knew herself. Xena was a good person who thought she was bad. Lucy liked her just as she was, and was astounded when people called her moody or grim.

A shrink might ask Xena what was her opinion of her ratings rival, Hercules? More interestingly, what was Lucy's opinion of Kevin Sorbo, the actor who plays Hercules? Lucy characterized their relationship as completely uncompetitive. Kevin was her big brother and Lucy loved him. Just because the warrior princess came from Hercules' rib didn't mean that she wanted to exterminate him.

And as if beating *Hercules* in the ratings wasn't enough, Xena was also whipping Hercules in online adoration. A preponderance of pages faithfully followed the mighty princess who was shaped in the heat of combat. *Ay-yi-yi-yi!*

Xena was in fact the subject of much online analysis. A mandate of the International Association of Xena Studies was "to encourage good, clean obsessive behavior towards anything remotely to do" with the television show. The association's online magazine, *Whoosh!,* contained full libraries of commentary, such as "Chain Mail and Its Uses on *Xena: Warrior Princess*" and "*Xena: Warrior Princess* and the Mortality Rate of Significant Others."

Bubba's Guide to *Xena: Warrior Princess* was the online abode of a group called the Texas Xena Mafia. One excerpt of Bubba's episode guide read: "Well, y'all ain't gonna believe this, but turns out Xena's got herself another shirt-tail relative that's the spittin' image of our warrior princess." The Texas Xena Mafia had their own private lyrics to "Warrior Princess Blues."

When Reneé O'Connor returned to Houston for her high school reunion, she was surprised with the overwhelming fan reaction she received. "There was this one girl who didn't know what to say to me," an amazed Reneé told *People*. "She was so excited that you could see her body shaking."

But Reneé could still stroll blithely through a busy hotel lobby without worry of touching off mob scenes. Dressed casually in a sky-blue turtleneck and jeans, riding in an elevator in Austin, Texas, with a freshly scrubbed kid, she was asked if she was with the student council convention. At twenty-six, she still had the look of a wholesome prom queen.

Reneé didn't fly north nearly as often as Lucy. She lived in New Zealand nine months of the year, and she remained fairly unrecognized there, too.

"New Zealanders are very English—they restrain themselves," Reneé told *People*. "If they recognize you, they're more likely to look at you with a funny expression, so you think you've got ink on your shirt!" Americans were much more extroverted and apt to approach the actress—that is, if they recognized her.

A BRAND NEW MERCEDES

Lucy traded in her Alfa Romeo for a brand new Mercedes—with a price tag of around $350,000. New Zealand's *Woman's Day* talked her into having her photo taken with the vehicle. Wearing a dressing gown to hide her breastplates, Lucy made a dash to the parking lot. She leaned proudly against the dark blue CL600 series three-door luxury model Mercedes. The photos in

Woman's Day showed her smiling hugely. However, her joy turned to annoyance as she bent nearer to investigate a mark on the vehicle's gleaming paintwork.

Her fame was snowballing, taking on a life of its own. She gave some healing tips, as did many other actresses, to *Natural Living Today* for the magazine's summer 1997 issue. July saw her appearing live at a New York City Fourth of July fireworks spectacular, along with Yankee shortstop Derek Jeter. She was really racking up the frequent-flyer miles with her flights north.

On July 10, she and Kevin Sorbo appeared live at Universal Studios' theme park in Florida to celebrate the opening of the new $10 million attraction, "Hercules and Xena: Wizards of the Screen." The dedication for the attraction took place on Thursday morning amid Florida's sultry summer heat. Lucy and Kevin came clad more like tourists than legendary warriors. According to the *Tampa Tribune,* Lucy wore a silk Oriental sheath that matched her azure eyes. She was slender and demure—but showed sudden eruptions of humor. Though *Femmes Fatale* had named her number thirty in the top fifty sexy women of science fiction, she seemed startled by female roars of "wooooo" that greeted her introduction. Even without her leather and metal bustier, Lucy's stunning good looks and stand-out figure would be hard to overlook. And she was tall, but not as tall as Kevin Sorbo. In black slacks and a knit shirt, Kevin proved tall enough to check the theme park's actors for male-pattern baldness.

The swords came out. "Schwing," Lucy said, sweeping her blade before her. Both actors took practice swings before severing the straps holding a cloak over a two-story sword marking the entrance of the Hercules and Xena attraction. Kevin dedicated the building to the hope of good's victory over evil. "Not that we have anything against evil," Lucy added in her natural New Zealand accent. Evil—at least the fantasy kind—kept them both employed.

The new theme park attraction brought visitors into the filmmaking process, showing how special effects on the show were concocted. The premise centered on a crossover episode that pitted the two lead characters against Ares and his hell-born army. Visitors were drafted to playact centaurs, operate a spidery monster, and furnish sound effects (a metal spatula hitting a pole for a sword fight, coconuts cropped against a counter for a centaur charge.)

After meeting with a mob of fans, Lucy and Kevin were subjected to questions, predominantly from British media representatives. It was a Detroit radio reporter, however, who asked which size action figure based on their characters they preferred: the four-inch or foot-long dolls.

Kevin deadpanned that from a male standpoint, he always preferred the twelve-inch. Lucy said that women always preferred the four-inch.

The reporter then asked Lucy if she was aware that the slippage of her top while singing at the Red Wings game earlier that year had created a big Detroit fan base for her. "Yes, thanks," she answered, blushing. But she recovered with true Xena form. She told the *Tampa Tribune,* "It was quite a hair-rais-ing experience, the scariest experience I've had since the accident." Was she referring to her worry about slipping on the ice, or about exposing herself?

Asked if there were any plans for Hercules and Xena to marry, Lucy said, "It will always be an unrequited passion. Once you get married, it's over." Was she referring to her own beliefs about marriage? Lucy had told the *San Francisco Chronicle* that she hoped to have more children one day. She wanted to be a very happy eighty-year-old, and for her, that meant having more of a family. But kids required time. And it was hard to imagine Lucy would follow the path of so many stars before her and have her children out of wedlock. Her reserved family and strong Catholic background still had a pronounced influence over her.

YOU CAN'T GET IT OUT OF YOUR BONES

Those long flights back and forth from New Zealand must have exhausted Lucy, but she told David Letterman that she felt she would make her home in New Zealand for the rest of her life—or at least one of her homes. "I will always have a home [there], yeah. You can't get it out of your bones."

> **"** I've even used it to change a few things in my life. I quit smoking, for instance, because I don't want the young women who look up to me to think it's OK. **"**

She was good-humored about the way Americans tended to confuse New Zealand with Australia, right down to the kangaroos (which they don't have in New Zealand). Americans tended to think one could surely just walk from one island to the next when the tide was out.

"Completely different country," she told David Letterman, "four-hour flight away."

Asked to choose her favorite episode of the show, she couldn't decide between "Is There a Doctor in the House" and "Warrior . . . Princess . . . Tramp." They stood out in her mind because she had been so busy in both. They had demanded really intense work—and the more pressure she was under, the better she liked it. She

wanted to be challenged, not just sit around on her backside.

The most physically difficult episode for her had been "Chariots of War," because of the biting cold. She'd suffered whiplash, black eyes, and loosened teeth, but it was the New Zealand weather that frightened her the most.

A reporter for *Parade* once guessed that she weighed about 135 pounds, but she corrected him: 140. And sometimes she put on five or ten pounds more. The reporter was astonished. Tennis star Gabriela Sabatini was the only other woman he had ever interviewed who had *added* pounds to his guess. Lucy told him she had modeled Xena on Gabriela. The tennis player was how Lucy had thought a warrior princess ought to look.

SUFFICIENT STAR STATUS

Lucy had finally accepted her place as a role model for others. "Now I find it a pleasure," she told *TV-Times*. "I've even used it to change a few things in my life. I quit smoking, for instance, because I don't want the young women who look up to me to think it's OK."

Lucy was being recognized so regularly in the United States that when she registered in a hotel, she used a false name. In New York's Four Seasons that summer of 1997, she was "Irma McHugh." Irma/Lucy was in New York to meet with Broadway producers about her role in *Grease!* Her appearance in the musical had recently been threatened due to a technicality of union qualifications. The Actors' Equity rules allowed foreigners to take roles in Equity productions only if they possessed sufficient star status, which they denied Lucy had. Because of the dispute, the producers of *Grease!* posted a notice that the play would be closing. But evidently Lucy's stardom was proved—the dispute was settled—and she would be on stage in New York come September 1997.

Even the Kiwis were beginning to realize what a star they had in their midst. New Zealand *Woman's Weekly* announced that Lucy was rapidly overtaking Rachel Hunter as the international New Zealander of choice. The magazine declared that it was Lucy's open personality that had intrigued and won the heart of the "Yanks." Unlike Rachel's glossy, impossibly perfect image, Lucy was not afraid to admit that her life had its dark patches. She was a natural, unpretentious figure, both on and off stage, as well as a good actress. Furthermore, *Xena* was "fast propelling Lucy into the NZ $1.5 million-per-week category with a hefty salary from the series, personal appearances, and earnings from merchandising.

The subject of her moving north to the United States kept surfacing. The New Zealand press speculated that Lucy's Kiwi roots would keep her home, and that she wouldn't want her daughter growing up as an American. New Zealanders seemed to be growing proud enough of her to want her to remain one of them.

Though Lucy maintained she was going to stay put, her relationship with *Xena* producer Rob Tapert might make the difference in the end. Lucy and Rob's personal alliance, like their professional one, had gone from strength to strength. Lucy evidently considered the connection permanent, for she no longer referred to herself as single. "I would hate to be single again," she told the *Mirror.* "Once you have become successful—especially in a small country like New Zealand—it's difficult to find a mate in real life. It adds a whole slew of new problems to building a relationship."

> " Once you have become successful—especially in a small country like New Zealand—it's difficult to find a mate in real life. It adds a whole slew of new problems to building a relationship. "

FROM GREECE TO *GREASE!*

Topps Comics gave Xena her own comic book in August. And Ru Emerson's Xena novels continued to sell briskly. A fourth Xena novel was written by Stella Howard.

Emerson, an Oregon-based writer, hadn't heard of Xena until her literary agent suggested she tune in. "The first show I saw opened with a hilarious scene in which Xena takes on fifteen goons and flattens 'em all," Emerson said in the *San Francisco Chronicle.* "I hadn't seen anything that good since Emma Peel in *The Avengers.*"

The thirst for anything Xena, Ru told the San Francisco *Bay Guardian,* is such that people often bought three copies of a book, "so they can have one sealed in plastic, one they read without bending the cover, and a third they lend to people who then go out and buy their own sets."

There was only one Lucy Lawless, however, and she was segueing from Greece to *Grease!* in September 1997, playing Rizzo in the revival Broadway production. She had only two weeks for rehearsals and previews, then she did the play for seven weeks. The revival was based on the book, music, and lyrics of Jim Jacobs and Warren Casey. It was directed and choreographed by Jeff Calhoun. The story concerns the lives of teenagers in the 1950s.

The play had become a way for actors from other media to make their Broadway debuts. Lucy's performance was scheduled to run from September 2 through October 19, at the Eugene O'Neill Theatre on West 49th Street. Ticket prices ranged from $30 to $67.50. Lucy's only worry about the appearance was her separation from Daisy during the six-week period.

According to the *San Francisco Chronicle,* she hesitated to talk about how she would portray the headstrong Rizzo. She would only say, "You can't help

but make choices with lines which are borne out of your own personality and history."

Did the idea of a Broadway opening and those savage theater critics intimidate her? No. She realized that she could fail completely—but she hadn't ever done that yet. She had studied hard—voice and dance and her lines—and she was prepared.

Xena fans were also set to hear Lucy's wonderful singing voice in the animated Hercules feature due out in October or November. In it, Xena sings about the loss of her Gabrielle.

By then, the *Xena* and *Hercules* series were airing in more than fifty countries every week. In the U.S. alone, *Xena* aired on some two hundred stations. Lucy's online fame also compounded daily. A *Denver Post* reporter's Web search elicited 7,271 entries for *Xena: Warrior Princess.*

Meanwhile, fans got all dressed up as Xena for the regular monthly screening of episodes at the New York City lesbian nightspot Meow Mix. All eyes were glued to the television screen over the bar as Xena plants "The Kiss" on Gabrielle. The horde of fans packing the place erupted in whoops and whistles. When Gabrielle discovers she's been kissed by a man carrying Xena's soul in his body, disappointed moans erupted in the bar, and full-throated cries of "Rewind!"

Meow Mix was just one more pulse point for the blooming cult of *Xena*. The once a month Xena Night meant a screening of three episodes, followed by a mock sword fight. "It's the one show on TV where I don't feel invisible," a lesbian library-science student told *Entertainment Weekly*.

"Of course, there's a big lesbian following," reported fan Tom Simpson to *Total TV*. "That's what always gets the press." But there were fans of every age, of every persuasion, all over the country. Lucy excelled at portraying a character whose popularity crossed barriers. Kids loved her, adults loved her, men loved her, women loved her—and all for separate reasons.

A REMARKABLE PERFORMANCE

Xena coexecutive producer R. J. Stewart told *Whoosh!* readers to stay tuned for the 1997 season premiere. The first episode was one of his favorites, called "The Furies." "Lucy gives a remarkable performance in that one. A syndicated show has never received an Emmy as far as I know, but Lucy deserves one for the consistently inspired and imaginative performances she gives every week."

Late September 1997 saw another convention with Lucy and Robert Trebor scheduled to appear in New York City, at the Marriott Marquis. In October, Reneé O'Connor and Michael Hurst appeared at a Convention in San Francisco. In November, Robert Trebor was to appear again at conventions in Chicago and in Houston.

Lucy assured her fans on America Online that she hoped *Xena* would continue for a few years more, but suspected that after it ended, she probably wouldn't choose to do a lengthy series again for some time. Instead, she hoped to do some film projects and some stage productions as well.

Regardless, fans could look forward to watching *Xena* episodes for a long time to come. In September 1998, the USA Channel would begin to rebroadcast earlier *Xena* and *Hercules* episodes.

> **"** It's not real to me. It's absolutely not real. It has nothing really to do with my daily life. You get up and put your pants on one foot at a time like everybody else. Then you go out and water the garden or clean up the dishes from the night before. **"**

much, it would be tough to ask her to do more," said Steven Sears in a live Universal Netforum chat, ". . . not that we won't."

XENA FOR THE REST OF HER LIFE

R. J. Stewart felt it was very likely viewers would get a fourth season of new episodes as well. Contracts were being signed. Money was being spent. Fans could count on it. Of course, it was up to the ratings—but there was not much to worry about on that front.

The Second Annual *Xena/Hercules* Convention in Burbank, California, was already planned for January 1998. As much as Rob Tapert would like to do a feature film or a video with Kevin and Lucy, their time schedules wouldn't permit it. "Lucy works so

A major attraction to becoming a performer is the dream of becoming the focus of everyone's attention, and many a bright star has let it go to her head. Lucy Lawless seems impervious to that foible. "It's not real to me. It's absolutely not real. It has nothing really to do with my daily life," she told Yahoo! Internet Life. "You get up and put your pants on one foot at a time like everybody else. Then you go out and water the garden or clean up the dishes from the night before."

She still felt a little amazed when she met hard-core *Xena* fans. She observed them rather like specimens and asked questions, hoping for answers to illuminate what drove them to such lengths of obsession. She felt as fascinated by them as they were by her.

No matter how confident she feels that she won't be typecast, it is bound to be a difficulty. She will be Xena in the minds of television watchers for the rest of her life. As David Duchovny pointed out, portraying an archetypical character creates a blending of actress and role. If you say "Superman," nine out of ten Americans will picture Christopher Reeve. Say "Wonder Woman," and Lynda Carter comes immediately to mind. Though Christopher Reeve was able to hide his cloak beneath the costumes of several other memorable roles (the lover in *Somewhere in Time,* for instance), Lynda Carter

never did move beyond her superheroine image.

Reverting to her natural hair color and New Zealand accent may help Lucy circumvent the problem. It is easy to believe, as she stares blue-eyed through the camera, that she can do and be anything she wants. She has already shattered several taboos, both as a woman and as an actress. And her rule-breaking portrayal of Xena assures her a place in whatever annals of television the future might write.

Meanwhile, "there are so many things out of my control . . . I'm just going to let them go," Lucy told Yahoo! "I'm more worried about my taxes and will the tomatoes [in my garden] rot than controlling my image."

SYGMA/GREGORY PACE

Lucy visited the United States frequently to promote her hit syndicated action-adventure show, Xena: Warrior Princess. *Such trips added to the challenge of keeping rested enough to give a good dramatic performance yet remaining flexible enough for the fights and jumps she must execute.*

Xena's popularity prompted a line of action figures. Lucy felt the Xena doll was sexy in a dominatrix sort of way.

Lucy Lawless and Kevin Sorbo at a January 1997 New Orleans convention. As if beating Hercules: The Legendary Journeys *in the ratings weren't enough,* Xena: Warrior Princess *was also whipping* Hercules *in online worship.*

It took Lucy longer to impress her native New Zealanders than it did to win the hearts of the "Yanks." Unafraid to admit that her life had its dark patches, Lucy was a natural, unpretentious figure, both on and off stage.

Here is a woman—an actress—who finds no need to create a myth about herself. She has lived honorably, has nothing to hide, and continues to hold the values instilled in her by a loving family.

Lucy Lawless and Kevin Sorbo mugged for the cameras at the unveiling of "Hercules and Xena: Wizards of the Screen." The $10 million attraction at Universal Studios in Florida opened on July 10, 1997.

Episode Guide

EVEN AS A SAVAGE WARLORD, XENA QUICKLY DEVELOPED A following. As a hero, she has attracted legions of fans of both sexes and all ages. They love her as much for her fighting skills and the glee she brings by flattening thugs as for her looks, her costume, her strength, and her ability to make her own way in a tough world.

XENA IN
HERCULES: THE LEGENDARY JOURNEYS

Warrior Princess

Xena's potential to do evil is highlighted in this must-see episode. Xena prepares an army to conquer the north. Certain that only Hercules can stop her, she plans to lure him to her stronghold and kill him. She seduces Iolaus, Hercules' strong but naive sidekick, and takes him north, knowing Hercules will follow.

Xena's men plan to attack Hercules. Aware of the trap, he warns Iolaus, who thinks Hercules is jealous and sends him away. Xena follows Hercules with one of her captains. The two men fight, and Xena kills the captain when he tries to surrender. Then she flees. Hercules pursues her. But Xena has returned, dirty and limping, to Iolaus. She tells him that Hercules murdered the captain and tried to kill her.

In a striking scene, Iolaus fights Hercules, but neither will kill the other. Iolaus learns the truth when Xena orders her men to kill

<XENAISM>

"I've just cut off the flow of blood to your brain. You'll be dead in thirty seconds . . . or, we can talk."

them both. Working together, the friends defeat the better part of her army. Xena flees with the remnants, vowing revenge.

To Look for The hot tub scene with Iolaus and Xena. According to the actors, the water was barely tepid.

The Gauntlet

Though dark, this episode does feature some light moments. When Xena captures a village, men bring her a prisoner: Hercules' friend Salmoneus disguised as a woman.

Xena's new captain, Darfus, rebels against her by breaking her rule of warning villagers before an attack—giving the peasants a chance to flee and killing only the males who stayed behind. When she goes scouting, Darfus stages a night attack on the next village, slaughtering everyone. Xena is sickened, especially after Darfus gives orders to put one surviving baby to death. Xena takes the infant, the son of Spyros, to safety.

She returns to find Darfus in command. He offers her one escape—through the gauntlet. She passes between the double line of men, some of whom beat her savagely, and though she makes it, Darfus orders her to be killed anyway. But no one will do it.

Hercules' cousin seeks him out in quest of protection from Xena and her army. They rescue Salmoneus.

Hercules asks Xena for her help. She refuses, saying she must kill Darfus and regain control of her army. The two fight. Hercules wins, but does not kill her. She leaves.

The men evade Darfus' ambush and reach the village. They evacuate the helpless and set traps. But the odds are against even Hercules, until Xena arrives unexpectedly. Darfus attacks Xena, and she kills him by plunging a sword into his chest.

Xena is unsure about her future as she and Hercules depart together.

In a final scene, a black-shrouded figure pulls the sword from Darfus' body. The warlord is given back his life—and two tasks: return Xena to Ares' service and kill Hercules. The god presents Darfus with a weapon to use against Hercules—the hellhound Gragus.

To Look for Hercules' cousin is played by the actor later cast as Homer in "The Athens Academy of Performing Bards."

Unchained Heart

This strong and dark episode picks up just after "The Gauntlet." As Darfus raids villages to obtain living victims for Gragus, one man is spared. The warlord shows the man the gaping wound in his chest and dispatches him to tell Hercules that Darfus is alive.

Neither Xena nor Hercules can believe it is Darfus, but they agree to stop the warlord. Salmoneus tags along. They catch up to Darfus and his army,

who are attacking miners. In the ensuing battle, Xena hurls a knife that buries itself to the hilt in the villain's chest. He smiles, pulls out the weapon, and rides away with what is left of his men. Xena wonders how he can be stopped.

Iolaus finds Hercules and is furious when he sees Xena. He is sure Hercules is being deceived, just as he was.

Darfus triggers a rock slide, burying the heroes, but Hercules holds up an enormous boulder while Iolaus and Xena dig themselves out. Salmoneus is terrified and, once they are safe again, he leaves. He hitches a ride with a blind peddler who inadvertently delivers him to Darfus' camp. Darfus orders him chained in the temple to await becoming Gragus' next meal. The hellhound has grown large from all the victims he has consumed.

Hercules, Xena, and Iolaus arrive. Iolaus fights Darfus' army while Hercules holds Gragus at bay and Xena attacks Darfus. Salmoneus is cut loose and helps Iolaus "flatten" the bad guys with a copper ladle. Gragus eats Darfus, and, as evil consumes itself, the hound vanishes back to Hades in flames.

Hercules and Xena are by now clearly fond of each other. But in a somewhat convenient finale, she decides she must go away, alone, to atone for her past deeds.

High Point Other warlords, in both *Hercules* and *Xena* have been bad, but no one has had that bad-to-the-bone look of the Ares-possessed Darfus.

XENA: WARRIOR PRINCESS—SEASON ONE

Sins of the Past

The first actual *Xena: Warrior Princess* episode offers plenty of light moments, thanks to the introduction of Gabrielle—and plenty of sexual tension stemming from the love-hate relationship between Xena and the warlord Draco.

Xena is burying her weapons and armor when armed thugs show up with local village women they have kidnapped to sell as slaves. Xena fights the thugs, and one of the girls, Gabrielle, starts inexpertly but enthusiastically thumping heads, which convinces the village men to fight. Once it is over,

Xena learns that thugs serve her old enemy Draco.

Gabrielle—who is bored with village life and does not want to marry the man chosen for her (Perdicas)—is fascinated by Xena's skills, but Xena wants no part of her. The village headman demands that the warrior princess leave. Xena warns Gabrielle not to follow her.

She finds Draco, and in a scene that crackles with their love-hate relationship, procures his promise to leave the village alone. Xena then departs for Amphipolis, her hometown. Draco lays plans for an attack on Amphipolis that will look as if it were her doing. He wants to prove to Xena that you can't go home again.

On her way, Xena runs into an old enemy—a cyclops whom she had blinded—and defeats him again. Gabrielle, who is on her trail, is caged by the cyclops, but she fast-talks her way out of the trap. Xena later takes out some of Draco's men who have been pursuing her. She now knows Draco is after Amphipolis but cannot convince the villagers, who hate, fear, and distrust her. Not even her mother will believe the truth. The villagers are about to stone Xena when Gabrielle appears and uses her powers of persuasion yet again.

When Draco arrives, Xena challenges him to a fight for the village. He chooses staffs as weapons, and she picks the setting—rickety scaffolding made of loose bamboo. The rules: First one to touch the ground will be killed. Once the fight begins, the village rallies around Xena. She finally knocks Draco to the ground, but agrees to spare his life if he will spare Amphipolis.

Xena reconciles with her mother, but she knows Amphipolis is no place for her. Gabrielle follows once again— but this time, Xena lets her tag along.

It's an extremely satisfying episode. Xena is still tough and defensive, though she is now warming in Gabrielle's presence.

Best Line   The blind cyclops says to Gabrielle, "Shut up. I hate chatty food."

To Look for   The ongoing confusion over the gender of Argo, Xena's mare. As Xena nears the cyclops and the horse gets nervy, she says, "Easy, boy."

Chariots of War

A good episode for the questions it raises: When and why do you fight? And when is fighting wrong for any reason?

Xena is wounded while protecting a farmer and his family. She grows close to the widowed Darius and his children, but Darius is a pacifist and confiscates her weapons. His neighbors know who she is and want him to send her away.

The warlord Cycnus is trying to turn his youngest son, Sphaerus, into a warrior with a killing instinct, but with little success. Meantime, Gabrielle has wound up (as usual in early episodes) in the wrong kind of tavern among the wrong kind of guys, in this case, Sphaerus' men. To get away from one of the uglier brutes, she takes refuge with Sphaerus, who is visibly pleased.

Xena tries to convince Darius that they must fight, but he disagrees. She understands his point, while he cannot see hers. She agrees to talk peace first, then thwarts a sneak attack by Sphaerus and his men. The villagers see this as proof that Xena cannot be trusted.

Cycnus tells the village headman that they soon will have eternal peace. The man realizes Xena was right. Cycnus then tells Sphaerus that Xena stabbed his brother in the back. Sphaerus swears vengeance.

Xena meets up with Gabrielle, and when two war chariots come after them, she forces Gabrielle onto Argo's back and sends them off at a dead gallop. Cycnus assumes the rider is Xena and pursues. Xena commandeers the second chariot, sparking a wild chase scene that ends when Gabrielle steers into Cycnus. Xena tells the warlord that his eldest son was murdered by his own men while seeking a truce. Sphaerus attacks his father but cannot bring himself to slay him. Xena kills Cycnus, and Sphaerus tells Darius they will negotiate a real truce. Parting on good terms with the two men—and with the villagers—Xena and Gabrielle leave.

Dreamworker

Though predictable—in that something had to check Gabrielle's intense desire to have Xena teach her to kill— this is a good episode. Xena refuses Gabrielle's request, saying that once you have killed, everything changes, and that there are ways to avoid fighting and killing. Gabrielle does not like the explanation. But moments later, when set upon by thieves, she learns firsthand. By picking up Xena's sword, she is immediately seen as a threat and is attacked. Xena flattens the thieves and kills their leader. Gabrielle is shaken, but is still not totally convinced.

Two priests of Morpheus, god of dreams, have witnessed everything. They want to present Gabrielle as their annual sacrifice to Morpheus because she is brave yet has never killed.

At the next village Xena encounters a blind ex-priest of Morpheus while Gabrielle vanishes. Xena learns that any village women who have never spilled blood are in danger this time of year, and that the priests must have captured Gabrielle. Xena seeks help from the blind ex-priest. He convinces her that a headlong attack will not save Gabrielle, and instead sends her soul on a dream-path, where she confronts specters from her past, including men she has killed, and her old, wicked self.

Gabrielle, in the meantime, is being tempted to kill. Xena comes to her rescue in the nick of time, and the ex-priest is restored as head priest of Morpheus once more.

Another step forward in the friendship between the two women. Each is concerned for the other, each learns from the other, and each succeeds only because of the other.

Best Line   Gabrielle asks Xena, after decking Manus, "Punches are all right?"

Cradle of Hope

In this middling episode, King Gregor's oracle informs him that a baby born to one of his slaves will eventually claim his throne. Gregor orders his captain, Nemos, to bring him the baby, whose mother died in childbirth. A servant saves the infant by putting him on a raft and sending him down river. Xena and Gabrielle find the castaway and set out to return him to his people. On the way, they join Pandora, who is

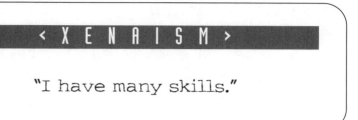

< X E N A I S M >

"I have many skills."

doomed to wander the world carrying a box containing Hope.

Xena learns that Gregor has recently lost his wife and child. She persuades him to raise the child as his own, so the boy will be his heir and the prophecy will come true.

Nemos starts a fight, intending to kill the baby and take the throne himself, but Xena defeats him. The king convinces Pandora to stay with him and the baby.

Gabrielle accidentally knocks over the box—and discovers it is empty. Xena tells her that Pandora was carrying Hope inside herself—as we all do.

Best Scene   The final battle against Nemos and his men, with Xena and Gabrielle hurling the baby back and forth.

Disclaimer   No babies were harmed during the making of this motion picture.

The Path Not Taken

The character of Marcus—adored by many fans—is introduced in this strong episode. Once Xena's lover, Marcus has tried to reform, as she did, but has failed.

Jana and Agranon talk about their wedding, which will unite kingdoms that have long been at war. They are attacked by armed thugs, who kidnap Jana. The event is designed to keep the war going, which means the arms dealer Mezentius is probably behind it. Agranon persuades Xena to rescue Jana.

Xena convinces Mezentius and his thugs that she is the old Xena, looking for profit and bloodshed—but she finds it more difficult to deceive Marcus, Mezentius' right-hand man. The chemistry is still there, but Xena does not dare trust him—and he is suspicious of her. Marcus has heard that Xena has "gone good." Failing to corrupt her, he feels bitter.

Xena is about to escape with Jana. Marcus learns what she has been up to and is angry because she did not trust him. She tries to convince him that he, too, can reform, that all it takes is one good act. He calls Mezentius instead. But when the arms merchant tries to shoot Jana with an arrow, Marcus tragically performs his one good act. He steps in front of Jana, and is fatally wounded. Xena kills Mezentius with her chakram and saves Jana.

Best Scene Gabrielle choosing a tavern with "atmosphere," then wandering inside, completely oblivious to Xena at her back, flattening leering brutes and thugs on all sides.

To Look for Marcus' funeral. The song was composed and sung by Lucy Lawless. Also, watch for Marcus, who turns out to be a man worth going to Hades for (see "Mortal Beloved" below).

The Reckoning

An OK episode, "The Reckoning" brings in Ares as both a solid character and Xena's would-be lover.

Ares frames Xena for the murder of four villagers, then creates a dreamworld in which he can seduce her into rejoining him. She refuses and is brutalized by Peranis, her jailer. Gabrielle talks the village elder, Benitar, into holding a trial, in which she will act as Xena's lawyer.

Ares thinks he has convinced Xena to serve him again by telling her he can bring back anyone she wants to soldier in her army—any hero from the past. But she calls for the four villagers who were killed. Ares is forced to comply, and the men testify that Xena was not their murderer.

Best Scene Gabrielle putting her life on the line to save Xena when vigilantes are about to kill her.

The Titans

Not one of the best episodes. As Xena tracks down the thug Hessiod and his followers, Gabrielle wanders into a nearby cavern, where a priestess is unsuccessfully reading a spell from a scroll. Gabrielle brightly explains that she is using the wrong pentameter and proceeds to read the spell using a different cadence. To everyone's surprise, she awakens three Titans—Crias,

< X E N A I S M >

"I like to be creative in a fight. It gets my juices going."

Theia, and Hyperion—old giants who had been turned to stone. The locals hope to use the Titans to protect themselves from Hessiod and his kind. The Titans will obey only Gabrielle—the "goddess" who awakened them.

Hyperion, the young male Titan, does not believe Gabrielle is a goddess. He is ashamed of having to labor for humans. When Gabrielle is unable to conjure a feast, the villagers are forced to take shelter in a temple. The Titans capture the village children, who were on an excursion. The kidnapping starts a rift between the Titans, made worse when Theia acts lovingly toward the older Crias and culminating with Hyperion killing Crias.

Xena and Gabrielle get into the Titans' cavern. Xena rescues the children and tries to hold off Hyperion until Gabrielle can read the spell that will turn the Titans back to stone. When Xena kills Hyperion, Theia agrees to be turned to stone.

What works in this episode is the growing bond between the two women, especially when Gabrielle is falling for the young priest Phyleus and Xena becomes fiercely protective of her companion's innocence.

Best Scene Gabrielle doing what the early Gabby does best—talking her way out of trouble. In this case, she deals with a very angry Hyperion, who wants her to recite the chant that will revive *all* the Titans.

Prometheus

The Greek myth is presented with an interesting twist in this entertaining episode. Hercules and Iolaus join up with Xena and Gabrielle to rescue Prometheus, a Titan who has been chained atop a mountain where a monstrous eagle comes regularly to feast on his liver. Hera wants Prometheus to turn his back on humankind, but he refuses. The vengeful goddess begins taking away the gifts that Prometheus has given to man, be-

ginning with the gift of healing. Even a small cut now results in death.

When Xena's mother falls ill, Xena and Gabrielle set out to free Prometheus. They meet up with Hercules and Iolaus. Iolaus is injured, and Gabrielle stays with him, knowing he will die unless Xena and Hercules succeed in freeing Prometheus. They do, and Iolaus is saved—as is mankind.

This episode is an interesting take on the myth of Prometheus and has some great special effects, but it does not give us much else, except the chance to see the two heroes and their sidekick teamed together against a common enemy.

Best Scene Xena and Hercules fight with lizard men for the sword of Hephaestus.

Disclaimer Iolaus was harmed during the production of this motion picture. However, the Green Egg Men went on to live long and prosperous lives.

Death in Chains

An interesting tale, this episode shows us that one of the most lethal forces around could be Gabrielle's love: When she falls for some poor guy, he is guaranteed to be dead by the closing credits.

< X E N A I S M >

"You see? I can play, too."

King Sisyphus is afraid to die, so he imprisons Death and steals her eternal candle. But the candle begins to burn. When it is burned through, Death herself will die.

They find men suffering deadly injuries caused by a rock slide, and Xena knows that the relief of death will not come for them. Gabrielle still does not understand why Death must be rescued. Sweet, handsome Talus shows up to help her attend to the wounded and tells wonderful stories to distract the men from their pain. Gabrielle falls for him hard. Talus tells her that he knows Sisyphus' castle well and can guide them.

Xena sends Talus and Gabrielle to help the wounded while she heads for the castle. While she's gone, Talus is injured by a warlord Xena "killed" earlier.

Karis, Sisyphus' wife, finds an injured bird. She sees that eternal life can mean eternal pain.

Gabrielle learns that if Xena touches Death or is touched by her in the rescue, Xena will die. Gabrielle heads for the castle, guided by Talus.

Xena falls into one of Sisyphus' many booby traps. Talus falls in with her after becoming separated from Gabrielle.

Karis tries to prove to Sisyphus that he has done wrong, but he is incapable of accepting this until Xena, Karis, and Talus all talk to him about the suffering he has caused. Sisyphus frees Death, who turns from Sisyphus to claim Talus.

Best Scene Any of the scenes involving the trickery Sisyphus has built into his castle. Look for Sisyphus later, in season two's "Ten Little Warlords."

Worst Scene Xena in a small space with rats.

Reality Check If all the injured are in such agony, why isn't the "undead" warlord?

Disclaimer No jumbo-sized cocktail rats were harmed during the making of this motion picture.

Hooves and Harlots

In this middling episode Xena and Gabrielle fall in with Amazons who are attacked, apparently by their ancient enemies the centaurs. Gabrielle picks up a walking stick—and is fascinated when Xena demonstrates how it can be used as a weapon. They are captured by four Amazons who decide to take them to Queen Melosa as trespassers. Gabrielle and one of the Amazons, Terreis, find they have a lot in common. Xena and another, Ephiny, distrust each other. They are ambushed. Terreis is wounded, and Gabrielle shields the fallen Amazon with her own body. To Ephiny's shock, the dying Terreis gives Gabrielle Right of Cast, making her an Amazon.

After they arrive at the Amazon village, Ephiny captures the centaur Phantes, whose arrow matches the one that killed Terreis. Phantes is the son of Tyldus, leader of the centaurs. Queen Melosa says he will be executed.

Xena confronts Phantes, but he will neither admit nor deny killing Terreis, saying only that he would like to kill all of them.

Melosa meets with Krykus, an arms dealer. Xena tries to keep the Amazons from killing Phantes and starting a war with the centaurs. She then appeals to Tyldus to avoid a war.

Gabrielle is angry that she has been told to keep the Right of Cast secret from Xena. Melosa names her Amazon Princess and tells Ephiny to train her. None of these women trusts the others.

Xena visits the centaurs and tells Tyldus that she has seen his son.

Gabrielle, dressed in Terreis' garb, convinces Ephiny to recognize her as a fellow Amazon. Ephiny shows her weaponry, and Gabrielle chooses the fighting staff.

Tyldus realizes he has to trust Xena in order to save his son. Phantes knows nothing of war except the glory of it. Tyldus will not see his son executed for something he didn't do.

Ephiny shows Gabrielle how to use a fighting staff to cripple a centaur. Gabrielle is appalled.

At the site where they were first attacked, Xena proves to Ephiny that the prints left are those of a horse, not a centaur. The arms dealer Krykus is behind Terreis' death.

Melosa tells Gabrielle that as Terreis' heir she is also her avenger. She must kill Phantes or die as a traitor. Xena confronts Krykus as Ephiny searches his belongings—and finds centaur arrows. Melosa will not accept the proof. Xena challenges the queen, and defeats her. At that moment, Tyldus' army appears, ready to fight the Amazons. Tyldus leads them after Krykus. The centaurs pull chariots full of Amazons, and together they trounce Krykus and his men.

There is peace—an uneasy one, but it's a start. Ephiny gives Gabrielle her fighting staff as a parting gift.

> ‹ X E N A I S M ›
>
> "It was just another village to conquer . . . nothing out of the ordinary."

Best Lines Gabrielle's, "I'm sorry. You must have mistaken me for a pet."

Disclaimer No males, centaurs, or Amazons were harmed during the making of this motion picture.

The Black Wolf

Another middling episode, a group of rebels are imprisoned by King Xerxes, who threatens to kill them to get their leader, the Black Wolf. Hermia's daughter, Flora, was taken with others who all claimed to be the Black Wolf. Xena promises to rescue the girl. She tells Xerxes she will enter the prison as a Black Wolf sympathizer. Once inside, she will learn the leader's secret identity for Xerxes.

Koulos, the king's chief advisor, reveals that he has his own spy working in the prison.

Gabrielle arrives in the village. The blacksmith working on Argo's shoes tells her that Xena is in prison. Gabrielle decides to get herself arrested.

Salmoneus is also in town, selling Black Wolf merchandise. Gabrielle lobs a tomato at one of the guards, but Salmoneus, caught holding a tomato, is hauled away.

Xena talks to Flora, who knew Xena as a child but no longer trusts her. Flora is sorry to have hurt her mother, but will not leave the Wolf Pack.

Koulos has Xena shoved into a grated pit. He tries to use her to force the Wolf Pack to talk. The water in the pit rises, but Xena escapes.

Xena and the prisoners haul themselves into a net near the ceiling so the guards will think they have escaped via a tunnel. The guards are shoved into the tunnel, which is then blocked with a boulder. Although Flora and the others are ecstatic, Xena is worried: It was too easy. Sure enough, Koulos and his men are waiting for them as they try to escape. The Wolf Pack suspects Xena has deceived them. She tells Xerxes that she would have learned the Black Wolf's identity had Koulos not gotten in the way. She goes back in.

One of the Wolf Pack, Diomedes, fights Xena. She could kill him but does not. She tells them there is a traitor among them.

Gabrielle finally gets arrested and is thrown in prison—wearing a sunbonnet in which she is hiding the chakram. Xena's whip is wrapped around her waist.

Xena now knows not only the identity of the Wolf but that the spy is crazy Parnassus, who walks around talking to a rock. The rock is hollow and holds messages. Found out, he is released. Koulos enters the prison with his guards. With Salmoneus' life in danger, Xena tells Koulos that Flora is the Black Wolf. Flora agrees and is hauled away for execution.

Xena and Xerxes prepare to watch the public execution. The other Wolves are chained together, along with Gabrielle, who convinces Diomedes to trust Xena. As Flora is about to be axed, Xena slices the shaft of the ax with her chakram, cuts the prisoners' chains, then attacks Xerxes. He is killed. Flora tells Xena that her group has members in government, so it should not be too hard to turn things around with Xeres dead.

Beware of Greeks Bearing Gifts

In this interesting take on the Trojan War, Xena comes to rescue Helen, at her own request, and stays to help defend the Trojans against Menelaus.

Helen is unhappy: Men are dying because of her. Paris seems to want her only for her beauty, Menelaus only to heal his hurt pride. And there is danger within Troy's walls that only Xena can cure.

Xena and Gabrielle fight their way to the gates of Troy, where Perdicas, Gabrielle's ex-fiancé, is standing guard. He opens the gates and comes to help. Gabrielle is stunned.

Menelaus plots against Xena with unseen men.

Xena gets in to see Helen, who wants to return to Menelaus so the war will end. Xena tells her this will not end the war.

Gabrielle realizes Perdicas is here because of her stories about war. She tells him he is not meant to be a warrior, but he ignores her.

Xena convinces Paris she is on their side. But she is suspicious of Deiphobus, Paris' brother.

Xena asks Helen what *she* wants. No one has ever asked her before. Xena discovers that Deiphobus is Menelaus' inside man. But Deiphobus claims he was trying to make peace and that Menelaus has decided to depart. The Greeks withdraw, leaving a gift at the gates: a wooden horse. Xena warns Paris to beware of Greeks bearing gifts. Paris, persuaded by his brother, has

< X E N A I S M >

"You got a snowball's chance in Tartarus with me. Ya got that?"

Xena thrown into prison. Paris' men haul the Trojan horse through the gates.

Paris continues to treat Helen as a prize of war. Meanwhile, Xena escapes from prison, Gabrielle and Perdicas make peace, and the Greeks emerge from the belly of the horse. Xena rescues Perdicas, Gabrielle, and Helen.

Deiphobus kills Paris and takes Helen. Menelaus wants the horse as a trophy. His men haul it back outside the gates—and discover Xena, Perdicas, and other Trojans are hidden inside. Perdicas is threatened, but Gabrielle saves him. Xena kills Deiphobus.

Helen departs, with Perdicas as her guard, to find herself. Gabrielle is stunned to learn too late that she has fallen in love with Perdicas.

To Look for   A different actor portrays Perdicas (first introduced in

"Sins of the Past"). He also plays the doomed Perdicas in "The Return of Callisto."

Disclaimer No oversized Polynesian-style bamboo horses were harmed during the making of this motion picture. However, many wicker lawn chairs gave their lives.

The Athens Academy of Performing Bards

A rare episode that centers around Gabrielle, featuring lots of fun clips from earlier *Xena* episodes and from old films, shown as various bards tell their tales. Xena persuades Gabrielle to enter a bardic competition. Gabrielle falls in with a collection of young males that includes Orion, who closes his eyes when he chants and is called the Blind Bard. His name is really Homer. Homer's father fears the boy will lose his place to Gabrielle. She sneaks in to the competition's auditions and persuades Homer to listen to his own heart when he does his own audition. Eventually, she decides she is better off with Xena, living the stories she will eventually set in verse.

To Look for Homer's competition piece is the tale of Spartacus, and the footage is from the classic 1960s Kirk Douglas film.

Disclaimer The producers would like to acknowledge and pay tribute to Stanley Kubrick, Kirk Douglas, and all those who were involved with the making of the film classic, *Spartacus.* Additional thanks to Steve Reeves.

A Fistful of Dinars

Among the early episodes, this is the most derivative. It was like *Indiana Jones* crossed with a spaghetti western.

Xena, the assassin Thersites, and Xena's ex-fiancé, Petracles, each have a portion of a clue to find an ancient treasure. Xena accompanies the hunt because along with the treasure is the key to locating ambrosia, the food of the gods. A taste of ambrosia will change even a mortal into a god. Xena wants to make certain it does not fall into the wrong hands.

Petracles courts Gabrielle, then accuses Xena of being jealous.

Once they find the treasure chamber, Thersites finds the key to locating the ambrosia and kidnaps Gabrielle. Thersites kills Petracles. Xena kills Thersites and disposes of the ambrosia.

Worst Scene Gabrielle getting kidnapped once again.

Disclaimer No ambrosia was spilled, spoiled, or harmed in any way during the production of this motion picture. (Thanks to the indefinite shelf life of marshmallows.)

Warrior . . . Princess . . . Tramp

Lucy Lawless had a fine opportunity to show her range in a dual role in this, one of the funnier episodes of the first season.

Xena is called to the palace of King Lias to protect his daughter, Diana. Amazingly, the princess is Xena's exact double. In appearance, that is. Diana is sheltered and very much a girl. After yet another attempt on Diana's life, Xena persuades King Lias that Diana's only chance is for the two women to trade places. Xena dons fluffy pink and does her best to act feminine, while Diana puts on the warrior's dark leathers and rides Argo (sidesaddle!) to find Gabrielle.

Complications abound. Diana has been courted by her fiancé's younger brother on the elder's behalf—and now she loves the wrong one. Not a bad choice, since the older brother—who is king of the adjoining kingdom—only wants to wed Diana so he can promote slavery in both realms. By the end of the show, both Xena and Diana have adapted so well to playing the other that they fool everyone.

This one is fun, as much for questioning what is feminine as for showing the notably tough Xena trying to adapt to pink, servants, ribbons, lapdogs, and having her hair brushed a thousand times a day.

Best Lines Diana (as Xena) says of Xena's chakram: "This? Oh, it's my round, killing thing."

Gabrielle: "That's a chakram."

Diana, clueless: "Bless you!"

Best Scene Xena (as Diana) and Philemon fighting off a pack of villains. He thinks he is protecting her, and be-

hind his back, she is clobbering the bad guys.

To Look for Philemon, Diana's future love, played the minor villain Brisus in "The Path Not Taken."

Disclaimer Neither Xena nor her remarkable coincidental identical twin, Diana, were harmed during the production of this motion picture.

Mortal Beloved

A two-hankie episode for Marcus fans. Marcus, returned from the dead, asks for Xena's help. Hades' helmet of invisibility has been stolen, and those who were condemned to the hell of Tartarus have invaded the Elysian Fields, chasing the pure-hearted into Tartarus.

Xena agrees to help. She dives into Lake Alcyonia—known to be exceedingly deep. She has to get to the Underworld one way or the other because the man she loves needs her.

Xena crosses the River of Death and enters Tartarus where she finds Marcus. They embrace. She has thought of him often. He knows this, because the dead can hear thoughts about themselves. He tells her that Atyminius, who has a penchant for chopping up brides, has stolen Hades' helmet of invisibility. He takes Xena to the Elysian Fields.

Xena believes he is among the good. Then Toxeus (killed in "Death in Chains") tells her that evil can move between Tartarus and the Fields. She realizes Marcus was put with the wicked. Why, then, has he asked for her help? He tells her that she moved him to die selflessly and it felt good.

The evil Atyminius plans his return to the living world so he can kill more brides. But he senses that one of the living is among the dead. Xena and Marcus escape past some lethal Harpies, into Hades' quarters.

Hades gives Marcus forty-eight hours of mortality to help Xena deal with Atyminius. They recapture the helmet and return it to its owner. Upon their return, the warrior princess kills Marcus in front of Hades, reminding Hades that Marcus must now be rejudged. She and Marcus re-

‹ XENAISM ›

"Hard times breed hard people."

unite briefly in the Elysian Fields, where Marcus now resides.

To Look for   Michael Hurst, who plays Hercules' buddy Iolaus, plays Charon, the ferryman who rows the dead across the river Styx.

Disclaimer   No winged Harpies were harmed or sent to a fiery grave during the production of this motion picture.

A Royal Couple of Thieves

An average episode with above average emphasis on Gabrielle. Xena and Gabrielle capture the master thief Autolycus. Xena "persuades" him to steal back a treasure taken from friends of hers. The island-dwelling warlord Malthus has the treasure chest and plans to auction it off as a weapon. Xena disguises Autolycus as Sinteres, a master assassin. She goes along as his

< X E N A I S M >

"Don't talk. Fight!"

"assistant." On Malthus' ship, Autolycus introduces her as his concubine, Cherish, and gives her a scanty costume to wear—to provide a distraction, he assures her. Xena reluctantly plays the part, giving her "Master" a look that promises revenge.

They are given a room in Malthus' castle, where Xena easily cools Autolycus' ardor. The stolen chest is booby-trapped and kept behind a locked door. Autolycus orders Cherish to dance for the men while he makes a wax impression of Malthus' key. But the chest is already gone—with Malthus lying dead in its place. The chest turns up in Xena's bed, but they manage to put it back before being caught.

Next morning, Arkel, Malthus' second-in-command, says the demonstration of the chest's powers will take place as planned, then introduces a surprise guest—the real Sinteres, who has

Gabrielle. Xena denounces Malthus' killer. He is executed by Sinteres. She, Gabrielle, and Autolycus escape. Xena then sends Gabrielle to find out where missing villagers are being taken—and, of course, Gabrielle is caught by Sinteres. Xena fights and kills Sinteres while Gabrielle frees the peasants. Arkel then opens the stolen chest while trying to run and is fried.

The chest, the Ark of the Covenant, is restored to the wandering Jews.

Best Scenes Autolycus continues his attempts to seduce Xena, who keeps decking him.

Worst Scene This is the early Gabrielle, once again getting kidnapped.

Disclaimer No ancient and inflexible rules governing moral behavior were harmed during the production of this motion picture.

The Prodigal

A seriously flawed episode. Gabrielle and Xena are ambushed. Gabrielle freezes.

In shame, she simply deserts her friend and heads for home.

She discovers that her village is next to be overrun by a marauding warlord—and that for protection the village has hired a depressed, hard-drinking old warrior named Meleager the Mighty. Meleager once froze during a fight (get it?) and has taken refuge in the bottle ever since.

Gabrielle is kidnapped (sigh) by the warlord, who urges Meleager to join him. As the warrior and Gabrielle escape back to her village, she disappears.

Gabrielle organizes the village's defense, and Meleager turns up in the nick of time. He skewers a bunch of bad guys, and the village is saved.

As Gabrielle returns to Xena, she is ambushed. She fights, Xena joins her—and everything is fine once more.

To Look for Meleager returns in "The Execution," season two.

Disclaimer Meleager the Mighty, the generally tipsy and carousing

‹ X E N A I S M ›

"Did I impress you?"

warrior-for-hire, was not harmed during the production of this motion picture.

Altered States

A twist on the biblical Abraham-and-Isaac tale that provides a backdrop for the growing bond between Xena and Gabrielle.

Xena and Gabrielle rescue a boy from a mob led by his older brother Mael. The boy, named Ikus, is supposed to be sacrificed to the god of their people. Xena leaves Ikus and Gabrielle in a cave while she talks to his father, Anteus.

Next, Xena finds Zora, Ikus' mother. She is terrified for her boy. She sends Xena away with nut bread for Ikus—a special bread that Mael has been feeding Anteus. The warrior princess smells henbane and realizes

< XENAISM >

"Oh, I'll do more for you than
that . . . much more."

that Mael has been drugging his father. She races back to the cavern to find Gabrielle drugged and delirious. Ikus has gone for his mother to help Gabrielle. He is captured.

Mael is using a bullhorn to impersonate the voice of God so Anteus will kill Ikus and make Mael his heir once again.

Xena and Gabrielle race to prevent the sacrifice. Xena confronts Mael, who falls to his death. Gabrielle retrieves the bullhorn from a tree so she can use it to halt the ceremony. Xena uses her chakram to knock the knife aside just as a voice tells Anteus that he has proven his faith and need not kill Ikus. Later, we learn that neither Xena nor Gabrielle spoke.

Best Scene   The opening teaser as the camera follows dropped articles of clothing and we hear Xena saying,

"Come on, Gabrielle. You've been wanting to do this for ages." At which point, Gabrielle finally catches a fish with her hands.

Disclaimer

No unabating or severely punishing deities were harmed during the production of this motion picture.

The Ties That Bind

An average episode showing the good and evil side of Xena. Xena rescues captured village women from the warlord Kirilus, who believes Ares is grooming him to take over the world. Ares pits him against Xena. Atrius, suddenly rides into the camp, also bent on freeing the slave girls. He is wounded. Gabrielle frees the girls and escapes with them, as Xena pulls Atrius to safety. He reveals that he is her father. He tells her enough about her childhood to make her trust him. Gabrielle takes the girls back to their village. When Xena and Atrius ride in, the villagers capture him. They tell Xena he tricked them before.

Meanwhile, Ares has been taunting Kirilus, telling him that Xena will take over his army. Kirilus fights her, and she beats him badly, then takes over the army and rides for the village. When they arrive, Atrius is strung up, dying, he tells her. She is enraged. She orders the army to attack the village.

Gabrielle, horrified, cracks Xena over the head. Xena comes back to her self. Atrius tries to persuade her to kill villagers. He is really Ares, of course, in a towering fury because he almost had her. He threatens to kill her if she will not join him, but she says she would rather die. He hurls a sword at her, stopping it just short of her throat. With a menacing promise of "next time," he vanishes.

Question of the Week   So who *is* Xena's father?

To Look for   When Xena leaps from Argo's back to confront Kirilus, the chakram falls off her belt, hits Argo's hoof, and rolls away. But as the scene cuts immediately to Xena striding across the grass, the weapon is on her left hip.

Disclaimer   No fathers, spiritual or biological, were harmed during the production of this motion picture.

The Greater Good

This is Argo's episode—a good horse story. Xena and Gabrielle ride to rescue Lord Seltzer and his village from Talmadeus, a warlord. Lord Seltzer turns out to be Salmoneus, now in the seltzer water business. He sold the warlord weapons and buckles that were made of talcus. When it rained, they dissolved. Xena drives off Talmadeus' thugs, but is ambushed and shot with a poisoned dart. We see enough of the body and armor to know it is Callisto. Xena becomes increasingly weak and disoriented. She is rescued by Gabrielle.

The warlord believes he scared her off. Xena has lost feeling in her legs and knows it will get worse. She persuades Gabrielle to impersonate her, right down to coloring her hair and riding Argo against Talmadeus. The ruse does not work well. Gabrielle cannot control Argo and must resort to using Xena's chakram to drive off the soldiers. She is eventually overpowered and tossed into a water trough, where the dye washes out of her hair. Talmadeus is ready to kill her, but Argo carries her to safety. Gabrielle finds Xena, apparently dead.

Salmoneus cuts a deal with the warlord. Talmadeus reneges. He prepares to kill Salmoneus, sell the villagers into slavery, and tear Xena's body apart using horses, one of them Argo. The horse refuses to move, even when the men beat her. As Talmadeus tries to kill Argo, Xena conveniently revives. The villagers take out the soldiers and Talmadeus winds up in the horse trough, cowering beneath a dozen swords.

Best Scene Actually an ongoing series of scenes in which Gabrielle comes to a truce with Argo.

Disclaimer Excessive belching can cause brain damage and social ostracism. Kids, don't give in to peer pressure. Play it safe.

Callisto

Two ongoing characters are introduced in this tense, dark episode: Callisto (Xena's dark side, with a vengeance) and Joxer (an inept, nerdy warrior).

The bloodthirsty warlord Callisto raids a village, sparing only one old woman to spread the word that Xena was responsible for the slaughter. Xena encounters the vengeful father of a boy killed by Callisto. She tells the man and Gabrielle why Callisto hates her: Xena's army once destroyed Callisto's village.

Callisto is taking out another village in her usual horrific fashion, when Xena rides in. The warrior princess hurls her chakram—which Callisto catches. They fight, but Callisto wounds Xena and escapes.

Meanwhile, Joxer, who desperately wants to be a great warrior (and imagines himself invincible) repeatedly attempts to capture Gabrielle, who keeps flattening him. He tries to join Callisto, who sneers at the idea.

Callisto intends to kill the oracle at Delphi. Xena defeats Callisto in a fight but hesitates to turn her over to a mob. Callisto grabs Gabrielle and races to her camp.

Xena arrives to find Gabrielle dangling from a rope, with Callisto's lieutenant ready to burn the rope and let her drop to her death. Callisto climbs into a maze of ladders. Xena follows—and an incredible battle between the two is on. Xena eventually rescues Gabrielle. Callisto nearly falls to her death, but Xena saves her as well. Her army is chained and ready to be marched off to prison, with Callisto at their head. Her last words to Xena, "You should have killed me."

Best Scene Beyond doubt, the fight on ladders. It is long and incredibly involved, with very impressive effects and stunts, and the music provides a perfect counterpart.

Disclaimer Joxer's nose was not harmed during the production of this motion picture. However, his crossbow was severely damaged.

Death Mask

In this serious episode we learn that both the king's first lieutenant and Xena's brother Torus are boneheads—

> **‹ X E N A I S M ›**
>
> "Come to bed when you finish with your sword. I'll be waiting."

and that Gabrielle is getting pretty good with the staff. Sporadically, at least.

As Xena and Gabrielle return to her old kingdom, they are attacked by iron-masked men. The masks are the same as those worn by the men of Centares, who sacked Amphipolis and were responsible for the death of Xena's brother Lyceus. She puts the pinch on a captured raider, who tells them that a party of the warlord's men are sacking the next village.

The women drive off the attacking lieutenant, Malik. The king appreciates Xena's help. Xena is cornered not long after by one of the death-mask raiders. It is her brother Torus, who has been trying to get close enough to the warlord, Cortese, to kill him.

> ‹ X E N A I S M ›
>
> "I want to wipe them
> off the face of the earth."

They argue, but Xena gets nowhere with Torus, who blames her for Lyceus' death. The two quarrel throughout the episode, very much like any brother and sister. Xena persuades Torus to take her as a prisoner to Malik, so she can learn what is going on and perhaps find a clue to Cortese's identity. Malik has the bound Xena tossed into his tent. Torus argues with him, gaining time for Xena to remove her bonds and search Malik's belongings. Malik drives Torus away, then attempts to take possession of his prize. She coldcocks him and leaves.

Torus is with Gabrielle. Xena shows up and asks him about Malik's messenger pigeons. Malik uses them to stay in touch with other raiders. Xena has also discovered he has royal seals. He is communicating with the king's castle.

Xena and Torus ask to see the king. The captain of the guard, who has the same boneheaded profile as Torus, takes their weapons and shows them into the throne room. The king reveals that he is Cortese. He tries to kill the visitors. Failing, he calls for guards to delay Xena and Torus while he runs.

Torus is determined to kill Cortese. He will not listen to Xena. He tries to kill Malik, who captures him. Xena lets herself be taken with him. They are brought to the castle. There, the second in command still refuses to believe his king is also the chief raider. Xena and Torus get free and find the king.

She, Torus, and the second in command enter the pigeon loft, where she sends a message to Malik from Cortese to attack the palace. He does. Xena captures Cortese. She and her brother attack Malik's men. Xena terrifies Cortese into ordering Malik to surrender. His men do, but only Cortese could convince Malik to surrender. The second in command finally gets it, kills Malik, and Cortese is taken prisoner. Torus wants to execute him, but when he tries to behead the terrified king/warlord, he can't bring himself to do it.

Torus plans to travel to Amphipolis to visit their mother. Xena says, "Tell her I . . . tell her you saw me."

Best Scenes Xena and Torus sniping at each other like a real brother and sister.

Disclaimer No messenger doves were harmed during the production of this motion picture. However, several were reported missing in action, and search-and-rescue efforts are under way.

Is There a Doctor in the House?

In an extremely intense season-ending episode, Xena shows healers in the real world that there is more learning gained on the battlefield.

Xena and Gabrielle, on their way to Athens, cut through some woods where men are pursuing other men and killing mindlessly in a civil war.

They stumble upon the Amazon Ephiny, who is very pregnant, wounded, grieving, and suffering her first birth pangs. The baby's father is Phantes, son of the king of the centaurs, but he was killed and now she is in danger from other Amazons. Xena will find a safe place for Ephiny to have her baby, then will end the war.

They reach shelter, along with the wounded warrior captain Marmax, in the temple of healing. Present is the young acolyte Hypocrates, an underpriest to a god's devoted fanatic. Gabrielle helps Xena in practical healing, enlisting men from opposite sides of the war to aid her as she splints breaks, reinflates punctured lungs and removes gangrenous legs. A Democratean leader Xena wounded earlier is starting to get a clue.

Gabrielle is sent out by a worried father to find his son. It is a trap, of course. She is seriously wounded, but Xena sets her aside to aid others, showing by example how a warrior/healer works in time of battle.

Xena helps deliver Ephiny's centaur baby by cesarean. Then all at once, Gabrielle is dying. Xena, in a moving

> < X E N A I S M >
>
> "You haven't heard
> the last of me, Hercules."

scene, brings Gabrielle back to life by breathing into her lungs.

To Look for The judge Arbus from "The Execution" (season two) is the priest of the healers' temple and Hypocrates' supposed teacher.

XENA: WARRIOR PRINCESS—SEASON TWO

Several episodes in the second season had to be shot around Lucy's October 1996 injury, accounting for an abnormally high number of episodes in which Xena does not inhabit her own body.

Orphans of War

An average episode, notable only for the revelation that Xena has a half-grown son.

Xena and Gabrielle are traveling through centaur country when they come up against Dagnine, who once served Xena. He has a wizard and is searching for the centaur's Ixion Stone (which supposedly holds all the evil power the centaurs refused).

Kaleipus, the centaur leader, reminds Xena she was never to come here again. A boy by the name of Solan drops from a tree, attempting to kill her for murdering his father, Borias, who sided with the centaurs against Xena and died in battle. He also fathered Solan on her.

Xena does not want Solan to become a warrior, and argues with Kaleipus about the way he is raising the boy. Dagnine also learns Solan is Xena's son. Dagnine's men then kidnap Solan.

Xena sneaks into Dagnine's tent, decks him, and steals the key to the boy's cage. But Solan, carrying his father's sword, falls into a hole in the ground with Xena.

This hole leads to the cavern where the Ixion Stone should be located. Solan is awed to find his father's footprints in the cavern dust, and Xena discovers the stone is gone. She makes a horn from a root and calls for help. The centaurs lower a rope just as Dagnine enters the cave. Solan drops his father's sword and the Ixion Stone falls out. Dagnine's wizard makes an elixir for Solan. He turns into one bad centaur.

Xena gets the centaurs to create a huge crossbow. When she fights Dagnine, he tells her he killed Borias (no surprise). He is skewed by the crossbow's bolt.

Solan throws his sword in a lake. He and Xena part as friends, her real identity still unknown to him. She leaves, fighting tears.

Best Scene We Don't See Dagnine does *not* kidnap Gabrielle.

Disclaimer No sleazy warlords who deem it necessary to drink the magic elixirs that turn them into scaly

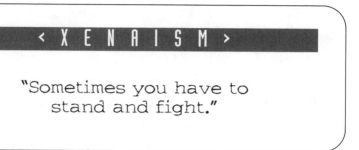

< X E N A I S M >

"Sometimes you have to stand and fight."

creatures were harmed during the making of this motion picture.

Remember Nothing

There are too many holes in the plot to call this a good episode, but its what-if theme offers interest. Xena and Gabrielle arrive at the temple of the Fates, so that Xena can pray for her brother Lyceus. The temple is attacked, but Xena fights to protect it and kills a boy during the battle. The Fates, grateful that the temple is safe, grant her a wish. She wishes she had never killed the boy or become a warrior. The Fates return her to the time before she first killed, but warn that if she sheds blood, everything will be as it was.

She is suddenly home, and Lyceus is alive; but her mother is dead and Gabrielle is a slave to Mezentius, who is dealing arms once more. Lyceus wants Xena to help him fight Mezentius, but she refuses. Gabrielle stabs Mezentius to death. Xena realizes that things could have been much worse if she had never become a warrior. She kills—*very messily*—and everything returns to what it was.

Disclaimer　Xena's memory was not damaged or . . . What was I saying?

Giant Killer

This is one of the weakest episodes of the second season. Xena and Gabrielle find themselves caught between the Philistines and the Israelites at the time of David and Goliath.

The Israelites don't trust Xena. The Philistines do. David is one of their slaves.

Xena tries to warn Goliath he is on the wrong side, but Goliath is doing it for the money. His family is dead and that money will help him find the giant Gareth.

Xena arrives in time to fight off a guard who has caught Gabrielle slipping food to David.

Xena then visits the Israelites, but the Philistines show up with their army and their giant. Xena persuades the enemies to let the champion of each side battle, winner take all, with the predictable outcome.

To Look for　Xena meets the giant Gareth in "A Day in the Life."

Disclaimer　No biblical myths or icons were irreparably mangled during the production of this motion picture.

Girls Just Wanna Have Fun

Even with all the blood (the Bacchae are vampires), this is a fun episode—one that leaves viewers asking more questions than there are answers.

Even though Orpheus still blames Xena for Eurydice's death, he asks for her help against Bacchus and his vampiric Bacchae. Joxer is attacked by wolf-Bacchae, but Xena chases them off with her whip. Gabrielle (surprise) is kidnapped.

Xena tries to recover Orpheus' lyre, stolen by the Bacchae, but during this raid she and Gabrielle may have been bitten by Bacchae. Joxer believes Xena was bitten, but it is Gabrielle who attacks them, then joins Bacchus. As she prepares to drink his blood, Xena hurls her chakram and shatters the goblet. A smug Bacchus tells her that only a Bacchae can kill him, however.

Xena arranges a distraction: Joxer plays Orpheus' lyre, and Orpheus sings. The warrior princess asks Gabrielle to bite her. Xena sprouts fangs, wings, and yellow eyeballs, then kills Bacchus. She and Gabrielle are restored to normal.

To Look for The special effects, especially the Dryads, are excellent.

Disclaimer No bloodsucking Bacchae were harmed during the production of this motion picture. However, a few Dryads lost their heads.

The Return of Callisto

The lesson of this episode is that no smart warlord ever lets his enemy escape alive, no matter how entangled in chains. Gabrielle meets up with a war-weary Perdicas, who now wants to marry her. They wed, but Callisto finds them and kills Perdicas. A grieving Gabrielle swears to kill Callisto and demands sword-training from Xena, who complies—even though she obviously knows her companion won't kill Callisto.

In a moving scene, Xena prays to the gods—something she seldom does—asking that they not let the light fade from Gabrielle's face. Gabrielle overhears, and agrees to return home and mourn, but before Xena wakes the next morning, Gabrielle leaves to find Callisto.

She finds her enemy and puts a sword to her throat, but is unable to kill her. Callisto has no such problems. She has Gabrielle tied to a stake to provoke Xena. Xena takes on Callisto's army, and rescues Gabrielle. Callisto escapes in a war chariot, and Xena jumps into another and chases her down the beach—another excellent chariot race. Xena finally gets her hands on the crazed warrior and leaps from the chariots with her. The two roll down an embankment into quicksand. Xena is able to pull herself out, but refuses to help Callisto, who sinks.

To Look for   Xena can't make a right move with Callisto. Now dead, Callisto is discovered by Ares, who allies with her and will pit her against Xena in "Intimate Strangers."

Disclaimer   Although Xena finally conquered her dark nemesis Callisto, it took her weeks to get sand out of her leather unmentionables.

Warrior . . . Princess . . . Tramp

Another light episode featuring multiple personalities (see "Warrior . . . Princess . . . Tramp," season one). This time Lucy gets three parts: Xena, Princess Diana, and Meg, a trollop.

King Lias sends for Xena. He is dying and wants to give his crown to Diana and Philemon, who are now married and have a baby.

Agis, Meg's sponsor, dresses Gabrielle just like Xena. Meg tosses her in prison saying, "You stay here—and trust me."

Meg has previously seduced Joxer while pretending to be Xena. He bragged about it, so when the real Xena rides in, she must fight off a bunch of men who have heard she is easy.

Meanwhile, Meg trades places with Diana. And Joxer makes a pass at the real Xena.

He and Xena overhear Meg and Agis talking, and they set out to rescue Gabrielle.

But now Diana is missing. So Xena dresses up as Meg posing as Diana.

Eventually everything gets sorted out. King Lias recovers, and Meg gets a job as the castle cook. Joxer still has the hots for her—and she feels the same.

Disclaimer   Neither Xena nor her remarkably coincidental identical twin were harmed during the making of this motion picture. Meg, however, suffered minor injuries while preparing Aardvark nuggets for King Lias.

Intimate Stranger

This is a very good episode, but quite dark, with Xena and Callisto inhabiting each other's bodies.

Xena and Gabrielle track Theodorus, Callisto's lieutenant; and Joxer follows them. Xena has terrible dreams, including one in which Callisto summons her to an eerie cavern. The dream turns out to be real: Callisto tells her that the guilt she feels for killing Callisto has left her open to danger. Callisto and Ares taunt Xena, who is suddenly flung into a huge stone and then vanishes.

Xena wakes in the real world. She tells Gabrielle that they must get to Amphipolis, because Theodorus plans to kill Xena's mother. It becomes clear over the course of this scene that Callisto has taken over Xena's body. Xena's horse, Argo, is very nervous. "Xena" tells Gabrielle that Argo has acted this way before. They continue to track Theodorus leaving Joxer behind.

The real Xena, now in Callisto's body, tells Hades what Ares and Callisto have done. He gives her one day back among the living to settle matters.

Ares warns Callisto, who tells Gabrielle that Callisto (really Xena) has returned and that Gabrielle must kill her. Gabrielle is sickened by this hatred

> ## ‹ X E N A I S M ›
>
> "My name is Xena.
> I'm a problem solver."

for Callisto. Callisto sends Gabrielle ahead.

Xena finds Argo, left wounded by Callisto. Xena tends to his injury. Joxer arrives, sees who he assumes is Callisto, and tries to defend the horse. Xena, unable to convince him what has happened, leaves him to guard Argo.

Callisto and Xena meet and fight. Gabrielle shows up, Callisto urges Gabrielle to kill Xena, who looks like Callisto. But Gabrielle realizes it really *is* Xena in Callisto's body. Callisto escapes.

She finds her old army and sends them to Amphipolis to capture all the villagers. Callisto plans to burn them when Xena arrives. Ares argues that all Callisto must do is wait out the time Hades gave Xena, but Callisto is mad.

Xena and Callisto fight for the lives of the captives, but Xena runs out of her allotted time. Just as she begins to vanish, she pulls one of Callisto's darts from her wrist-guard and hits Callisto with it.

The two are suddenly back in the cavern. Eventually, Callisto vanishes into the same rock as Xena did earlier.

Back among the living, Callisto is seen on the floor—but is it really Callisto or Xena in Callisto's body? She tells Gabrielle: "It's me—Xena." So far as they can tell, Xena will be trapped in Callisto's body forever.

Disclaimer Argo was not harmed during the making of this motion picture. However, she is undertaking intensive psychotherapy to help her work through her resentment and feelings of distrust toward Xena.

Ten Little Warlords

Several nice twists to the Agatha Christie *Ten Little Indians* plot, including Xena in Callisto's body, and Ares as a drunk and depressed mortal.

Xena, in Callisto's body, receives an invitation from Ares to attend a party on an island. Of course, Ares did not really send it—he knows Callisto is Xena. But Xena is curious. She and Gabrielle arrive at the village where nine other warlords are waiting for the ship to take them out to the island. Oddly, the warlords are courteous to each other—but ordinary people like Gabrielle are showing high levels of anger. Xena learns why when the two enter a tavern to find a very drunk—and mortal—Ares. Someone stole his sword when he was dallying with Callisto, in Xena's body. Xena is persuaded to help him get his godhood back when she realizes that the lack of natural order is why Gabrielle and the others are so angry. People like Xena know how to channel anger.

Xena and Ares dispose of a warlord, steal his invitation, and get aboard the ship. The ship's captain sets a top in motion which plays a message, supposedly from Ares, saying he plans to retire and name one of them God of War. On the island, Sisyphus tells them they must draw lots to kill the Barracus, a monster howling in a pit below. Whoever kills it will become the new God of War.

Ares knows Sisyphus stole his sword, but without his godhood, Ares is a lousy fighter. He has never been injured and never felt fear. He is nearly killed while battling Sisyphus, but Xena rescues him. Weapons are distributed to the warlords for the impending competition.

As the warlords kill each other for first crack at the monster, Xena discovers Ares' sword on one of the dead men. Xena kills the last surviving warlord, who is about to skewer Ares. Ares regains his godhood. Sisyphus, who had made a deal with Hades to get out of Tartarus in exchange for killing ten warlords, returns defeated. Ares leaves, but he keeps his word and gives Xena her body back.

Disclaimer No one was harmed in the making of this motion picture. However, Xena's ability to recover her body was severely impeded by Lucy Lawless' unexpected mishap.

A Solstice Carol

A fine episode featuring a toymaker named Senticles. This is Dickens' *Christ-mas Carol* with some fun Greek twists and a donkey.

Gabrielle and Xena separate to buy each other Solstice gifts. A boy steals Xena's chakram. She catches the thief at an orphanage, where the children have set the weapon atop their solstice tree. When soldiers arrive to collect back taxes for miserly King Silvus, Xena shows the orphans what the chakram is really for.

The king plans to close the orphanage. Xena and Gabrielle learn from Senticles, an ex-toymaker turned King's scribe, that the King has banned Solstice celebrations since his wife "went."

Xena sneaks in on the sleeping king and warns him he will be visited by the Fates. Leaving his chamber, she stumbles into a cobwebby room with a solstice tree, wrapped presents, and a picture of Queen Analia. (It's *Great Expectations* XWP-style.)

‹ X E N A I S M ›

"Go. Make me proud."

Xena, pretending to be the Fate of the past, takes the king to the cobwebby room where Gabrielle floats (on a hidden rope) pretending to be his dead wife.

Gabrielle has discovered that Senticles was a maker of wonderful toys and was forced to retire. She persuades him to put on a red suit and white beard and take the toys to the orphans.

Xena as the Present Fate, takes the king to the orphanage. His guards arrive to foreclose on the tax debt. While Xena battles the soldiers, he passes out.

Just then, Gabrielle and Senticles drop into the orphanage via the chimney. Senticles, Gabrielle, and the children fight the guards in an absurd scene, using everything from marbles, to a hula hoop, to stars from the solstice tree.

When the king wakes, he thinks the hooded figure hanging over him is the third Fate. He vows to change his ways—and to his astonishment, the hooded figure is his wife, who forgives him.

As Xena and Gabrielle leave town, they encounter a couple with a baby. Gabrielle gives the woman a donkey she has acquired, so they can travel more quickly. The camera pulls back from the softly glowing baby, pans to the sky, where an enormous star is shining in midday.

Best Line When Gabrielle has no present for Xena, Xena replies, "Gabrielle, you *are* a gift."

To Look for The fight with toys, which starts when Xena tosses out a handful of marbles, uses a Hercules puppet, and ends with a wild pillow fight.

Disclaimer Senticles was not harmed in the making of this motion picture. However, several chimneys are in dire need of repair.

The Xena Scrolls

An episode inspired by *Indiana Jones,* with plenty of action, flashback scenes, and fun insider jokes. When first aired at the Xena Convention in Burbank, California, January of 1997, many fans were rumored to have lost their voices cheering.

It is 1942 in Mycenea. Janice Covington—who looks a lot like Gabrielle—is digging for the Xena Scrolls originally sought by her father. She is joined by Mel Pappas, a glasses-wearing, suited, Southern Belle who claims to be the daughter of another famous archaeologist—and *she* is a dead ringer for Xena. A John Smythe shows up with two gun-toting thugs to steal Mel's briefcase, but Janice runs them off. She has a whip, an attitude, and a Gatling gun. She knows the Xena Scrolls will prove that Xena was a historical character. Even though Mel can read the scrolls, Janice does not want her help.

Lieutenant Jacques S'Er shows up, supposedly to provide the protection of the French government. Jacques looks just like Joxer with a mustache. Smythe returns with a plaque he claims is the key to the tomb, and Mel opens the tomb. Smythe and his thugs then pull their guns and take Mel, Janice, and the lieutenant hostage.

Mel finds the scrolls by accident, and part of Xena's chakram as well. Janice cannot pull the broken chakram from the stone in which it is embedded, but Mel does, easily. Janice turns away to load the scrolls in her backpack. When she and the lieutenant turn back, Mel is gone.

Down a darkened hall, Mel is pulled along by her half of the chakram, which is drawn to its other half in Smythe's possession. The lieutenant and Janice rescue Mel and seek a safe haven in the wrong room. Fire pots spontaneously combust. Smythe and his thugs find them and demand the other half of the chakram and the scrolls. Mel is thrown halfway across the chamber as the chakram reunites its two halves. She is knocked out cold.

Now the lid of a sarcophagus slides open, and Ares appears, after being trapped for centuries. Smythe orders his guards to shoot Ares, but the bullets bounce off the God of War. Ares smiles and forces the men to shoot each other, then hurls three daggers at Smythe, killing him. The lieutenant offers to fight Ares—and is revealed to be

> ‹ X E N A I S M ›
>
> "Making war is simple.
> Making peace is never easy.
> If it was, everyone would do it."

a brush salesman from New Jersey (and a descendant of Joxer).

Ares has been awaiting a descendant of Xena to release him. Janice is certain that she is the descendant. Ares tells her that she is Gabrielle's descendant.

Ares then turns to Mel, awakening from her faint. She comes to her feet, sword in hand—as Xena. She yells at Janice and Jack to run, then fells Ares with a *very* low blow.

Xena finds Janice despondent. Xena tells her how important Gabrielle was to her life. They retrieve Jack from a mummy case and try to find a way out—but Ares captures Jack and Janice and tells Xena that either she uses the chakram to free the stone that holds him prisoner, or the two die. She agrees. The chakram strikes the stone, and the door opens. But Xena makes him mad enough to fight her. Jack and Janice escape through the door. Xena hurls the chakram at a chain holding a spiked ball, which lands on Ares. The chakram breaks in half—and she is plain Mel Pappas again. The door is closing. Janice gets Mel out. Janice dynamites the hilltop to entomb Ares for good.

Jack rides off on his motorcycle with the scrolls. Janice remembers everything, though Mel seems to have no memory of being Xena. Janice asks Mel to join her.

Shift the scene to fifty years later: A grandson of Jack's is pitching stories to a television producer but getting nowhere, until he offers scrolls that his grandfather translated. The producer, who looks amazingly like a well-groomed Ares, wants to know more about this warrior princess.

Best Lines Ares teases Janice about her relationship to someone in the scrolls: "I'll give you a hint. Think 'irritating blonde.'"

Disclaimer No Hollywood producers were harmed during the production of this motion picture.

Here She Comes . . . Miss Amphipolis!

A light episode with a rather heavy-handed message. Xena and Gabrielle reach a coastal land that was at war, but for a full year there has been peace. On their arrival, a bevy of scantily clad beauties run at them, chased by slavers. Xena defends the women, and they flee as Salmoneus arrives. The girls are there for a beauty pageant to celebrate the year of peace. Salmoneus tries to enlist Xena's help. The rulers of the three former enemy kingdoms are each making threats against the others for the crown of Miss Known World. Xena agrees to become a contestant for herself.

Xena saves one contestant from a booby trap, discovers that Miss Artiphys is actually a young man, and learns that none of the girls wants to be there.

The kings realize that someone is trying to kill off the competitors and each accuses the other. Accidents continue but the contest goes on, with Miss Amphipolis winning her first two events.

The king sponsoring the contest, who was neutral during the war, reveals to Xena that he is behind the accidents. His kingdom has suffered during the peace. War will make it prosperous again. Unfortunately, Xena has bound and gagged the three rival kings and hid them under the table. They have heard the confession of the host king.

A frantic Salmoneus waits for Miss Amphipolis so he can announce the winner, but Xena, out of costume, announces that she is bowing out. The other contestants quit, too, leaving only a wildly thrilled Miss Artiphys.

Best Look The one on Salmoneus' face after Miss Known World is crowned. As Salmoneus praises the winning beauty, he is answered by a *very* deep voice.

Best Scene A rehearsal for the fancy costume event, with wild headdresses and winged gowns colliding, women tripping over each other, and Salmoneus doing an *almost* tuneful Bert Parks.

Disclaimer No ribbons were harmed during the production of this motion picture. However, several experienced severe motion sickness.

Destiny

An extremely bleak episode. After Xena is injured, she insists that Gabrielle must take her to a distant healer. Meanwhile, Xena's mind slips back to when she ruled a ship of pirates who captured a noble Roman named Julius Caesar. There is also a stowaway on the pirate ship, M'Lila, who possesses all of the fighting skills Xena knows in her life. Xena seduces Caesar, who wants to rule the world. Xena makes M'Lila teach her a remarkably effective "pinch." Xena sells Caesar for ransom. He then comes after her with his own ship, kills most of the pirates, and brutally crucifies Xena.

M'Lila rescues Xena and takes her to a mountain healer. Caesar's soldiers track and kill M'Lila—whose fighting talents transfer to Xena as she dies. Xena kills the soldiers in spectacular fashion.

Moving ten years forward, the healer is unable to save Xena this time. M'Lila comes to assure Xena that it is not her time to die. Xena then hears Gabrielle grieving for her—and realizes M'Lila is right. She has to return.

To Look for Julius Caesar is played by the actor who portrayed the equally arrogant and driven Mael in "Altered States."

Disclaimer Julius Caesar was not harmed during the production of this motion picture. However, the producers deny any responsibility for any unfortunate acts of betrayal soon thereafter.

The Quest

This story continues the arc begun in "Destiny" with the same bleak undertones. Gabrielle swears to take Xena home to be buried. She batters thugs who want to steal Xena's body—several warlords will pay well for it. Iolaus initially helps Gabrielle, but then leaves to give Hercules the bad news of Xena's death. Gabrielle is discovered by Amazons, led by Ephiny. Queen Melosa is dead, killed by her adopted daughter Velasca, who will be the next queen unless Gabrielle claims her Right of Cast. (See "Hooves and Harlots.") Velasca also plans to start war with the centaurs. Gabrielle agrees to let Xena's body be burned, and to become Queen of the Amazons.

> **< X E N A I S M >**
>
> "Don't change, Gabrielle. I like you just the way you are."

Meanwhile, Autolycus attempts to steal the Dagger of Helios from its temple. Someone takes over his body, forcing him to also steal a book. Xena's spirit has entered Autolycus' body. He was the one person who could steal the dagger and the book. The book will show her where the ambrosia is, and the dagger is the key to release it.

Autolycus agrees to let her stay in his body, so long as he is in charge. She agrees, then tells him he has to rescue her body from the Amazons.

He dresses in Amazonian drag and gets into the chamber with Xena's sarcophagus, but he's caught by Gabrielle, who believes he is out for reward. She has him confined, but Xena takes over and rescues her body. Gabrielle realizes Xena is in his body. She renounces her queen's mask to help Xena. Velasca is furious, calls her a traitor, jails Ephiny and her allies, and starts after Gabrielle.

Gabrielle and Autolycus find the cavern where the ambrosia is hidden. The floor is lined with vicious spikes, and flames roar up as Autolycus steps into the opening. The only way to reach the ambrosia is via hanging ropes.

Velasca arrives. Autolycus tries to let Xena take him over so she can attack Velasca, but Xena has left him. Velasca takes them prisoner and beats Autolycus to learn the final key to getting the ambrosia. She realizes the dagger is the key and heads back to the cave.

Gabrielle breaks out and goes after Velasca. As Velasca climbs the ropes toward the ambrosia, Xena takes over Gabrielle's body. Gabrielle/Xena defeat Velasca, who is impaled on the spikes.

The ambrosia falls into the flames—but a bit is stuck in Gabrielle's top. She feeds it to Xena, who revives.

Another stray piece drops to the floor. Velasca's hand creeps toward it.

To Look for The "kiss" scene where Xena, in Autolycus' body, comforts Gabrielle.

Disclaimer Xena's body was not harmed during the production of this motion picture. However, it took Autolycus weeks to get his swagger back.

A Necessary Evil

A third part of the continuing plot arc, and an intense episode that left as many questions as it answered. Velasca eats the small amount of ambrosia she has recovered and becomes a god. She wants to kill Gabrielle, who "stole" her queenship. Even Xena and an entire army of Amazons cannot stop her, but Ephiny agrees to slow Velasca's progress. Xena tells Gabrielle they need help from another immortal—Callisto.

Xena hauls Callisto from the temple where Hercules has imprisoned her, and strikes a deal. If Callisto will delay

Velasca, Xena will give Callisto ambrosia. Callisto demands that Xena tell a prosperous village how she killed everyone in Callisto's village and destroyed Callisto's life forever. Callisto momentarily looks like a woebegone child, but quickly regains her fierceness.

Xena leads Callisto and Gabrielle to a high-walled canyon. Velasca will follow, Callisto will distract her, and Xena will drop a rockslide on Velasca. But Velasca has grown too strong to be held by a rockslide. Velasca destroys a temple of Artemis, patron goddess of the Amazons, proclaiming herself Artemis' enemy.

Xena cuts another deal with Callisto: Callisto will draw Velasca onto a bridge over a river of lava, and Xena will cut the ropes. Velasca will fall, and Callisto will get the ambrosia. In reality, Xena plans to also drop Callisto into the lava.

Velasca forms a whirlwind and uses it to catch up with Xena and company.

Gabrielle acts as bait to draw Velasca toward the bridge. Velasca knocks Xena aside, nearly sending her into the lava, then prepares to stab Gabrielle. Callisto demands ambrosia *now.* She cuts the pouch containing Velasca's supply from Velasca's belt. Gabrielle seizes the pouch and runs for the rope bridge, but slips and dangles over the lava flow. Meanwhile, Xena tries to rescue herself so she can rescue Gabrielle.

Callisto demands the pouch. On Xena's advice, Gabby throws it to her. Callisto eats the ambrosia, then turns to fight Velasca as an equal. Xena fashions a "bungee" cord and uses it to help her cut the ropes, so the two goddesses fall into the lava. She also catches Gabrielle.

To Look for Callisto truly is a "Barbie on Acid." Even Ares calls her a "psycho."

Disclaimer The reputation of the Amazon Nation was not harmed despite Velasca's radical adherence to an otherwise valid belief system.

A Day in the Life

One of the best lighthearted episodes, with plenty of insider jokes for fans.

< X E N A I S M >

"Be careful. I am in a bad mood!"

Xena and Gabrielle spend most of this show sniping at each other like an old married couple.

They are wakened by an attack by armed men. Gabrielle uses her staff, feet, and fists to fight them off, but Xena uses pots and pans. She puts the pinch on one, and learns that Meleager has sent them. He intends to destroy a nearby village and does not want her to interfere.

Not long after, they encounter a peasant named Howar who needs help for his own village. The giant Gareth is on his way to destroy it. Howar's girlfriend, Minya, is the only other person still in the village—and she is a fawning fan of Xena's. At least until she realizes that Howar is in love with Xena.

Xena plans to divert the giant through Meleager's army, then she invents a kite, drawing the giant away from the village as a thunderstorm

> < X E N A I S M >
>
> "No one should pass up their dream."

starts. He is the tallest object around, and he gets fried.

Meleager's army is destroyed, and now Xena takes him out as well. Meantime, she talks to Minya, who soon after lures her wayward boyfriend home—in homemade Xena-leathers.

Best Line In the bath, Xena asks Gabrielle, "Are you sitting on the soap?"

Best Scenes Gabrielle snarls at Xena for ruining her pans; Xena catches fish by hand and tosses them into Gabrielle's face; Xena and Gabrielle walk down a path while aiming kicks at each other's backsides.

Second-Best Scenes Gabrielle repeatedly tries to catch Xena by surprise with her staff.

Disclaimer No eels were harmed during the production of this motion picture despite their reputation as a fine delicacy in select cultures.

For Him the Bell Tolls

This episode gave Ted Raimi a good chance to flex his acting muscles.

Aphrodite decides to break up a royal marriage arranged by her son Cupid, because the fathers of the pair have decided to destroy two of her temples. She picks Joxer as her tool. She hypnotizes him and gives him a small bell to give the bride as a wedding gift. When it rings, he is suddenly a swashbuckling hero—until the bell rings again. Then he reverts back to klutzy Joxer.

As the heroic Joxer, he wows the bride and infuriates the groom, whose father is outraged and humiliated. He has Joxer hauled out to be executed. Gabrielle hurls a rock that hits the executioner's ax and makes it ring like a bell. Joxer turns into the hero again and fights the king's men. He takes the fight into Aphrodite's temple, where Aphrodite's adored vases and other knickknacks get broken. Gabrielle tells the goddess that she will take Joxer from temple to temple unless the goddess restores him to himself. Cupid reunites the royal lovers and all is well.

Disclaimer The producers wish to acknowledge the inspiration of Danny Kaye and pay tribute to the motion picture *Court Jester.*

The Execution

This is a much better trial episode than "Reckoning." Meleager has been convicted of murder and sentenced to hang. He claims he is innocent and tells Gabrielle that a one-eyed man can testify that he was elsewhere during the murder. Xena says the judge has a reputation for honesty. Gabrielle still refuses to believe the accusation and helps Meleager escape. She is caught and nearly lynched herself. Xena agrees to recapture Meleager, and takes Gabrielle with her.

When they catch up with Meleager, Gabrielle plans to attack Xena. She then learns that Meleager did commit the murder and that there was no one-eyed man. He was so drunk at the time, he does not remember what happened.

After returning to the court, Xena suddenly realizes that Meleager did not kill the man—she did. She found an enormous man attacking a small man one night and cut him badly. Apparently the injured man dropped his blood-covered sword. He then died. Meleager later picked up the sword.

As Xena searches for proof, Meleager is hung. His body is brought to the judge's chambers. The judge is about to sign the death warrant when Meleager sits up and accuses him of executing an innocent man. Meleager is not dead because Xena was under the gallows trapdoor when he fell, and she braced his feet on her shoulders. The judge, however, is not as honest as his reputation claims. Xena tosses him in the cell, letting an astonished Gabrielle out.

Best Line "Gabrielle, you put people on pedestals, and they are gonna' fall off."

Disclaimer By popular demand, "The Executioner" will bring back his comfortable, light-weight cotton-flax blend robe in a variety of spring colors.

< X E N A I S M >

"Act, don't react."

Blind Faith

In this middling episode a scarred lone scamp named Palaemon kidnaps Gabrielle as a way to get Xena to fight him. He figures to win and gain a huge reputation. He tells Xena that Gabrielle is dead, and in the resulting brawl, Xena's eyes are sprayed with oil that has sumac in it. She begins to go blind.

Xena eventually subdues Palaemon, forcing him to lead her to Gabrielle. Along the way, he realizes she can not see.

Gabrielle, meanwhile, is forcibly married to a dead king. The law of the land states that if the king is not married when he dies, the kingdom falls to a brother in a distant land. If the king marries and then dies, the advisor becomes ruler. The advisor shams the wedding, then pronounces the king dead. The "newlyweds" are to be cremated together.

Though still blind, Xena rescues Gabrielle from the flames at the last possible moment, and Gabrielle is able to restore her vision. Palaemon is impressed by the love that drove Xena and decides he will try to do good instead of evil.

Most Toe-Curling Scene Gabrielle's coffin sliding slowly toward the cremation fire.

Disclaimer Once again, Gabrielle's luck with men was harmed during the production of this motion picture.

Ulysses

A visually satisfying but otherwise weak episode, due to some massive holes in the story. Xena and Gabrielle come to the aid of a lone fighter battling pirates on the beach. The two-sworded, bare-chested hunk turns out to be Ulysses on his way home from Troy to reclaim his kingdom of Ithaca. Unfortunately, the only way to get there is through the realm of his dire enemy, Poseidon, god of the sea (seen in the opening credits). Poseidon warns Xena not to get involved.

But Xena is charmed by Ulysses and she and Gabrielle help him recover his ship from Poseidon's pirate allies. Xena helps him sail to Ithaca; Gabrielle is seasick the entire voyage. Ulysses gets home, strings his bow—with a little help from Xena—and regains his kingdom and his bride. Xena takes the ship and, with Gabrielle, sails into the sunset.

Worst Scene Ulysses hands Xena a variant on the old saw, "My wife doesn't understand me"—and Xena puts up with it.

Disclaimer Despite Gabrielle's incessant barfing, Ulysses' ship was not harmed during the production of the motion picture.

The Price

This is a grim, unwavering episode. Xena is confronted by an old enemy, the cannibalistic Hoard. She and Gabrielle escape them to fall in with a company of Athenian guards manning

an outpost. The men have all given up hope of a rescue. In order to rally them, she becomes the old Xena— much to Gabrielle's horror. When Xena takes a prisoner, Gabrielle talks with him and finds a way to impose a brief truce. Xena sets up a battle between her and the enemy chief. She defeats him and he is killed by his own men. Then they vanish into the woods—but not forever.

Spookiest Scene Xena and Gabrielle paddle downstream. In the water near the shore can be seen the slowly emerging head of a glowering cannibal.

Disclaimer To show sympathy for the Horde, "Kaltake" was served only upon request during the production of this motion picture.

The Lost Mariner

This weak episode seems to pick up right after the end of "Ulysses," as the ship in which Xena sailed from Ithaca is wrecked in a storm. Gabrielle and one of the sailors are hauled aboard a wreck of a ship belonging to Cecrops, once First Citizen of Athens, now cursed by Poseidon to remain at sea until he learns to love. Athena has given him eternal life, to give him the chance to learn the secret of love. The curse—and the eternal life accompanying it—extends to anyone on Cecrops' ship. Anyone who jumps overboard is killed by Poseidon. Xena, who washed ashore on a nearby island, leaps aboard Cecrops' ship to be with Gabrielle. He is impressed by her sacrifice From her he learns that it is not how much he loves, but how much he is loved—that is the secret to break his curse. He sails into the whirlpool Charybdis, and the ship is destroyed. Xena, Gabrielle, and the sailors make it to shore—and so does Cecrops, who has apparently become mortal once more.

To Look for Gabrielle devouring raw rubbery squid with gusto.

Disclaimer Cecrop's "Joie de Vivre" was not harmed during the production of this motion picture.

A Comedy of Eros

Probably the lightest episode of the whole second season. Cupid puts his son Bliss down for a nap so he can party with Bliss' mommy—and maybe make him a baby brother or sister. The moment he leaves, Bliss wings over to grab a bow and love-arrows, giggles happily, and vanishes—reappearing in a village where Xena and Gabrielle have come after hearing a rumor that Draco is on his way to sell the virgin-priestesses of Hespia to the slaver Pinullus.

Whoever Bliss shoots with his love-arrows falls in love with the first person—or animal—he or she sees: a boy buys flowers for his blushing girlfriend, then hands them to another boy; a man falls in love with a cow. Xena turns to confront Draco just as she is hit. To Draco's astonishment, she puts a full-throttle liplock on him.

He is dubious, but his hormones churn. Still, despite a bad case of the giddies, Xena does not intend to let him steal the virgins.

Draco captures Joxer and Gabrielle, and Xena agrees to give up the virgins to keep both alive. Bliss' arrow strikes Gabrielle, and her eyes light on Joxer. Complications follow when Draco is hit and sees Gabrielle.

The last chunk of the show takes on all the seriousness of a Three

Stooges scene, with virgins chasing Draco, Draco chasing Gabrielle, Xena chasing Draco, Gabrielle chasing Joxer (who remains clueless but willing to be adored).

Xena finally hauls Cupid from his warm bed to retrieve his errant son and return things to normal. Cupid reverts Gabrielle, but cannot fix Joxer. Xena won't let Cupid fix Draco because the warlord has sworn to go clean in order to prove his love to Gabrielle. In the end, only Joxer is left miserable, and clearly in love with Gabrielle.

> ‹ X E N A I S M ›
>
> "No, we can't kill them. They're the good guys. Remember?"

Best Scenes Draco climbs out of his bath to find Xena lounging on his cushions, eating a banana. And Gabrielle is zapped by a Love Arrow as Xena releases her and Joxer from the stake. Just before the eye contact that would create true love between the women, Joxer stumbles between them.

Disclaimer No cherries were harmed during the making of this motion picture.

An Encyclopedia
of the Xenaverse

ambrosia   the food of the gods; when a mortal consumes ambrosia, he or she becomes a god.

Ares   the god of war; son of Zeus and Hera; Xena was once Ares' protégé

Argo   Xena's horse

Bacchae   wild, soulless creatures whose only allegiance is to Bacchus, god of wine; Bacchae women take many forms and sometimes roam the forest as wolves.

bard   narrative poet; Gabrielle is a bard.

blood innocence   a state in which one has never killed another.

Callisto   Xena's arch enemy, sworn to make Xena suffer before her death; she is sometimes called "Psycho Barbie" by Xena fans.

centaur   strong, noble creatures who are part human, part horse.

chakram   razor-edged, discus-like ring used by Xena as a weapon.

dark side   evil side of Xena.

demigod   offspring of a god and a mortal, such as Hercules.

flame   (1) a fighting skill used by Xena in which she swallows combustible liquid and spews it through a lit torch, shooting flames into the faces of her enemies; (2) term describing verbal abuse of or by internet users.

Gabrielle   a bard; Xena's best friend and traveling companion; Amazon princess.

gaida   Eastern European bagpipe used in the *Xena* soundtrack, producing a dark, exotic sound.

gauntlet   form of punishment in which two lines of people facing each other and armed with clubs beat a person forced to run between them; Xena was forced to run the gauntlet when she left her army.

Hard-Core Nutball   a fan who has watched *Xena* from the very beginning, through the good and the bad.

Hercules   son of Zeus; demigod known for his prodigious strength.

I.A.X.S.   International Association of Xena Studies, an online publication.

Iolaus   Hercules' best friend and traveling partner; also known for his bravery, gallantry, and martial arts skills.

Joxer   warrior-wannabe.

kaval   shepherd's flute of Bulgarian origin used in the *Xena* soundtrack.

M'Lila   mysterious, Gaelic-speaking girl, probably Egyptian, who taught Xena the "Xena touch" and her acrobatic style of fighting.

neck pinch   see "Xena touch."

Nicklio   healer on Mt. Nestus who saved Xena's life.

stunt breasts   refers to Xena's remarkable ability to launch a knife from her bustier without the use of hands.

Tyldus   legendary king of the centaurs.

Unco   nickname for Xena's alter ego; abbreviation for un-coordinated.

warlord   military commander exercising power by force of arms.

Warrior Princess haze   state of bliss experienced by *Xena* fans after a good episode.

whoosh   rushing sound; special effect employed when Xena whips out her sword, throws her chakram, does a back-flip, turns her head, bats her lashes, etc.

Xena   a warrior princess who after doing much evil in the world has dedicated her life to protecting the innocent from other evil doers.

Xena scrolls   ancient manuscripts, rediscovered in 1932, telling the story of the Warrior Princess and her traveling companion.

Xena touch   both a weapon and a healing technique; it can kill instantly, but when used humanely it only anesthetizes; Xena also uses it to extract information.

Xenabilia   memorabilia based on the *Xena* television series, such as miniature action figures, trading cards, autographed photos, etc.

Xenafest   fan-organized gathering to celebrate the television series.

Xenaholic   someone who is addicted to *Xena*.

Xenaphile   a fan of the television series and its main character.

Xenaphobe   someone who is fearful or contemptuous of all things relating to *Xena*.

Xenastacked   term describing what happens to actresses after they visit the Wonderbra trailer on the set of *Xena*.

Xenathon   watching six or more episodes of *Xena* in one sitting.

Xenawatch   a small gathering of Xenites to watch a new episode.

Xenite   a fan who never misses a single broadcast; also called a Hard-Core Nutball by Lucy Lawless.

XWP   abbreviation for *Xena: Warrior Princess.*

Y.A.X.I.   Yet Another Xena Inconsistency, referring to the anachronistic touches on the series, such as steel swords and American accents in ancient Greece.

yi-yi-yi-yi   Xena's war cry; often startles and frightens her opponents.

Zeus   father of all gods, and lover of Lysia (played by Lucy Lawless in *Hercules and the Amazon Women*).

QUICK FACTS:
THE WOMEN OF *XENA*

LUCY LAWLESS

Born   March 29, 1968, in Mount Albert, New Zealand

Mother   Julia Ryan

Father   Frank Ryan, former mayor; currently Chairman of Finance for Auckland City

Siblings   five brothers and one sister

Height   5 feet 10½ inches (180 cm)

Weight   140 pounds (plus 5 or 10 pounds more, on occasion)

Physique   medium-boned, slender

Hair   honey brown

Eyes   icy blue

Accent   pure New Zealand

Comfort with nudity   somewhat uptight about taking it all off

Occupation   starring actress in *Xena: Warrior Princess*

Previous Occupations   grape picking in Germany; gold mining in Australia; acting in New Zealand—ASB bank advertisements, comedy series *Funny Business,* hostess of *Air New Zealand Holiday,* guest roles in *Hercules: The Legendary Journeys*

Marital History   Married to Garth Lawless at age nineteen, now divorced

Children   Daisy Lawless, eight years old, who resides primarily with father

Known Lovers   *Xena* executive producer Rob Tapert

Special Skills   singing, horse riding, elementary martial arts
Weapons   1,000-megawatt smile, ice-blue eyes
Languages   English, German, French, Italian
Favorite Flowers   champagne roses
Favorite Colors   Tiffany colors, such as rust brown and emerald
   green
Favorite Musicians   Fats Waller, Nina Simone, Lyle Lovett, k.d.
   lang
Leisure Pursuits   spending time with daughter, Daisy; gardening
Best Line About Xena   "Xena's agenda is just to get through the
   day without killing someone."

XENA

Age   timeless
Born   Amphipolis
Mother   Cyrene, innkeeper, of Greek heritage
Father   unknown, left the family in Xena's youth
Siblings   elder brother Toris, and younger brother Lyceus, both
   now dead
Height   6 feet
Physique   big-boned, muscular
Hair   black
Eyes   icy blue
Accent   American Midwest
Comfort with Nudity   completely comfortable displaying her
   body
Present Occupation   Warrior Princess, fighting for the rights of
   the downtrodden
Previous Occupation   evil warlord; pirate captain

Marital History   single, never married

Children   son, Solan, fathered by Borias, left to be raised by the centaurs

Known Lovers   Hercules, Marcus, Petracles

Special Skills   acrobatics, martial arts, pressure-point training, healing, battle strategy, sailing, fishing

Weapons   chakram, sword, whip

Best Friend   Gabrielle, a bard

RENEÉ O'CONNOR

Born   February 15, 1971 in Houston, Texas (raised in Katy, Texas)

Mother   Sandra Wilson, co-owner of Threadgill's restaurant in Austin, Texas

Step-Father   Eddie Wilson, co-owner of Threadgill's restaurant in Austin, Texas

Siblings   none

Height   5 feet 6 inches (169 cm)

Physique   medium-boned, slender

Hair   golden blonde

Eyes   green

Occupation   supporting actress in *Xena: Warrior Princess*

Previous Occupations   acting debut in 1989; played in *Teen Angel* and *Match Point* series; had key roles in television films including *Hercules: The Legendary Journeys, The Flood, Changes,* and *Follow the River;* guest roles on *NYPD Blue, The Rockford Files,* and *Tales from the Crypt;* appeared in the video release *Darkman II: The Return of Durant* and the theatrical film *The Adventures of Huck*

Marital History   single, never married

Leisure Pursuits   jazz dancing, horse riding, sports

HUDSON LEICK

Born May 9, 1969, in Cincinnati, Ohio (raised in Rochester, New York)

Height 5 feet 8 inches

Occupation Supporting actress on *Xena: Warrior Princess*

Previous Occupations modeling; roles in the *Canadian University Hospital* television show, in plays at the Neighborhood Playhouse in New York City, in an after school television showcase series called *Sexual Considerations,* in a video movie titled *After the Game*

LITTLE-KNOWN FACTS ABOUT THE XENAVERSE

Xena had a relationship with Julius Caesar.

Xena was crucified by Julius Caesar.

Xena helped Ulysses string his bow of kingship.

Xena wanted to have a relationship with Ulysses.

Xena has a son being raised by the centaurs.

Xena has died and returned from the dead.

Xena has inhabited the bodies of Callisto, Autolycus, and Gabrielle.

Xena invented bungee jumping.

Xena and Gabrielle rescued the Lost Mariner.

Xena was a personal friend of Goliath, but was tricked into helping David kill the giant.

Xena invented kite-flying.

Xena avenged the death of Goliath.

Xena harnessed electricity, by flying a kite to attract lightning, to avenge the death of Goliath.

Xena saved the Ark of the Covenant from those who would use it wrongly.

Xena inspired David to write a Psalm for her.

Xena and Gabrielle provided Mary and Joseph with the donkey that took them to Bethlehem.

Xena and Gabrielle met Santa Claus.

Xena taught Hippocrates much of his medical skills, including how to perform a tracheotomy.

Xena invented CPR.

Xena unchained Prometheus.

Xena defeated the Sirens.

Xena strung Ulysses' bow.

Xena rescued Helen of Troy.

Gabrielle's poetic works influenced Homer and Tyldus.

Joxer invented Joxer shorts, later known as boxer shorts.

THE SECRET SIGNS AND SYMBOLS OF LUCY LAWLESS

LUCY LAWLESS WAS BORN MARCH 29, 1968, IN THE SOUTHERN Hemisphere, under the cardinal fire sign of Aries. Generally speaking, those born during this time manifest a great enthusiasm for life. Their energy is exceptional in initiating projects, and their ability to endure and adapt is noteworthy. Usually more extroverted than introverted, they tend to heavily influence their immediate environment. They like to share their thoughts, creations, and productions; and they are, more than those born under other signs, in need of fairly consistent appreciation and approval. A desire to be free distinguishes many born in this time, and they may not respond well to restrictions. They need to expand and make their mark on the world.

They often carry an ingenuous air about them all their life. Innocence, spontaneity, and impulsiveness are their character traits. Generally positive in their approach, they may shy away from highly serious attitudes and show little patience for negative orientations.

THE ARIES PERSONALITY

Aries is the first and most elemental sign of the zodiac, representing the beginning of all things. Aries depicts ego and resolve in their purest form. Like children, persons born under Aries are spontaneous, frank, and open. They apprehend the world with wonder. They have a strong urge to be a star and to shine brightly, as well as to explore the world. They need to explore their physical limits, much as children do, in order to develop properly.

Aries notables include Jane Goodall, Billie Holiday, Sarah Vaughan, and Bette Davis.

THE MARCH 29 PERSONALITY

This personality tends to study life minutely before taking action. March 29 people are not ones to let others down; they take their commitments very seriously. Idealism permeates almost everything they do.

Early in their lives, March 29 people form concepts of the world that will remain with them always. For them, life simply means continuing along a personally defined path—steadily, unassumingly, even relentlessly.

They are among that rare company of humans who can laugh at themselves. They see life's ironies all too clearly. In fact, very little escapes their attention, as they are attentive observers of society. They are alert to the foibles and flaws of others, as well as themselves.

Even if they live distant from their birthplace, they will never forget their heritage. Many, however, live in one area their entire lives, collecting memories and old friends in a living album.

Notables born on March 29 are Pearl Bailey, Jennifer Capriati, Alene Bertha Duerk, Vera M. Dean, and Ronia Lhevinne.

THE FIRE PERSONALITY

Fire is the combustive element. It can refer to acute inner feelings, and to their public display. Fire must be kept carefully controlled to maximize its effectiveness.

The cardinal fire sign, Aries represents fire in its plainest and most basic form. Aries is childlike in nature and enjoys being the center of attention. Those persons born under a fire sign apprehend their world primarily via their intuition and have a strong sense of themselves. But because of their impulsive disposition, they are accident-prone.

ASTROLOGICAL INDICATIONS

Element   fire

Quality   cardinal

Ruler   Mars

Symbol   the Ram

Mode   intuition

Motto   "I am"

Image   child

Stones   diamond (enhances self-confidence), ruby (raises a fighting spirit), emerald (helps communication), amethyst (relieves headaches)

Colors   all shades of red

Body Areas   head, face, upper jaw, cerebrum, cerebro-spinal system

Musical Keys   A-Major and F-Sharp minor

Musical Compositions   Beethoven's Seventh symphony, Shubert's Trout Quintet, Mozart's Twenty-third Piano Concerto, Franck's Sonata for Violin and Piano, J. S. Bach's F-sharp minor preludes and fugues from *The Well Tempered Clavier*

Plants   poppy, thistle, fern

Trees and Shrubs   alder, pomegranate, dogwood

Attractions to   Gemini, Leo, Libra, Scorpio

Medieval Condition   hot
Medieval Temperament   choleric
Medieval Humour   yellow bile
Psychological Orientation   subjective
Physical State   combustive
Strengths   idealistic, ironic, loyal
Weaknesses   opinionated, unambitious, aloof

NUMEROLOGICAL INDICATIONS

Ruling Number   2
Ruling Planet   Mars

TAROT INDICATIONS

The second card of the Major Arcana is the Priestess, shown seated on her throne, calm and impenetrable. A spiritual woman, she reveals hidden forces and mysteries, empowering us with that information. Favorable qualities are silence, intuition, reserve, and discretion.

Unofficial Dictionary of Lucy Lawless' English

First, a note about New Zealand pronunciation: According to *Whoosh!*, as a corollary of the First Law of Thermodynamics, the Linguistic Law of the Conservation of R's states that r's are neither created nor destroyed. Thus the extra "r" in "Xener" (New Zealand phonetics) is taken from words like spider, which then becomes "spiduh."

A&E   accident and emergency room of a hospital.

adverts   television commercials.

agro   aggressive, aggression.

all Beverly   all out of line; crooked, as "My backbone was all Beverly."

arse   rear end, as "a pain in the arse;" a coarser word than *bum*, which refers to the buttocks.

Baby Blue   ending of a sentence, equivalent to "Sorry, Charlie," as in "It's all over now, Baby Blue."

banger   sausage.

basin   bathroom sink.

bench   kitchen counter.

berm   shoulder of the road.

big bickies   lots of money.

biscuits   cookies (note: *cookies* are crackers, and *crackers* means crazy).

blinked   blind or blinded, as in "I've been going around blinked."

bloke   man; similar to *chap* (guy, male friend).

bloody   darn, or damn.

bludge   to live off the generosity of others, to sponge.

Bolshie   extreme radical, derived from Russian *Bolshevik*.

bonk   to have sexual intercourse.

bonnet   hood of a car.

boot   trunk of a car.

box   a cuplike device to cover and protect male genitalia (not a *carton*).

box of birds   an easy task, same as "a day at the beach."

Boxing Day   public holiday celebrated on December 26th.

buggered   exhausted, also known as "bushwagged," "knackered," "bushwagged," or "stuffed."

bum   buttocks.

bum bag   fanny pack, also known as "belt bag."

bush   forest or scrub wilderness; "going bush" means dropping out of sight.

bush shirt   woolen outdoors shirt.

candyfloss   cotton candy.

caravan   small mobile home or trailer.

carked   died, "kicked the bucket."

carpark   parking lot.

carton   box (not a *box*).

chat-up   to flirt using chat-up lines (come ons).

cheeky   humorously impertinent.

cheers   same as "good-bye" or "thank you."

chemist's   drugstore, pharmacy.

cheerios   cocktail wieners.

chilly bin   portable insulated cooler.

chips   french fries.

chippy   carpenter.

chook   chicken.

chrissy   Christmas.

chuffed   pleased.

chunder   to vomit; also known as "spew."

cinema   movie theater.

college   high school (not a university).

collywobbles   upset stomach, sometimes causing one to chunder or spew.

cor blimey   exclamation of disbelief, derived from "God blind me."

corker   very good.

cot   child's crib.

cotton buds   Q-tips.

courgette   zucchini.

creche   daycare center.

crisps   potato chips.

crook   sick.

dairy   convenience store.

ding   small auto accident, a fender bender in which the auto might sustain a car dent (see "prang").

dolly   doll.

does me up a treat   same as "suits me fine."

draughts   checkers game.

dummy   baby pacifier.

Eketahuna   similar to "Timbuktu," a backwater town where nobody knows anything; may instead use "Waikikamukau" (pronounced "why kick a moo cow"), a place so remote it makes Eketahuna look like a metropolis.

Enzed   N.Z., New Zealand.

fancy   to like something.

filled roll   subway sandwich.

fizzy   carbonated soft drink.

flannel   wash cloth.

footpath   sidewalk.

forms   grade levels at intermediate or secondary school.

fortnight   two weeks.

French letter   condom (not to be confused with "rubber").

fringe   bangs.

frock   dress.

gallops   a kind of horse racing.

g'day   good day, hello.

get off the grass   exclamation of disbelief, equivalent to "no way."

give it heaps   to try hard.

good nick   in good condition.

good on ya   "good for you," "congratulations."

grotty   run-down, worn-out, dirty.

ground floor   first floor.

gum boots   rubber boots.

guts for garters   in big trouble.

headmaster/mistress   school principal.

hokey-pokey   a kind of candy, also called "sea foam," covered in chocolate; also, an ice cream flavor.

holiday   vacation; one goes on holiday to relax and have fun.

home and housed   safe; also, completed successfully, as in "the episode was home and housed."

hoon   rough person, or gang member.

hooray   good-bye.

hotdog   corn dog (as opposed to "an American hot dog").

hottie   hot water bottle.

ice block   popsicle.

icing sugar   powdered sugar.

intermediate school   junior high school.

jam   fruit spread for bread (not to be confused with "jelly").

jandals   flip-flops, thonged sandals.

jeeze, Wayne!   an exclamation, usually said to someone acting or speaking foolishly.

jelly   gelatin dessert, like Jell-O.

jellymeat   canned pet food.

jersey   sweater; also known as "jumper."

judderbar   speed bump.

jug   kettle.

Kiwi   a native of New Zealand.

kiwi   a flightless New Zealand bird with a long, slender bill and brownish hairlike feathers.

kiwifruit   the fruit of the kiwi tree, formerly known as Chinese gooseberry.

knickers   panties or underpants; to get "one's knickers in a twist" is to suffer a state of anxious irritation.

kornies   corn flakes.

lavatory   toilet; also called a "bog," "dunny," or "loo" (see also "long drop").

lemon squash   lemonade.

lemonade   lemon-flavored soft drink, such as 7-Up or Sprite.

lift   elevator.

lolly   candy.

long drop   outhouse.

lounge   living room, usually furnished with a "lounge suite" (sofa).

lovee   term of endearment similar to "honey."

Maori   the indigenous people of New Zealand.

mate   friend.

metal   gravel, which is used to pave "metal roads."

mince   hamburger.

money for jam   easy money.

motorway   freeway.

Mr. Whippy   ice cream truck.

mum, mummy   mom, mommy

nana   grandmother.

nappy   diaper.

netball   a game similar to basketball.

nought   zero.

no wuckas   no worries.

O.E.   Overseas Experience; a prolonged period of traveling, working, or vacationing overseas.

Oz   Australia.

paddock   field.

petrol   gasoline; a "petrol station" is a gas station.

piece-of-piss   easy.

pissing down   raining hard.

plaster   adhesive bandage.

plonked   drunk.

pottle   small container.

prang   dent in a car.

primary school   elementary school.

primmers   grades 1 through 4 at primary school.

propelling pencil   mechanical pencil.

pudding   the dessert course of a meal.

push bike   bicycle.

pushchair   baby stroller.

quencher   ice cream bar.

queue   line of people.

rack off   go away angry.

ratbag   contemptible person.

rattle your dags   to hurry up.

rellies   relatives.

rice bubbles   breakfast cereal.

ring   to call on the telephone.

rock melon   cantaloupe.

roundabout   circular intersection.

rubber   eraser (not to be confused with "French letter").

rubbish   garbage, which is kept in a "rubbish tin."

rucksack   backpack.

sammies   sandwiches.

sandshoes   canvas sneakers.

scrogum   trail mix.

serviet   napkin.

shandy   a drink made with lemonade and beer.

shank's pony   walking.

shift   to move, as in "I'm shifting to a new house."

singlet   sleeveless undershirt.

skiting   bragging.

skivvy   a type of shirt.

skull   to drink beer rapidly, to guzzle.

smoko   short break from work.

solicitor   lawyer.

spotcha   "see you later."

standards   grades 1 through 4 at primary school.

state house   rental house owned by the government.

stirrer   troublemaker, agitator.

'strewth   "honestly," from "God's truth."

stubby   a small bottle of beer.

swimming togs   swimsuit, often shortened to "togs."

ta   "thank you."

take-aways   take-out food.

tasty cheese   sharp cheddar.

tea   dinner; "teatime" is dinnertime.

tea towel   dish towel.

telly   television set.

terraces   bleachers.

tertiary education   education above secondary school; university.

throw a wobbly   to have a temper tantrum.

tiki tour   roundabout way to get somewhere; scenic tour.

tin   can, as in "a tin of beans."

toll call   long distance call.

tomato sauce   catsup.

torch   flashlight.

trad   rigidly traditional.

tracksuit   sweats.

tramping   hiking.

traveling jones   the urge to travel.

trots   a kind of horse racing.

tucker   food.

twink   white-out.

unwaged   unemployed.

ute   pickup truck, abbreviated form of "utility vehicle."

walkshorts   dressy shorts for men's business attire.

wally   incompetent person, a loser.

wanker   jerk, an unpleasant male.

wing   car fender.

windscreen   windshield of a car.

wonky   crooked.

wops   rural areas.

whinge   whine or complain.

Yanks   Americans (large American-made automobiles are known as "yank-tanks").

yonks   a long time ago.

zed   "z," last letter of the alphabet.

zimmer frame   walker used by the injured or elderly.

ADDRESSES

Official *Xena: Warrior Princess* Fan Club
411 North Central Avenue, #300
Glendale, CA 91203

Lucy Lawless
P.O. Box 279
Pendleton, IN 46064

The Reneé O'Connor Fan Club (ROC)
P.O. Box 180435
Austin, TX 78718-0435

Hudson Leick
c/o Innovative Artists
1999 Avenue of the Stars, Suite 2850
Los Angeles, CA 90067

Hudson Leick Official Fan Club
P.O. Box 775
Fair Oaks, CA 95628

BIBLIOGRAPHY

America Online, "Lucy Lawless on AOL!" December 6, 1996

Area 52 Web Site, "Xena and Heard," John Walsh, June 1997

Baltimore Sun, January 1997

Black Belt Magazine, "What Puts the Punch in *Hercules* and *Xena*?" September 1996

CelebSite, "Lucy Lawless Biography," Starwave Corporation, 1997

Chicago Tribune, "Xena Usually Has a Fight on Her Hands," Allan Johnson, March 11, 1997

Cleo Magazine, "Wild at Heart," Eirik Knutzen, January 1997

CNN, "The Hollywood Minute," October 18, 1996

Crimson Castle Web Site, "Interview with Steven L. Sears," Catherine M. Wilson, February 25, 1997

Cult Times, "I Fought the Lawless," John Binns, December 1996

Daily News, "Lawless' Success All Greek to Her," Christy Slewinski, November 11, 1995

Daily Variety, "Meidel Snaps Up McNamara," Jim Benson, March 5, 1995; "MCA Sets *Hercules* Spinoff," Jim Benson, May 3, 1995

The David Letterman Show, "The Lucy Lawless Interview," 1997

Denver Post, "Fallen Star," Joanne Ostrow, November 20, 1996

Detroit Free Press, "Xena Gets It Off Her Chest," John Smyntek, May 8, 1997

Entertainment Tonight, "Interview with Lucy Lawless," September 13, 1996

Entertainment Weekly, "Toys in Babeland," A. J. Jacobs, November 24, 1995

BIBLIOGRAPHY

Entertainment Weekly Online, "Xena-phila," Mike Flaherty, March 7, 1997

Evening Post (Wellington, New Zealand), "New Age Hercules Still Flexes His Rippling Pecs," January 29, 1996

Femme Fatale, January 1996; June 1997

Frontiers Newsmagazin, "The (Lesbian) Adventures of *Xena: Warrior Princess,*" Laura Federico, June 1997

Gannett News Service, "TV or Not TV," Mike Hughes, December 29, 1995

The Globe, "Xena's Back in the Saddle," April 15, 1997

Independent, "Roseanne Barr, the Lottery Loser of All Time," Daniel Jeffreys, February 17, 1997

ITV Guide Entertainment Network, "Singing a Different Toon," June 28, 1997

KTLA Morning Show, "Interview with Lucy Lawless," September 27, 1996

KTLA Radio, "Interview with Lucy Lawless," January 26, 1996

KYSM Radio (Mankato, Minnesota) "Interview with Reneé O'Connor," April 24, 1997

Los Angeles Times, "Lucy Lawless Did Have to Pray to the Goddess of Spinoffs," N. F. Mendoza, October 1, 1995; "Not Even a Horse Can Throw Xena for a Loop," Candace A. Wedlan, March 3, 1997

Lucy Lawless Fan Club Newsletter, "Letter from Lucy," December 12, 1996; "Letter from Lucy," January 15, 1997

Michigan Live, "Russian Unit Back in Force," May 7, 1997

The Mike and Matey Show, "The Lucy Lawless Interview," February 13, 1996

The Mirror (Great Britain), "Lucy Pays the Price of Fame," July 25, 1997

Mogul (New Zealand), "*Xena: Warrior Princess,*" June 1996

Mr. Showbiz (a service of Starwave), "Lucy Lawless Interview," Gillian G. Gaar, January 28, 1997

BIBLIOGRAPHY

Ms., "Xena: She's Big, Tall, Strong—and Popular," August 1996

Natural Living Today, July/August 1997

Netforum Xena Mailing Lists, November 21, 1996

The News Times, "*Hercules* and *Xena* Racing at the Front of the Fantasy Pack," Dennis Anderson, February 7, 1997; "New Zealand Actress Lucy Lawless Is a Star on the Strength of *Xena,*" Christy Slewinsky, September 5, 1996; "Lucy Lawless Lays Down the Law as *Xena,*" Eileen Glanton, September 17, 1996

New York Times, "A Woman Wielding Many Weapons, Among Them a Sneer and a Stare," William Grimes, May 19, 1996; "There's Nothing Conservative About the Classics Revival," Celia McGee, February 16, 1997

New Zealand Radio, "Interview with Lucy Lawless," April 12, 1997

The Official Lucy Lawless Fan Club, "Interview with Lucy Lawless," 1996

Orange County Register, "Lucy Lawless Interview," October 3, 1996

Parade, "In Step with Lucy Lawless," James Brady, July 27, 1997

People, "Xena-Phile," Karen S. Schneider and Kirsten Warner, April 8, 1996

People Daily, "The Daily Dish: Smoochin' Warrior," June 29, 1996

People Online, "The Gods Have Spoken," "Tube," and "Lucy Lawless, Down Under on Top," June 1997

Philadelphia Inquirer, "She's a Kick in More Ways Than One," Jennifer Weiner, January 30, 1996

Playbill Online, "*Xena: Warrior Princess* to Join *Grease!*" Robert Viagas and David Lefkowitz, July 21, 1997

Playboy, "Twenty Questions," David Rensin, May 1997

The Province, "She is Xena (Hear Her Roar)," May 1997

The Regis and Kathie Lee Show, "Lucy Lawless Interview," January 17, 1997

The Rosie O'Donnell Show, "Lucy Lawless Interview," August, 1996

BIBLIOGRAPHY

Salon, "Who Owns Xena?" Andrew Leonard, July 3, 1997

San Francisco Bay Guardian, "Ain't Myth Behavin'," Gillian G. Gaar, May 14, 1997

Satellite Times (Germany), "Feminist Warrior?" Alex J. Geairns, March 1997

Sci-Fi Buzz, "Lucy Lawless Interview," February 20, 1997

Sci-Fi Universe, "*Xena: Warrior Princess* Follows *Hercules* into the Treacherous Ground of First-Run Syndication This Fall," Dan Vebber, Vol. 2, No. 10

SFX, No.19, "Hip or Myth," Joe Nazzaro, December 1996

Sky TV Guide (New Zealand), "On the War Path," February 1997

Spur (of Montgomery College), "Renee O'Connor Interview," Malaurie Hotier, May 12, 1997

Star Ledger, "Girlfriends Offers Gender-Bending Short Subjects," Henry Cabot Beck, July 20, 1996

Star-Telegram (Fort Worth), "Is She or Isn't She? Only Xena Knows for Sure," Ken Parish Perkins, March 14, 1997

Sunday Star-Times (Auckland, New Zealand), "Roberts Stepping Down as Communicado Boss," Linda Herrick, February 16, 1997

Tampa Tribune, "Mythical TV Heroes," Wal Belcher, May 25, 1996

Televizier (Germany), "Expected: A Hype Around Xena," May 10, 1997

Total TV Magazine, "Web-Wide Warriors," Karen Winter; "Lucy Lawless Uncut," Scott Barwick; "Hercules and Xena: A Modern Marvel," "Xena Rank and Philes," Kirk Miller; "The Power of Myth," June 1997

TV Guide, "Xena-phobia?" Glenn Kenny, September 30, 1995; "Mything Links," Peter Richmond, November 9, 1996; "Wounded Warrior," Mark Schwed, February 8, 1997; "The Woman Behind the Warrior," David Rensin, May 3, 1997; "Two Who Trounced Trek," Elisa Zuritsky, May 3, 1997; "Fourth of July Fireworks Spectacular," June 28, 1997

BIBLIOGRAPHY

TV Guide Online, "*Xena*'s Lucy Lawless," John Walsh, April 24, 1997

TV Hits (New Zealand), "Lucy Lawless," March 1997

TV-Times, "My Mum's Got Real Power!" Gill Pringle, July 1997

Universal Channel Web Site, "Lucy Lawless Stars in *Xena: Warrior Princess,*" June 1997

Universal *Xena: Warrior Princess* NetForum, "Lucy Lawless," March 3, 1996; "Rob Tapert," 1997; "Steven Sears," April 22. 1997

Us, "95 Biggest Stories of 95," January 1996

USA Channel, "Blockbuster Action Series *Hercules* and *Xena* to Team Up on USA Network," press release 17, July 22, 1996; "Lucy Lawless," July 1997

USA Today, "TV's Mythical Heroes," Jefferson Graham, February 15, 1996

USA Weekend, December 27-29, 1996

Vancouver Sun, "She Is Xena, Hear Her Roar as She Evens the Score," "75 Reasons Not to Give Up on TV," Alex Strachan, February 17, 1997

Waikato Times, "New Act for Xena's Stunt Double," Geraldine Jacobsen, September, 1996

Washington Post, "Woman of Steel," Elizabeth Kastor, September 21, 1996

Weekly (New Zealand), "Lucy Was Always Popular with the Boys!" Rowan Wakefield

WGN Radio, "Interview with Lucy Lawless," August 14, 1996

Whoosh!, "An Interview with Kevin Smith," Bret Ryan Rudnick, May 6, 1997; "Exploring Lucy Lawless Hair Color Myths," Kym Masera Taborn, September 1, 1996; "Mysteries Surrounding the Creation of the Syndicated Television Show *Xena: Warrior Princess,*" Kym Masera Taborn, November 1996; "*Xena: Warrior Princess*—The CD," Bret Rudnick, December-January, 1996-97; "Unexpected Turbulence,"

Michael Evans-Layng, February 1997; "Just Marry Her, Will You?" Cynthia Ward Cooper, February 1997; "An Interview with Sandra Wilson," Jacquie Propps, February 1997; "Adventures in an Autograph Line," Diane Silver, February 1997; "Women at the Convention: A Survey (Part I)" Catherine M. Wilson, February 1997; "Women at the Convention: A Survey (Part II)," Catherine M. Wilson, March 1997; "An Interview with Robert Field, Part I," Bret Ryan Rudnick, May 15, 1997; "Why We Like *Xena: Warrior Princess,*" Christine Schinella; "Plot Development and Fun Facts I Learned from *Xena: Warrior Princess,* Season Two," Christi Clogston, 1997; "Encyclopedia Xenaica," May 5, 1997 edition; "I'm Guilty!" Ephany, May 1997; "An Interview with R. J. Stewart," Bret Ryan Rudnick, June 1997

Women's Weekly (New Zealand) "Big Bonus for Xena," Neil Blincow, February 10, 1997; "Lucy Outshines Rachel," Tony Brenna, July 7, 1997

Xena Media Review, No. 21, "Why I Watch XWP," "Convention Report: Dallas StellarCon 12/27-29/96," Cynthia Ward Cooper, January 23, 1997

Yahoo! "Xena, Web Princess," David Sheff, May 1997

INDEX

INDEX

Also from Prima

Wonder Woman
Gods and Goddesses

John Byrne

U.S. $20.00
Can. $26.95
ISBN 0-7615-0483-4
hardcover / 320 pages

Religious tolerance and bigotry violently clash in this gripping novel. Wonder Woman, molded from clay and brought to life by ancient, pagan deities, threatens the self-righteous in the modern world by her very existence. A powerful televangelist, aided by a mysterious ally, incites her followers against the superheroine. The disruption extends even to the realm of Wonder Woman's birth—Themyscira, the home of the Amazons. Author John Byrne packs this, his third novel, with all the excitement and story-telling skill that he brings to DC Comics' Wonder Woman series as writer and artist.

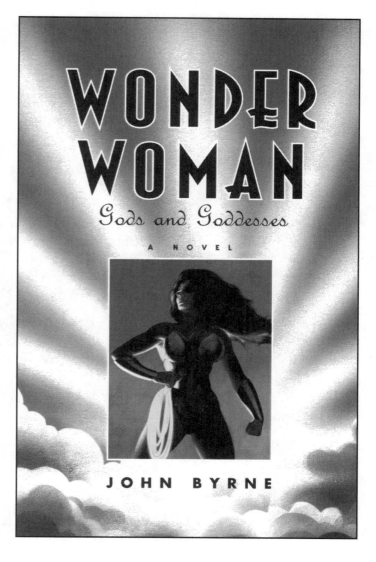

To Order Books

Please send me the following items:

Quantity	Title	Unit Price	Total
_____	Scully X-Posed	$ 16.00	$ _____
_____	Wonder Woman	$ 20.00	$ _____
_____	_____	$ _____	$ _____
_____	_____	$ _____	$ _____
_____	_____	$ _____	$ _____

Subtotal	$ _____
Deduct 10% when ordering 3-5 books	$ _____
7.25% Sales Tax (CA only)	$ _____
8.25% Sales Tax (TN only)	$ _____
5.0% Sales Tax (MD and IN only)	$ _____
7.0% G.S.T. Tax (Canada only)	$ _____
Shipping and Handling*	$ _____
Total Order	$ _____

*Shipping and Handling depend on Subtotal.

Subtotal	Shipping/Handling
$0.00–$14.99	$3.00
$15.00–$29.99	$4.00
$30.00–$49.99	$6.00
$50.00–$99.99	$10.00
$100.00–$199.99	$13.50
$200.00+	Call for Quote

Foreign and all Priority Request orders:
Call Order Entry department
for price quote at 916-632-4400

This chart represents the total retail price of books only
(before applicable discounts are taken).

By Telephone: With MC or Visa, call 800-632-8676 or 916-632-4400. Mon–Fri, 8:30-4:30.

WWW: http://www.primapublishing.com

By Internet E-mail: sales@primapub.com

By Mail: Just fill out the information below and send with your remittance to:

**Prima Publishing
P.O. Box 1260BK
Rocklin, CA 95677**

My name is _____

I live at _____

City_____ State_____ ZIP _____

MC/Visa#_____ Exp._____

Check/money order enclosed for $ _____ Payable to Prima Publishing

Daytime telephone _____

Signature _____